BODY OVERBOARD

RUSSELL WATE

CRANTHORPE
—MILLNER—
PUBLISHERS

First published by Cranthorpe Millner Publishers (2024)

ISBN 978-1-80378-243-0 (Paperback)

www.cranthorpemillner.com

Cranthorpe Millner Publishers

Printed and bound by CPI Group (UK) Ltd
Croydon, CR0 4YY

FSC
MIX
Paper | Supporting responsible forestry
FSC® C013604
www.fsc.org

Foreword

This is a story about a detective, his skills, and the process involved to investigate homicide. It shows us that detective as a man, his family, and his life. The book is also a travelogue as seen through his eyes.

∞

The investigation branch within the Foreign, Commonwealth and Development Office described in this novel is fictional and is not currently, or will ever be, real in the format I have described within the story. They do have very gifted police superintendents who work there on a seconded basis as liaison officers, and they do all they can to support families and police forces. They work with a murder and manslaughter team within the FCDO.

∞

My sincere thoughts and wishes go to all those families who have lost loved ones abroad and the nightmare they face in trying to come to terms with and understand it, as well as having to plan for their loved ones to be returned to the UK.

Chapter One

DCI Alexander (Sandy) McFarlane was not sure what he needed to do next. He had just taken a phone call telling him that the Oscar-winning actress, Vivienne Jones, was missing having gone overboard from a yacht just off the coast of Barbados. Her husband, Adam Scott, himself a well-known actor, had asked a mutual friend if Sandy could help in some way.

He glanced around the room looking for his girlfriend Hannah Tobias, who had been with him and others in the room which was above a pub in Fleet Street in London. He couldn't see her and presumed that she must have gone to make a call to her father. As he looked more closely around the room, he saw that everyone who had been at the meal following a court case they had all been involved in had gone home. With a sinking feeling he realised that he couldn't see Hannah's coat, handbag or laptop case anywhere. Hannah, who had been a barrister in the case, had only just told him that she was very keen to take their relationship to the next level, but before he could reply to her, he had received and taken the call about Vivienne.

With this anxious, sinking and depressing feeling not going away and sitting in the pit of his stomach, he sprinted down the stairs of the pub and out into Fleet Street. At that time of the evening, there were hardly any pedestrians or vehicles moving about, but what he did see was a black London cab just moving off up the road. Sandy wondered whether to race after it, he instead quickly made a call to Hannah's phone but received no reply.

As he went upstairs again to retrieve his jacket and backpack, his phone buzzed to tell him he was receiving a call. He happily and swiftly answered it, saying, 'Hannah, where are you? I was hoping you were going to stay in the flat with me tonight so that we could talk.'

'It's not Hannah. What have you done to upset your relationship again?' commented Juliet Ashton, the DS he normally worked with at the Foreign, Commonwealth and Development Office (FCDO). 'Gosh, you can be such an idiot when it comes to love. I only left you both less than thirty minutes ago as well.'

Looking at his phone screen Sandy saw that he had an incoming call from Hannah, but he had no chance to answer it, because Juliet just kept on talking.

'Have you heard the news about Vivienne Jones? My family in Barbados are all calling me.' Sandy sadly saw that Hannah had stopped her call. 'They are saying it is all over the news there, that Adam Scott is in custody for killing Vivienne.'

Sandy urgently interrupted. 'Juliet, I have to go and make a call to Hannah. I have just missed a call from her.'

'Yes, you must give her a call, but talk to the boss straight afterwards. Sandy, we have a chance of a trip to Barbados here. It's my dream to get a chance to work back in my home.'

Even though Juliet had lived in England since she was a

2

toddler, she had been born in Barbados and regarded it as her home. Sandy didn't tell Juliet that he had already had a call about the case, indirectly from Adam Scott, who was asking for his help. This would have just led to him spending much longer on the phone to Juliet.

Before he could make his call, Sandy saw that he had a WhatsApp message from Hannah: *I am sorry I went off without talking to you, but I didn't want to distract you. Why don't you come and spend the weekend with me in Cambridge, my house mates are both away and we can talk through what the future means for us. I am in court until late Friday so Saturday probably best.*

He didn't phone Hannah but just sent her a message back letting her know that would be great and he would be with her first thing Saturday morning. He then messaged his team captain for the Ely Tigers 2nd rugby team, to let him know he wouldn't now be available to play that Saturday. One thing he didn't do was call Detective Superintendent Jane Watson, who was his and Juliet's boss. Tomorrow morning was soon enough to talk to her about Vivienne Jones and Barbados.

Sandy wandered back to the London flat he shared with his father, taking a slight detour to walk around St Paul's Cathedral on Ludgate Hill, marvelling at the architecture which was over three hundred years old. Having walked around it he looked at his favourite footbridge in London, the Millennium Bridge, beautifully lit all the way across its span over the Thames to the South Bank.

∞

3

After an uncomfortable, restless, in fact sleepless night, Sandy made his way into the office area in the FCDO where the consulate investigation support team were based. Even though he was in the office fairly early, lots of civil servants were already at their desks, and there waiting for him was Juliet and Clare Symonds who was the lead Crime Scene Manager for their team.

'Sandy, you didn't call the boss, did you!' Juliet admonished him, before he could even sit down. 'She wants to see you though as soon as you get in. I am sure she wants to send us to Barbados.'

'I am not so sure,' Sandy said, trying to calm a very excited Juliet down. 'You know that Jane will only deploy if we have had a request from a police force or a coroner.'

As he walked off to see Jane Watson in her office, he heard Juliet saying behind him, 'Don't you dare, Sandy McFarlane, come back into this office without having got the permission for us to deploy to Barbados.'

As usual D/Supt Watson was peering at her laptop screen and typing away on her keyboard. For once though she wasn't also on her phone.

On seeing Sandy enter her office and take the seat in front of her, Jane said, 'Late last night, I had a long conversation with Seymour Garner, the Assistant Commissioner for the Royal Barbados Police Force.' Sandy started to feel hopeful as to what Jane may say next. 'He has put in a formal request for your assistance in the case of Vivienne Jones going missing.'

'Is that what they are saying that she has gone missing rather than going overboard from her yacht?'

'They don't know what happened and are treating her as a missing person.'

'I have scoured the internet and looked at all of the press reports and they are saying that Adam Scott is in custody having been arrested for killing Vivienne, and throwing her body overboard,' Sandy commented, outlining what he had done with his time during his sleepless night while trying to take his mind off Hannah.

'That is not what I am being told, and Mr Scott has asked for you personally to assist with the investigation. He is of course the neighbour in Eaton Square to Viscount Peveril and his sister Arabella Montague, both of whom you know so well and have had so many dealings with during the last eighteen months.'

'So, can I be clear Jane, am I assisting here in London or going to Barbados?'

'Both. We are sorting out a flight for you and Juliet to go to Barbados tomorrow. They are paying for you to assist, but Miss Jones's sister is here in London at the Eaton Square house and you are to be her liaison officer. Make sure you see her before you fly.'

Jane's phone started ringing and their conversation was now almost over, but to make sure he had got it right, Sandy asked as he was leaving the office, 'You, did say Juliet is to go with me?'

'I wouldn't dare send someone to Barbados and not Juliet,' a laughing Jane replied.

As Sandy got back into the office and as Juliet was walking straight over to him. 'I am so sorry Juliet, I tried really hard, so hard, but it is only me that is going to Barbados, not you as well.'

'Don't you dare think for one moment Sandy McFarlane that you can wind me up like that. You are just no good at it,' Juliet said, trying to look stern and trying not to smile. 'We have just had an email from business admin telling us that we are on tomorrow morning's British Airways flight from Heathrow to Bridgetown, Barbados.'

'We had better get on with going to see Vivienne's sister and then getting home to pack. What time is the taxi picking me up or is that still to be organised?'

'Five a.m. for you and mine is coming at six a.m.'

Shaking his head whilst picking his backpack up again and realising that he hadn't even sat down yet, and had missed having a cup of tea or any breakfast for that matter, Sandy wondered if he could persuade Juliet to take a detour to a nearby Prét a Manger.

∞

As they walked into Eaton Square in Belgravia, Sandy was always impressed with the beautiful classic style of the houses in the square's 19th century architecture. They were all very large houses, and he knew that Vivienne and Adam's would be no different.

They had no sooner knocked on the door when it was opened by a woman who was extremely pretty with short, brunette hair and was wearing oval shaped glasses and a blue trouser suit. There was no mistaking that she was Vivienne's sister, but quite the opposite in how she wore her hair and clothes and she had on very little, if any, make up. Well, she was not the movie star, that was her sister.

'You must be DCI McFarlane, and who is this with you?' Imogen Jones asked as she escorted them through the large reception hall and into a small lounge area.

As they sat, Imogen offered them both a drink, and Juliet introduced herself.

'I am DS Juliet Ashton, and I will be working with the DCI to try and help to find your sister. What do you know of what has happened as the media has gone crazy with its stories? Most of which imply that Adam has killed her.'

'I am not surprised, as they have a very volatile relationship. I presume that you know that this is the second time that they have been married to each other.'

Sandy, who was pleased that Imogen was talking in the present tense about her sister, asked her, 'Before we get into their relationship can you tell us about what you know about your sister's movements, please?'

'Well, that should be easy, but it is not, I am afraid as my sister is a free spirit. I am a combination of her manager and personal assistant, which means I try to organise her diary. Her agent gets in the way as he is always trying to milk her to act in unsuitable films, endorse expensive products, promote herself in whatever way he can get her to do.'

'Are you older or younger?' Juliet asked, not wanting to presume, even though she thought that Imogen was older.

'I am her older sister, there are just the two of us now. Both our mum and dad have died.'

'How did they get to be on a yacht and in the waters near Barbados?' Juliet asked.

'Vivienne had just finished filming in America and had

flown to Antigua where she met up with Adam. I had charted a yacht with a skipper whose job was to take up to six days to get them from there to Barbados where they have a villa in Sandy Lane. Vivienne and Adam were going to have a week together there before they both went off to do different film-related promotion work, then they were coming back here to Eaton Square in three weeks or so.'

'Why were they still on the yacht then, having reached Barbados and not in their villa in Sandy Lane?' Sandy asked.

'They must have got there a day early as they had let one of their friends stay in the villa and they were only due to leave yesterday, I believe.'

'When was the last time you heard from your sister?' asked Sandy.

'Spoke to, or do you really mean heard from her?'

'Let's try heard from her first?' Sandy said.

'Lots of emails sent by her on Tuesday evening that I picked up Wednesday morning here in London. She was at some sort of harbour club where they had moored for the night. Don't ask me the name as I don't know it. She was dealing with all of our business and correspondence really well.'

'When did you last speak to her?' asked Sandy.

'She was at Miami airport just about to fly to Antigua. The after-filming party had left her a bit fragile. She was looking forward to seeing Adam and having a holiday as she had been filming for months.'

'Has she ever threatened to harm herself or has her state of mind caused you to worry about her mental health?'

'Not worried for her mental health.' Imogen said whilst

8

adjusting her glasses, 'When I just said fragile that was through too much drink. My sister does everything in excess!'

'Do you think Adam could have harmed her?' asked Juliet.

'Not to my knowledge, but you don't know what could happen behind closed doors. I am rarely here when they are, and I never travel abroad with them when they are together. Who wants the big sister or sister-in-law tagging along?' Imogen said, shrugging her shoulders.

'What could have happened to your sister then?'

'No idea. I just hope it is not some whizz kid's marketing ploy to promote her films.'

After exchanging contact details, Sandy and Juliet left the house. Ideally, they should have considered carrying out house to house enquiries to see if any of the nearby neighbours had seen anything that could assist with their investigation, in particular any sign of domestic abuse between Vivienne and Adam. They didn't have time to do this at the moment and because Sandy knew the Peveril's who lived next door he let Juliet know he would call them. Juliet said she would contact the Met Police to see if they had any reports of incidents at the house or relating to Vivienne and Adam.

As they waited for a cab to collect them and take them to their railway stations, Juliet said, 'Is it just me wondering why Imogen showed no concern that anything had actually happened to her sister? Do you think she knows more than she is telling us?'

With a shrug of his shoulders, Sandy got into his cab and told Juliet that he would see her at Heathrow Airport in the morning.

Chapter Two

Long before the train that Sandy was travelling on from London to his home in Ely had reached Cambridge, he had made the decision to leave the train there so that he could go and see Hannah.

He rushed off the train and out into Cambridge, walking extremely quickly, almost running, down Hills Road to Hannah's House. He had not told her that he was going to Barbados the next day as he thought it best to do that in person.

One of her housemates opened the door and looked at Sandy quizzically. 'What are you doing here?' she said, 'Hannah left about half an hour ago to go to Birmingham for her court case tomorrow.'

'I thought she might still be here,' Sandy replied dejectedly, turning to head back to the railway station.

He had a sinking feeling as he walked along, very slowly this time, that Hannah had just got on the train he had been on and would be changing trains at Ely where they would have definitely seen each other.

This was confirmed when he rang her. 'Hannah, are you able to wait at Ely train station for me?'

'Sorry Sandy, I have just this minute changed trains and I am heading to Birmingham. Why, where are you? I thought you were still in London until tomorrow.'

Having no opportunity to tell Hannah in person where he was going to, Sandy blurted out. 'I can't see you this weekend as I am flying to Barbados in the morning.'

There was a long silence. Although he hoped this was due to a loss of signal, he knew that in all likelihood Hannah was sad about what he had just told her.

She eventually replied, 'I wondered if you would end up going to assist in finding Vivienne Jones. Have a great time and let me know how it is going.' She promptly ended the call.

After Sandy walked into his home in Ely, he could see his youngest sister Isla sitting on the sofa being comforted by their mum, Katherine. He was surprised to see her as she lived in Durham and although he wanted to know what was going on he said nothing and putting his bags down he walked up to her and just gave her a big hug.

His dad Gregor, who was in the kitchen making what looked like a pasta dish, shouted out to him, 'What are you doing here Sandy? I have only made enough food for us.' He gesticulated with the wooden spoon in his hand to the others in the room and not Sandy.

Before Sandy could reply, his mum shouted back, 'Sorry Sandy, I got your message but I have been distracted and forgot to tell your dad you were coming home this evening. Why don't you go to the pub with your grandad he is having to fend for himself as Grandma is not at all well.'

As soon as he got in his room Sandy called Grandad Tom and arranged to meet him in the Cutter Inn, which was extremely close to where they lived, just off the Great River Ouse foot path. His grandad was delighted that he had called, and this lifted Sandy's mood. He felt very emotionally unsettled not just about his and Hannah's relationship but even more so seeing his youngest sister so upset.

When he had packed his suitcase, he went and found on the bookcase a guidebook to Barbados to take with him, which they had from a family trip they had taken there a few years ago. The McFarlane family had stayed in a wonderful resort called Sandy Lane. His father had paid! As he knew the weather was going to be hot, Sandy packed short sleeved shirts and shorts just in case he got any off-duty time.

While he was packing, he heard the front door open and then heard his other sister, Aileen, arrive. She lived locally with her husband and two boys. So, everyone in this family knew what was going on, but not him! He hadn't even known that his grandma was not well, if he had, he would have called to find out how she was. He knew that they were all aware that he had had a big trial coming to a conclusion that week and that might have meant no one wanted to bother him. He made a vow to himself that he must not be so self-absorbed with his work from now on. What was that training he had had a few years ago when he was in the Met Police, something to do with being more emotionally intelligent? Well, that was his project for himself from now on. He promptly sent a message to Hannah, checking she was OK as he walked to the Cutter Inn.

∞

On getting into the Cutter Inn, Sandy saw that his grandad was already there and had on the table in front of him two freshly poured pints of beer and also two menus.

Before they ordered their food, Sandy asked, 'Grandad, what is wrong with Grandma?'

'Not sure, but she hasn't been able to get out of bed all week and I couldn't get her to agree to going to the doctor's,' Tom replied, taking a long sip of his beer. 'Nothing for you to worry about though, your grandma is made of steel and will soon be back on her feet.'

After ordering their food, Sandy told his grandad that he needed to look after himself; he had put a lot of weight on and was prime heart attack age.

Ignoring his grandson completely, Grandad Tom said, 'You are back home early for the weekend, are you taking a bit of time off after your busy court case?'

'I am not staying home this weekend; I am off to Barbados in the morning.'

'Are you looking into Vivienne Jones being missing?' Tom asked. He had been a Detective Inspector in the Cambridgeshire Police and was always fascinated by Sandy's cases. 'When I have been reading about it in the media it sounds just like the Natalie Wood case, the actress that went missing from a yacht off the coast of California. Her husband Robert Wagner was suspected of being involved in her death, but nothing was ever confirmed.'

'I don't know too much about that case but will read up on it.' Sandy said, thinking that it sounded all a bit too similar and suspicious. Was it a big marketing ploy after all?

'What are your different hypotheses then?' Tom asked, with his mouth quite full of sausage and mash.

'Did you say hypotheses?' Sandy said, laughing. 'The media are saying that Vivienne fell overboard from the yacht. If that is the case then she could have fallen into the sea accidently, she could have been pushed, she could have been murdered and then thrown overboard.' Sandy suddenly realised he should probably write all of this down.

'If she has gone in the water, it might take a few days before she surfaces,' Tom said, deliberately not taking another mouthful of his food. 'I had a couple of cases where a missing person went in the River Nene near Wisbech, and they both took twenty-eight days to surface. Very tidal and very cold water there though.'

'Does the cold water change things then?'

'Yes, so I was given to understand that the warmer it is the quicker that a body would re-surface. I suspect the Caribbean Sea will be like a hot bath in comparison to the River Nene, so possibly only a few days.'

'If she has been pushed or murdered there can only be one suspect,' Sandy said, looking around to make sure that they couldn't be overheard. 'Adam Scott.'

'The media already have him convicted anyway. Any more hypotheses?'

'We must keep an open mind that she could have gone off in a small boat that I presume the yacht must have to get to docks or the shore. This may also be a big publicity stunt.' Sandy thought about his conversation with Imogen earlier. 'When I saw Vivienne's sister this morning, I felt she wasn't worried and maybe wasn't telling us everything.'

'What is your gut feeling then, Sandy? What in your judgement do you think has happened?'

Sandy considered the question for a few moments, sipping his beer. 'Hmm, I just don't have enough information as yet. I don't know what the police in Barbados have found out from Adam Scott or the skipper of the boat to even start to make a

14

judgment. Hopefully, by the end of this weekend I will have. What do you think, Grandad?'

'All of your hypotheses are reasonable, and I agree, until you speak to the last person who saw her before she was reported missing you can't rule anything out. There might be CCTV or phone data that could help. Your only key focus of the investigation though must be to find Vivienne Jones. Treat her as alive until the evidence tells you otherwise. Good luck. I wish I was coming with you.'

∞

The taxi arrived far too early, in fact it was in reality still the middle of the night, but it made good progress and got Sandy to Heathrow in plenty of time to check in, have breakfast and then find Juliet, who was beyond excited about their trip to Barbados. Sandy was pleased that this was not just about going home, but also Juliet was showing her passion to do everything that she could and make use of all of her years of experience to try and find out what happened to Vivienne. Two days had almost gone by with no sign of her.

The two detectives set about making phone calls to complete what UK-based enquiries that they could before they left for the Caribbean. Sandy also set about writing in his enquiry book all of the hypotheses he had discussed with his grandad last night, then what actions and investigations were needed to develop them further. He had been too tired to do this last night after talking to his parents and two sisters, still not finding out what was going on, but happy to just be part of the family and supporting them.

He had sent a long message to Hannah last night just

15

telling her about his grandma being ill and having dinner with his grandad and not knowing what was happening with his youngest sister which was worrying him. Hannah had sent an equally long reply expressing her concern. On re-reading their messages this morning Sandy frowned, as not once had the messages involved anything about their relationship. He sent a message wishing her luck in court before Juliet and him made their way to the boarding gate.

After the drinks trolley had been round and the pretty woeful meal had all been cleared away, Sandy got out his notebook again. He wrote a title on a fresh page: "Domestic abuse-relationship conflict enquiries".

'I have spoken this morning to both Viscount James Peveril and his sister Arabella Montague who live next door to Vivienne and Adam in Eaton Square,' Sandy said. 'They say that in the three or four years that they have been neighbours they have never heard any disturbances next door and Viscount Peveril has never heard any arguments or any conflict between them. He says that they are only there a few months of the year.'

'What about their housekeeper?' Juliet asked with her own notebook open on her lap and with her pen poised to write.

'James put her on the phone to me and I must say I have the feeling that she is quite starstruck by them and is probably infatuated with Adam.'

'I am not surprised, he is a gorgeous looking man, and he always portrays a leading romantic male role in the movies I have seen him in,' Juliet said with a knowing smile.

'More than a bit infatuated yourself – I had better steer him clear of you!' Sandy chuckled. He was sadly unable to avoid the thump to his arm from Juliet. 'What she did say though, was that sometimes when they came out of the house and no one was about in the street, they were always arguing with each other as they either went off walking or waited for a taxi.'

'Two big personalities clashing, most probably,' Juliet said. 'I saw a photo on the internet of Vivienne with a bruise on her cheek from about three years ago, didn't anyone see her with this?'

'Yes, Arabella said she did and asked Vivienne about it. She replied it happened whilst filming. Arabella had no reason not to believe this was true. Anything from the Met Police to assist us?'

'Nothing on any of their IT systems at all, either for them as individuals or for the address.' Juliet consulted her notes. 'I managed to speak to the neighbourhood police inspector whose name I can't seem to find at the moment,' she said, as she flicked through her note pages quickly. 'I can only find the name of the sergeant and he is called Brian. They cover that area of Belgravia, and got the impression that when Vivienne and Adam were at home they were model residents, and they had in fact helped out with a couple of fundraising campaigns that the police have had in the recent past.'

As there was nothing further that they could do, watching a film and probably having a bit of a sleep was now the two detectives' priority and they put their notebooks away.

Chapter Three

Waiting for them in the arrivals hall of Grantley Adams International Airport, Barbados, were two uniformed officers, one of whom was holding up a big cardboard sign which said DCI McFarlane. Without Sandy even acknowledging them, they had clocked that he was most probably the one they were waiting for. Police officers, like no doubt other professionals, seem to have an innate sense of being able to recognise a fellow officer, or at least having a good idea when they see a fellow officer. Likewise, if they see someone who they believe may have a criminal record.

The police officers were smartly dressed in their uniforms and the taller one, who was in fact very tall, was called Paulette and the shorter, stockier one was called Garry. He clearly worked out in the gym as they saw his bulging bicep muscles in his short-sleeved shirt as he placed their bags in the back of the minibus that they had brought to collect them in.

Their first stop was to meet Assistant Commissioner Seymour Garner. Sandy left Juliet with the officers when he went alone into the office at the police headquarters in Lower Roebuck Street, Bridgetown. There he was met by a slight man with greying hair and a pencil thin moustache wearing uniform, and Sandy was straight away made to feel very welcome.

'DCI Alexander McFarlane, we are delighted to have you and your colleague come all this way to join us. We are so honoured to have you working with us on this missing person enquiry. Anything that you want, please do not hesitate to contact me immediately.'

Smiling back and feeling totally at ease, Sandy went to sit down, but before he could, Seymour had jumped to his feet, grabbing Sandy by the arm, saying, 'Sorry, no time to sit down. I have been asked to introduce you on your arrival to the Deputy Commissioner, Carlos Bishop.' Escorting Sandy out of the door and down the corridor, he added, 'Let's go catch him before he leaves to go home.'

On entering an even bigger office than the sizeable one that Seymour had, they were met by a man at least six foot six tall with dark, greying hair wearing, not a uniform, but a smart cream-coloured possibly linen suit. On seeing Sandy, he seemed to growl and sigh at the same time.

Looking directly at Sandy, he said, 'You are not even as old as my son!' He then gestured for them to sit down, taking his own place behind the desk in front of them. 'I need to be very clear with you, you are here at the request of our police force. You are not the next great white hope that has landed in Barbados who is going to solve everything for us. You have one role and one role only, to support us in managing this international media story that is engulfing us.'

As Sandy went to respond, Seymour very discreetly but firmly grabbed Sandy by the arm.

Carlos Bishop kept on talking. 'If I hear for one moment that you, or your sergeant, are doing anything without our permission, you will not stay one moment longer on this island, nor ever have the opportunity to return. I think I have made myself clear, now good day to you and try to enjoy yourself while you're here without getting yourself into trouble.'

Without saying a word to each other, they returned to Seymour's office, where he put his hand on a completely shell-shocked Sandy's shoulder. 'Don't worry about him, you will be working with one of my detective inspectors and his team and only be required to liaise with me. Mr Bishop has been taken up with all the fervour of Barbados becoming a republic next month, and that we are going to be re-named as the Barbados Police Service at the end of November.'

As Sandy went back downstairs to re-join Juliet and their police escort, he felt more than a little confused about what he was now supposed to be doing.

∞

Twenty minutes later Sandy and Juliet had entered a small meeting room in Holetown Police Station. Waiting for them there was a slightly built man who was not much older than Sandy, probably in his early thirties. He had a similar pencil-thin moustache to the assistant commissioner, but his hair was very black and had tight curls. He was immaculately dressed in a light blue linen suit with a colourful blue tie.

The room had no air conditioning, so it was a bit humid in there, and as Sandy took off his jacket, the man introduced himself as Detective Inspector Richard Ambrose.

'Mr Alexander and his esteemed Detective Sergeant colleague have come all the way from London, England to help us.' Looking straight at Sandy he said, 'We are delighted that you are here with us.'

Before Sandy could reply to correct him about his name, the uniform officers, Paulette, Garry, and another man who was in plain clothes and wearing a short-sleeved shirt said, almost in unison, 'Yes, we are delighted.'

Again, before Sandy could say anything, Juliet and the plain clothes man started hugging and giving each other a kiss. Sandy decided that the best thing he could do was to take a seat and let all of the noise, mayhem and confusion settle down before he tried to speak. He was pleased that the warm glow of being in the Caribbean was now returning after his stern lecture and warning by Deputy Commissioner Carlos Bishop.

Juliet gestured to the man she had been hugging. 'Sandy, this is my cousin Dave Ashton. My dad is his uncle. He is a Detective Sergeant who is going to be working with us.'

Before Sandy could speak, DI Richard Ambrose asked, 'Why are you being called Sandy?'

Standing quickly to try and gain some control of the room, Sandy responded, 'We are also delighted to be here. Good to meet you DI Ambrose.' He shook the DI's hand. 'Great to see you too Dave. Juliet did tell me she had cousins working in the police here. How wonderful for her that we will be working with you.' Juliet and Dave gave each other big booming smiles. Sandy looked again at Richard. 'Is it possible for us please to have a briefing about what has happened and what has been done so far?'

'What I think we should have is a cup of tea, a nice cup of tea before we do that. Don't you think Mr Alexander?' DI

Ambrose suggested, nodding at the two constables to go and make the tea.

'What you need to do, Sandy, is relax. All in good time,' Juliet said. 'We are in Barbados now.'

'Why does DS Ashton keep calling you Sandy?' DI Ambrose asked again, looking confused.

'Which DS Ashton?' both Juliet and Dave said almost in unison, laughing loudly as did the whole room, including the two constables who had made little effort to go and make any tea.

'Sandy can be used as a shortened name for Alexander, if you have Scottish roots, which Sandy has,' Juliet said, still smiling widely.

As if a switch had been turned on in him, DI Ambrose stood and started the briefing. 'We had a call at approximately eight a.m. on Wednesday morning that Vivienne Jones had gone missing from the yacht called *Magnificence*.'

Sandy and Juliet, having been taken by surprise with the sudden shift into a briefing, were scrambling to get their notebooks out of their bags.

'Who made the call, and have you got a recording of the call?' Sandy asked, as he wrote furiously to catch up.

'Adam Scott called, and yes, to having a copy of the recording. He had woken up and Vivienne was missing. He sounded very distraught, worried and upset. There has been no trace of her ever since. So, at least two and half days now. We have taken statements from him and Theo Le Tissier, who is the skipper of the yacht *Magnificence*. I have copies for you both to read.'

'What search enquiries have you made so far?' Juliet asked.

'There have been extensive searches of the water in the breakwater, lagoon and marina dock. Enquiries with all boat owners and in the clubhouse and restaurant. I thought we would start there tomorrow morning. CCTV has started to be checked. Her phone was left on the yacht which we found when we searched through. I have that in our store here.'

'Where is Adam Scott now?' Sandy asked.

'He is at his home in Sandy Lane,' Dave Ashton added. 'I have spent time with him every day. His manager actually flew in on the same flight as you did. I am his liaison officer, and he is looking forward to seeing you tomorrow.'

'One last question,' Sandy said. 'Where have we got the idea that Vivienne has gone overboard? That is what the world's media are saying and that is what I was first told by Arabella Montague, a neighbour in London of Adam and Vivienne, but how do we know that is what happened?'

'That is what Adam told us in the call and it is in his statement that she must have fallen overboard,' replied DI Ambrose. 'It is my main theory of what happened.'

'Excellent. I look forward to seeing you all in the morning,' Sandy said, before being surprised by the reactions of all present.

'We don't work weekends here. We will see you on Monday,' Paulette said, echoed by the other Bajan officers before she started laughing followed by the rest of them.

The Bajan sense of humour and friendliness was so lovely that as long as Sandy avoided the deputy commissioner, he was going to enjoy working with them.

∞

There was no time to unpack, only time to have a quick shower and a change into shorts and tee shirt before Juliet, who was staying with her parents, arrived at Sandy's hotel in Holetown. He was ready and waiting when an old, battered, maroon Kia saloon car arrived. A slim woman in her mid to late sixties dressed in a leopard print jumpsuit, ankle boots and with long, straightened, dyed blonde hair got out of the passenger side door and embraced Sandy.

'I am Juliet's mother and I have heard so much about you from Juliet over the last couple of years that I feel I know you.'

They sped off down the road in the direction of Bridgetown. Sandy, sitting in the back, with Juliet driving, looked at the two women in front of him, although a definite resemblance, their stature was different with mum slim and Juliet a large lady. Presumably she took after her father as Dave Ashton, her cousin, was an almost identical build to her. As they drove along, the mum, who was called Josephine never stopped talking. There was no scenery to be seen as it was dark outside and in fact had been since they arrived in Barbados. It was though still hot and humid, and the car thermostat showed twenty-nine degrees Celsius.

The journey seemed to by-pass most of Bridgetown, and they ended up parking near a fishing village on the south coast which was near to the capital. The place was absolutely buzzing with people and was called Oistins. It was fish fry Friday. There were two sets of live music playing, one was the inevitable Bob Marley and similar reggae music and the other seemed to flip between calypso and country music.

Oistins Bay Gardens was full, not only of tourists but also locals. Sandy was loving the whole atmosphere of the place. When he had visited Barbados before, he hadn't visited here and this fish fry Friday was always on his list of things to do if he ever visited again. Josephine almost danced down the road and through the gardens.

'My mum is incredible, isn't she?' said Juliet. 'Gosh I miss her and my dad so much with me living in England.'

The road was full of endless kiosks or most probably locally called shacks, with seating outside, and the smell of the fish they were frying was intoxicating and making Sandy realise how hungry he was. The flames of the grills were lighting up the evening sky as much as any of the lights. Sandy would have stopped at the first shack he came to, but Josephine and Juliet obviously had a favourite to visit.

As they walked along Sandy could just about make out the white sand beach and a pier stretching out to sea in the distance. There were also a number of stalls selling crafts, and even though food was at the forefront of his mind, Sandy went with Juliet and bought an aquamarine blue bracelet for Hannah.

They caught up with Josephine where she was holding court with some old men who were playing dominos. Josephine was telling them that her daughter and her friend were important London detectives who had come to find the missing British actress Vivienne Jones. They were near "Uncle George's" shack, where they bought beautiful, tasty looking and smelling sword fish and flying fish, chips and Banks beers. The beat of the music made it almost impossible for them to sit still and they moved along to the beat.

What an evening they had. Sandy had thoroughly enjoyed himself revelling in the heady mix of the atmosphere, the people, the music and the food and drink. However, as they drove back to drop him off at his hotel, Sandy did start to wonder what it was that he could do to actually find out what had happened to Vivienne, which was the real reason that he was in Barbados.

Chapter Four

After only a few hours' sleep, which was most probably due to jetlag with the UK being five hours ahead, Sandy found himself wide awake. He exchanged a few messages with Hannah. He found out from his mum that his grandma was still not very well and that his sister Isla had headed home to Durham.

Surprised that it became light shortly after five a.m. Sandy headed out to have a run on the beach. The west coast of Barbados now he could see it was, in his view, stunning. The Caribbean sea that morning was azure blue. He ran happily for half an hour or so before the weather changed from an increasingly blue sky to overcast, and a heavy shower drenched him as he ran for cover back into the hotel.

Holetown Police Station was a short walk for him from his hotel and Sandy arrived just as DI Ambrose did.

'Good morning, Mr Sandy.' Richard had remembered that he wasn't usually called Alexander. 'Lovely tie you are wearing this morning!'

The morning briefing was led by Richard, and he laid out the key duties for that morning. He and Sandy were going to visit the marina restaurant and clubhouse. The two uniformed officers were going to go round all of the villas fronting the marina and also talk to anyone working on the boats in the

27

marina. The two Ashton's were going to check CCTV at the clubhouse, webcams and any CCTV footage around the marina.

The drive to Speightstown Marina took less than five minutes. The marina was stunning, nestling on the Caribbean Sea. There was a large lagoon with boats moored within it. Sandy looked at the boats; some of them were huge, so huge that they must have each cost multiple millions of dollars. The sunshine helped make it look an absolutely idyllic spot. What there was for visiting boats like the enormous *Magnificence* was a breakwater facility that had six boats moored there at present. At the briefing Richard had told them that this mooring had been full on the day that *Magnificence* had arrived, so *Magnificence* was allowed to drop anchor and stay within the breakwater area overnight, as did another boat, a fifty-five-foot catamaran that Richard had told them was being sailed by two Americans.

As they pulled up in the car at the clubhouse and restaurant, even though Sandy was looking everywhere, he wasn't able to work out which of the boats was the one that Vivienne and Adam had been on. He had forgotten his sunglasses and was squinting a bit in the Bajan sunshine, but he was sure he couldn't see it. There was also no sign of the catamaran. Sandy presumed that they had been moved into the marina itself.

'Richard, where is Vivienne and Adam's yacht and also the catamaran?'

'They have gone,' Richard said, with a big smile on his face. 'The catamaran left on Wednesday itself, not long after Miss Jones was reported missing, and I am not sure about the yacht, I think it might not have gone until Thursday.'

'Please tell me that your officers searched them both,' a now worried Sandy said, but seeing a frown develop on Richard's face, he quickly added, 'I know the catamaran would most probably not be a crime scene, but we just don't know if anything untoward happened on the *Magnificence* as yet, do we?'

'Good point,' a now less than confident Richard replied, 'but we did search them both and could find no trace of Vivienne on board either of them. The two Americans were very reluctant and quite assertive of where we could search. Our constable, Miss Paulette, is very persuasive as you have by now, or will soon, find out. She takes no messing from anyone; she ensured that a thorough search was carried out for anywhere Vivienne could be.'

'What about the yacht?' Sandy asked as they were about to enter the clubhouse. 'I know you told me you have possession of Vivienne's phone but what about a laptop and any other documentation, have you got these?'

'No laptop seen but some other documentation was taken. They are all in the store at Holetown police station. A few of her clothes and other belongings we helped take to her villa in Sandy Lane, so, if need be, we can look at anything you want there.'

∞

Juliet and Dave had arrived before them and were heading off with a lady who, Sandy presumed, was the manager as that was who they were there to see. As they entered the restaurant and bar area, they saw that the room was fairly empty except for a few tables which were taken with people having breakfast.

The two waiters/barmen who had been working on the Tuesday night took them to a table in the corner of the room which had a great view over the marina and out to sea. *How beautiful it is*, thought Sandy. That Saturday morning a number of boats were going by and heading out to enjoy time on the Caribbean Sea.

The two men were called Benjamin and Royston. Both of them started talking at the same time, one of them saying how distressing it was that such a thing could happen to such an incredibly beautiful person, and the other said how much they hoped that she could be found soon and safely. This was what they had been telling the media who had been visiting over the last few days. They both said with a smile that they had done a lot of interviews and were starting to be quite the celebrities as people were now recognising them from the TV.

In order to take some control over the direction of the conversation, Sandy said, 'I am thinking about splitting you two up so that we can get your separate accounts of what happened on Tuesday night.'

Richard looked at Sandy, then back at Benjamin and Royston. 'They are not suspects though, are they?'

'They are though likely to be significant witnesses aren't they, DI Ambrose?' Then, shrugging his shoulders and smiling at both of the men, Sandy added, 'OK, let's just hear what you have to say and remember only one of you talk at any one time.' He got out his notebook and with his pen ready said, 'What time did you notice Vivienne and Adam Scott arrive?'

'It was eight thirty p.m.,' Benjamin said, responding first. 'They had booked in for a meal at eight p.m. but turned up late.'

'How did they seem?'

Benjamin continued doing the talking. 'They were happy to start with and they had clearly had quite a bit to drink before they arrived. I did say to Royston that he should try not to serve them too many drinks so as not to get them drunk.' He then looked at Royston. 'See now what has happened!'

Royston responded angrily, 'They weren't drunk Benjamin when they left here. Don't you go saying that to these two policeman.'

'OK you two,' Sandy said, regretting that they hadn't spoken to the two men separately. 'Benjamin, just tell us what you remember of the evening.' As he said this, he frowned at Royston to make sure he kept quiet. 'They ordered drinks. They were both drinking rum cocktails and the man that was with them had a coke.'

Royston then butted in. 'The man was called Theo, he was the yacht skipper. He had sailed them from Antigua to Barbados and was then going to head back to Antigua to meet another skipper that works for their company. They were then both going to sail back to the UK for some boat repairs and refurbishment.'

'Did they have anything to eat and much more to drink?' Sandy asked, looking at Benjamin.

Royston answered, 'They both had fish tacos and another cocktail. They were then bought a couple of drinks by two

Americans who were staying on a catamaran. They were inviting them back to the catamaran to continue the party when they all left together.'

'I noticed earlier,' Sandy said, consulting his notebook, 'that you said they were happy to start with. What did you mean by that Benjamin?'

'When they started talking to the Americans, Vivienne was flirting with them.'

'She wasn't,' Royston butted in. 'She was captivating them like she was all of us.' As he said this, he seemed to have dreamy eyes. 'I do agree that Mr Scott seemed to get a bit jealous and was starting to get cross with Miss Jones. Nothing out of hand or too loud and she just ignored it and brushed him aside.'

Richard then added, 'He must have got used to it though over the years, men and women were just captivated, I think that was the word you used, by her beauty, charisma and personality.'

Benjamin and Royston showed them on their phones a number of selfies that they had taken with Vivienne and Adam. Sandy then took Royston's statement and Richard did the same for Benjamin and both of them sent the photographs to Richard via a WhatsApp message.

∞

As they headed back to the police station, they had to go round a stationary car that had all of its doors and its boot open. Constable Paulette Weekes was going through the car, searching it.

Garry was standing watching but keeping a careful eye on the crowd that was assembled, in particular, a scruffily dressed young man who was shouting abuse at Paulette.

'What is happening Garry?' Richard asked, pointing to the car with all of its doors open.

'He,' Garry said, pointing at the man making all the noise, 'wasn't wearing a seat belt, and when Paulette pulled him over and advised him, he gave her a bit of back chat, and this is the result.' Garry shrugged as if resigned to what was happening and said, 'Apparently Paulette is looking for drugs!'

It would appear that Constable Paulette was not a person to mess with. Richard told Sandy that Paulette represented Barbados at netball and would most likely be at the commonwealth games in Birmingham next summer.

Having left them to it, they got back earlier than the others. Sandy took the time he now had to read the statements of Adam Scott and Theo Le Tissier. It became clear from what they were saying in the statements that they had both gone to bed on returning to the yacht and left Vivienne to stay up and carry on drinking.

When the others returned to the police station, Garry went to the sink and moaned that there were no clean cups and no hot water, and he would need to boil a kettle to wash up.

Paulette shouted to him, 'Better boil that kettle then, Garry, and no sugar in my tea.'

There was no doubt who was in charge of this partnership!

Richard stood up and started the briefing. 'Sandy, tell us what you are thinking and what we know so far.'

'What we know so far, is that the last time Vivienne was

seen was approx. eleven p.m., Adam Scott realised that Vivienne was missing at 7.30 a.m. That is our time gap. It is huge, eight and half hours.' Sandy looked around the room at the officers. 'That is the gap we need to fill and find out what happened to Vivienne during that time.'

Having sat down, Richard stood up again then thought better of it and sat down again. 'I think it is Theo who says in his statement that not long before he went to sleep, probably just before midnight, he thought he heard the motor of the small boat, the one the yacht used to get to shore and which they had used that night to go to the clubhouse. That might narrow the time down slightly.' He paused. 'That is if it was Vivienne who took the boat.'

'Maybe. I know the boat was adrift and found that morning on the shore, but you told us,' Sandy said, looking directly at Richard, 'you thought that Vivienne had gone in the water, and this was an accident. Have you changed your opinion, as that changes our priorities for our investigation, doesn't it? If she went off on the boat, Vivienne may have gone to the Americans' catamaran to continue the party, or, it might fit the possible hypothesis that it is all a huge marketing ploy, and she went ashore and is hiding out somewhere.'

Richard was squirming. 'I stick by my original hypothesis,' he said. 'We do though need to keep an open mind on other possibilities, don't we?'

Paulette and Garry hadn't got anything to add, and Juliet and Dave had nothing from the CCTV and webcam footage that could help with anything that was seen of Vivienne and Adam after ten thirty. The yacht and catamaran were not in view. However, they had some great photos from the clubhouse of them both and also of the Americans who they had found out were Bradley and Michael Lewis. Plus, they saw for the first time a picture of what Theo, the skipper of *Magnificence*, looked like.

'There is no proof of life for Vivienne now for the last three and a half days,' Dave Ashton said. 'Obviously a key way to have confirmation of this is if her phone was with her, but we know that it was left on the yacht. Don't get me wrong, there have been numerous sightings worldwide, sometimes using old photos that people are now posting all over social media. More than a nuisance to our investigation. there has been no activity on her email accounts, bank accounts, etc.'

Richard said very quietly and sombrely, 'We have to assume the worst then, don't we, that Vivienne Jones is no longer alive.'

Chapter Five

Before Dave and Sandy went to see Adam Scott in his villa, they clarified with DI Richard Ambrose what status he had for Adam. Obviously, he was one of the victim's family members, but what other category of person was he: a witness, a significant witness or even a suspect? Richard was clear with them that at this stage, from all that they knew so far, he was being categorised as a significant witness, so as to ensure, if possible, they made special allowances in order to capture his account of events.

They drove through Holetown which, with its authentic Caribbean small town feel and with the sun shining, was, Sandy thought, captivating. On their way to Sandy Lane, they went along the coast but before they went to the villa itself, they parked on the road outside the Sandy Lane Hotel and walked down the alleyway onto the white sand of the beach. The hotel's blue sun umbrellas were set out in neat lines and in the beautiful blue sea a variety of water sports were taking place. The McFarlane family had had such a happy time on this beach and was still for Sandy a significant memory. Dave pointed out the apartment blocks that the rich, famous and many other celebrities had homes in. Sandy told Dave about the holiday when his parents had taken him and his two sisters to the hotel there the year before the elder of his two sisters had got married.

As they pulled up outside the villa, Sandy recognised the large home. He had played a few rounds of golf with his dad during their holiday, and they had passed this villa a few times as it overlooked one of the golf course's greens.

There were two TV cameramen and half a dozen or so other photographers stood outside. Two security men were standing just inside the gate. They waved them through and ignoring the pleas for a comment from the reporters they walked up to the door. Before they had a chance to knock, the door was opened by a small lady, probably aged in her early sixties. Celia Longstaff, she introduced herself as, adding that she was Mr Scott's long-suffering personal manager. Celia had a cigarette in her mouth and blew out smoke away from them as she escorted them both back out into the sunshine and onto the terrace that overlooked a kidney shaped swimming pool. What an amazing place to have as a home.

Adam in a pair of matching red shorts and tee shirt who was without doubt devastatingly handsome, was lounging on a reclining chair with his phone in his hand. On seeing them he jumped up to greet them.

'DCI McFarlane, any news? I am terrified I have lost Vivienne.' Adam looked visibly exhausted. 'Celia, can you organise cups of tea for the DCI and Dave. I will have another rum and coke. A large one!' As Celia left the terrace and went back into the house, no doubt to find the housekeeper, he continued, 'How can anyone just vanish into thin air. Especially someone as famous as Vivienne?'

Dave had with him a body-worn video camera. 'Mr Scott, please can we have your consent to video record our conversation today?'

'Of course, as you know I do my best work in front of a camera,' he laughed, as did Sandy and Dave, the intensity of the mood lifted almost immediately.

After they had taken their seats and Dave had switched on the camera, Sandy said, 'Can we go way back and ask you when you and Vivienne first met and got together?'

Adam's left hand went through his hair and then after pausing for a moment, he said, 'We acted in a film together. Vivienne had another film coming out that was about to make her a star. She was nineteen and I was totally and utterly transfixed by her.'

'How old were you?'

'He was twenty-six and a much bigger star at the time and a married man,' Celia said, as she came back onto the terrace. 'He left his then wife, caused a huge scandal, which the gossip columnists loved, then he very quickly married Miss Jones, in fact the day his divorce came through.'

'Who is telling this story, Celia?' Adam said, smiling at his manager. 'We were married for less than three years. We were both busy with our careers so saw too little of each other and our bright flame of infatuation with each other had dimmed.'

'He then quickly got married again and had two children. I have never known anyone fall in love as quickly as him,' Celia added, pointing at Adam while exhaling a deep plume of cigarette smoke. 'No one likes wedding cake more than Adam. I did the invites for this third wedding and some of the responses were that they were sorry they couldn't come, but they said that they we will try and be at his next wedding!'

Both Sandy and Dave spluttered into their tea as they laughed. Even Adam smiled whilst shaking his head at Celia.

'Almost ten years to the day after we got divorced, Vivienne and I met at the British Academy Film and TV awards in London. Vivienne won best actor and we have been inseparable since. Over six years now,' Adam said, avoiding looking and turning his back away from Celia.

This didn't stop Celia talking though. 'And a fourth wedding. No wedding cake this time, as only the pair of them went and got married in Capri, Italy.'

'Might have been four weddings but only three women though Celia,' Adam said, as if to somehow justify all of his weddings.

Sandy sincerely hoped it wasn't going to be a case of four weddings and a funeral. The funeral of Vivienne.

Sandy and Dave looked at each other, fully aware that they had asked almost no questions.

'Obviously we have an open mind,' Sandy interjected, 'but a consideration we must have is that someone may have harmed Vivienne. Is there anyone that could have done this to her?'

'Other than me you mean!' a now clearly distressed Adam said. 'Everyone seems to think it is me. We have a stalker. Well, it is Vivienne who has the stalker, but it affects me as well. He slashed the tyres on my car on regular occasions. Vivienne is terrified of him. Who can blame her?'

'What is his name?' Sandy asked, thinking they may now have a lead.

'Adam Jones,' Celia replied, puffing on probably her fourth cigarette since they had arrived. 'As you can imagine darling, that is not his real name. It is Roger Forbes. He is in prison. Wormwood Scrubs in London, I believe. He received four years for his third conviction of stalking and harassment of Vivienne.' Celia took another deep draw on her cigarette. 'The first two slaps on his wrist amazingly didn't work.'

∞

When Celia had left the terrace to make a couple of phone calls and send emails, Adam continued their discussion. 'Celia has been with me for twenty years, not just as my manager, agent and also a bit of a mother to me, mostly though as my friend. She is incredibly fond of Vivienne as well.' As he mentioned Vivienne's name Adam started to sob softly. 'We are missing her so much. I feel frightened, empty and at a loss without her. Please find Vivienne for us, she is the centre of our universe.'

After giving Adam time to compose himself, Sandy asked, 'Shall we now focus on what happened during the last few days?'

'What, since she went missing? They have been full of tears, despair, no laughter, so much quiet. Vivienne was the light and spark in any room,' Adam said, brushing away his tears.

'I want to go back to the time before Vivienne disappeared. Her sister Imogen tells me she hired a yacht with a skipper to take you both from Antigua to here in Barbados,' Sandy said, consulting his notes. 'The company is based in Guernsey, one of the Channel Islands.'

'Yes, Imogen sorted it all out. We originally wanted to sail from Miami, but it would have taken too long with a single crew, so we opted to meet the yacht in Antigua. This worked out fine and was a glorious time for us. It was a holiday, a break from our busy schedules, away from the limelight. Away from always being recognised everywhere you go. Don't get me wrong, fame is what both Vivienne and I crave, but it is exhausting. We had been apart for a few weeks, with Vivienne finishing a film in the States and me doing some film promotion work in New York. Theo, the skipper, got us here in Barbados a day early, hence we stayed a night on the boat at the Speightstown Marina. He had tried to get us in the one at Bridgetown, but it was full, as was the one at Speightstown really, but they let us drop anchor within the breakwater.'

'What did you do after you arrived at the marina?'

'Nothing too much, other than a bit of sunbathing. Theo then took us across to the marina clubhouse for something to eat.'

'Was this in the small boat that the yacht had?' Sandy asked, and showed Adam a photograph that Richard had given him of the boat on the shore where it was found the next morning.

'Yes, that's the one. I occasionally used it as we sailed around the Caribbean to get us to various beaches.'

'Would Vivienne have used it as well?'

'I don't think so. I am not sure that Vivienne would know the first thing about operating it.'

Sandy and Dave looked at each other. This information, taking account of Theo's statement, meant that the time gap was now most probably back again to ten thirty.

41

'Talk us through the time at the marina clubhouse. We have statements from there that you and Vivienne had had a lot to drink, and you were upset with her when she was getting too friendly with the two Americans from the catamaran.'

'I accept we both had more to drink than we normally do. We had dinner and then I was tired and wanted to go back to the yacht. Vivienne, however, wanted to continue the night, and when the Americans who, like everyone always is, were captivated by her, invited us back to their boat, I lost my temper.'

'You then went back to the yacht, and you said in your earlier statement that you went to bed, but Vivienne stayed up wanting to carry on drinking. Do you think she may have gone across to see the Americans and kept the night going?'

Rubbing his face and putting his hand through his hair a number of times, Adam said, 'I don't know what to think anymore. I am at a loss.' He looked like a man who was beaten, deflated and not in control of anything. He finished the rum and coke in a gulp. 'I don't know everything about my wife, but I don't think she would have got there herself. I do accept that they may have collected her in their own small boat, but I never heard anything.'

As Adam started to sob again, Sandy made a decision to stop their conversation there. He left Adam on the terrace telling him that DS Dave Ashton would call and see him tomorrow.

As they were about to leave the villa, Celia came out of a side room and silently gestured with her head for them to step inside.

Chapter Six

The room had air conditioning, which Sandy was pleased
about as he had spent at least the last thirty minutes in direct
sunlight. In his shirt, suit and tie he felt and looked distinctly
hot.

Having taken up a position behind a desk that had on it
a large computer screen, Celia asked, 'What are you going
to do about the vile social media trolling of Adam and also
this lot.' Celia indicated to the now much larger group of
reporters and photographers outside who they could easily
see as the window of the room faced out onto the front of the
villa. 'They have not only convicted Adam but are saying
total untruths about his and Vivienne's relationship.'

'Can I ask a question, Miss Longstaff?' Dave asked.

'You just have, DS Ashton. Isn't that a question, can I ask
a question?'

They all couldn't help but smile, but it didn't lessen the
bubbling anger that Celia clearly felt.

'DS Ashton,' she continued, 'the Barbados Police have
made no comment whatsoever about this. By keeping
silent they are fuelling the fire of this horrible, awful and
revolting social media and press reporting. It is quite frankly
disgusting.'

'The question I wanted to ask was this, are you, or

someone that works for you, able to share with us the social media feeds and any press cuttings or links to online media interviews please?'

'I would hope that you have someone already looking at this,' Celia said, peering at Dave through her overlarge round rimmed glasses. 'I have a couple of part time assistants who I will get to do it. One is in London and the other in New York. Imogen Jones also has someone that leads on Vivienne's social media, who I will ask to do the same. Vivienne has fifteen million followers on Instagram and twenty million on TikTok.'

'Do you think they would be able to say if a user logged into an account?'

'You mean like Vivienne? I will ask Imogen, but I would say of course.'

'I will speak to DI Ambrose and Assistant Commissioner Garner straight after we leave here to try and organise a more detailed press statement,' Sandy said, with the threatening words of Deputy Commissioner Bishop still reverberating in his head about what he saw as Sandy's "role in the investigation" – handling the media.

'Not good enough,' Celia said firmly. 'There needs to be a police media conference not just some bland statement.'

They all crowded around the computer screen while Celia showed them some of the social media feeds and press reporting. She was right, it was all quite shocking and in some cases as she described, vile.

'A further consequence is that nearly everything Adam was lined up to do has been cancelled and I have no new offers of work at all this week, which is unusual. No one wants to be in the slightest bit associated with a domestic abuse perpetrator, even if they are not!'

Both Dave and Sandy understood the predicament that Celia and Adam had, and possibly would always have, especially if Vivienne was never found.

'Another problem we have is that Adam can't act!' Celia smiled as she said it.

'What do you mean, I can't act?' Adam had suddenly appeared in the doorway behind them. 'What about the millions of pounds my acting has earned for you as well as me. I even went to drama school.'

'What drama school? It doesn't even exist now. It is your good looks that is keeping you in films. Luckily, you appear to be holding onto them like George Clooney and Sean Connery.'

'Now Vivienne, she could act!' Adam said in a soft melancholic voice.

'Oh yes, an actor at the top of her game. A once in a generation talent,' Celia agreed.

As Dave and Sandy left the villa, Dave commented, 'If he has done something to her, well, in my view he most certainly can act.'

'Did you notice how he said in the past tense "could" rather than "can" act,' Sandy added.

They avoided the large throng of reporters, refusing to make any comment, and walked straight through them to their car.

∞

As Dave drove them back to Holetown, Sandy made calls to both Richard Ambrose and Seymour Garner. Just as they pulled up and parked outside the police station, Seymour Garner confirmed with Sandy that a media briefing would take place at nine a.m. the next morning at the police HQ in Bridgetown, and Sandy was expected to play a key role.

As soon as they walked into the meeting room, Richard came up to them. 'Mr Sandy, I am so worried about the media briefing tomorrow. I won't be able to sleep tonight. Is there anything you can suggest?'

Not being very experienced himself in media briefings let alone the likely magnitude of this one, Sandy remembered a few words from his media training when he was in the Met Police. 'Richard, make a note of exactly what you are going to say and just stick to that.'

It was clear that Richard was in no state to lead the briefing and, as everybody was looking at him to take over, Sandy started it by turning to Juliet and Dave. 'Can you both look at finding out where the yacht *Magnificence* is now? We need to search the yacht and speak to Theo Le Tissier again. Also, can you find out where the Americans, Bradley and Michael Lewis, and their catamaran are.'

Juliet and Dave nodded in understanding, and Sandy looked at his notes from the meeting with Adam.

Before he could say anything, Dave spoke up. 'Boss, should we check which prison that stalker is in?'

'What stalker?' Paulette asked.

'Vivienne Jones had a stalker who was sent to prison for four years. He called himself Adam Jones.' Smiling to himself at the wordplay, Sandy went on. 'His real name is

Roger Forbes. Juliet, check with prison intelligence back in the UK to find out where he is.'

The largest task they had at the beginning of the next day was a proper systematic search of the water throughout the whole of Speightstown Marina. Richard had organised this so Sandy looked at him to outline the tasks required of the team in the morning.

'We have a dive team and a couple of boats with sonar arriving first thing in the morning,' Richard said, now forgetting his media briefing worries and clicking into professional mode. 'I had tried to close the marina down for the next few days, but I didn't get permission from Deputy Commissioner Bishop to do this.' He sighed and shrugged. 'We are using an area right next to the marina clubhouse as our main forward control point. Paulette and Garry, can you make sure that the area is kept clear of any members of the public and in particular the press.'

Everybody seemed tired, it had been a long week and with no clear idea when any of them was likely to get a day off, Sandy sent them all home to enjoy the rest of their Saturday. He couldn't believe what a busy week he had had himself. He and Juliet, and of course Hannah, had been in court at the start of the week and then here in Barbados the last couple of days. Pretty exhausting!

∞

One thing he did do as he sped off quickly to his hotel to get changed before being taken out by Juliet, was call his grandad.

47

'How is it going in Barbados, Sandy?' Tom asked as soon as he answered the phone.

'Tell me about Grandma first, please?'

Tom sighed. 'She's not too good I am afraid. Her oxygen levels are not what they should be.' Tom paused, getting tearful. 'We were pleased that the doctor came and saw her at home, as it is the weekend. She has been prescribed some steroids as well. However, if no improvement by tomorrow they want us to take her into the emergency department at Addenbrookes. Your mum and I are not so sure she will be well enough to travel.'

Feeling a large lump in his throat, and a bit tearful himself, Sandy relayed his own news. 'All is going well here, Grandad. Incredible island and lots of sunshine. No sign of Vivienne Jones though. Vanished without a trace. We have a huge media briefing tomorrow morning, and it might be on TV there in the UK on newsclips.'

'Don't forget the purpose of a media briefing is to only give out information to reassure the public and work out what information you want to generate from it.'

Having now got back into his hotel room, Sandy wished his grandad goodnight and told him to give his grandma a kiss from him and to ring him at any time, day or night, if there was any change.

There was one person Sandy desperately wanted to talk to after hearing the news about his grandma, and that was Hannah Tobias. As he waited in the reception area of his hotel for Juliet to arrive, he made a WhatsApp video call which was answered straight away. Just seeing her face made his heart leap.

'How has your Saturday been, Hannah?' Sandy asked.

'Very quiet. I have come home to Harrogate for a few days. Dad and I are going for a walk tomorrow and then I have some court preparation work and a few video conferences over the next few days. No court hearings next week though.'

Sandy explained about his grandma not being well, before changing the topic to something lighter. 'Barbados is a beautiful island. I'd love us to visit someday.'

Hannah paused, a grim expression on her face. 'When you get back, we should… sit down and discuss our future together.'

'We do have a future together though, don't we?' Sandy asked, almost pleading with her.

'I don't want to get into this now and certainly not on a video call.'

Recognising that he was probably in grave danger of losing Hannah, and just as he was about to plead some more, Juliet seemed to arrive from nowhere.

Looking into the screen, she shouted to Hannah, 'How are you doing girl?'

It was amazing how quickly Juliet had adopted the local accent after getting to Barbados.

'I am good thank you, Juliet,' Hannah said, now with a beaming smile on her face.

'Your boyfriend and I have to go now, or we'll miss what I want him to see.'

With no further conversation other than to say goodbye to each other, that was it. Was he really still Hannah's boyfriend, Sandy wondered to himself as they left Holetown and headed north up the coast road.

Juliet was driving her parent's car and as they went through various typical Bajan villages, she told him that both she and Dave had sent off requests for information for the tasks he had set them at the briefing.

They parked alongside a number of other cars that were already there, with more still arriving at a place that seemed to be right at the top of the island.

They got out and walked to the rocky edge. The view was breath-taking.

'This place is called the Animal Flower Cave,' Juliet told him. 'We are too late to have a tour of the cave. It is an incredible natural rock formation and cave. The sea up here would probably have been too rough for a visit today anyway.'

Sandy looked around. It really was an incredible sight, and so different from the peaceful beaches that were further south around Holetown and Sandy Lane beach. Barbados was an island of brilliant contrasts.

Very soon after they arrived, the sun started to set over the Caribbean Sea.

'This is why I have brought you here Sandy, not to see the cave and the rock pools, but to see this unbelievable sunset,' Juliet said.

The sun came down very quickly and became at first vivid orange then, after a few seconds orange and red strands mingled together and streaked off to the sides from it and started to paint the whole sky. This glorious painting was only completed when the sun had finally dipped down out of sight into what felt like the nearby horizon. Sandy lost count of the number of times he took photos on his phone of the Barbadian sunset.

Dinner that night was in a restaurant in one of the quaint villages closer to Holetown. The owner and his family seemed to know Juliet. She ordered for them. She said they had to have a local dish, Cou-Cou which in the restaurant they were in was especially good at the weekend.

'What is Cou-Cou?' Sandy asked. He didn't remember having it when he had visited before with his family.

'Cou-Cou in Bajan cooking is made in many different ways depending on the family recipe, but here it is made from a combination of cornmeal and okra. The two ingredients are combined to make a sort of savoury type porridge. They put in some green bananas and other veg that is to hand and it goes perfectly with some of the spicier Bajan dishes – like flying fish. Which is what we are going to have with it.'

Juliet was right, it was absolutely delicious and after being presented with a local rum, not the well-known Mount Gay rum, but something that on drinking it was a lot more potent, Sandy felt that he was falling over the cliff of exhaustion from a combination of work and jetlag. Sleep was without doubt the next item on the menu for him.

Chapter Seven

There was no time for a run on the beach, only a snatched breakfast before Richard turned up outside the hotel reception to take them both to police HQ in Bridgetown.

Because it was a Sunday there was no traffic build up heading into Bridgetown, so they got there very swiftly. Richard had already been working for over an hour that morning, briefing and getting the search teams started at the marina. He had left Juliet in charge as he left for the media conference.

He seemed much more relaxed and confident about the conference than he had been yesterday. Richard patted his pocket and told Sandy he had his notes typed and ready to read out.

The conference room was empty as they entered, apart from Assistant Commissioner Garner who was waiting for them. They took their seats with Seymour Garner sitting in the middle, Richard to his right and Sandy to his left. The doors were opened and in came a throng of reporters. The people with the TV cameras moved into the area that the Barbados police media department had allocated for them, which was on Sandy's side of the room. They were from all over the world including CNN, Fox News, the BBC, as well as Japanese, Italian and local TV. The photographers were placed on the opposite side. The reporters then jostled for position into the rows of chairs.

As soon as nine a.m. arrived, even though not everybody who wanted to be there had taken their seats, Seymour addressed the assembled crowd. 'Thank you all for coming. The Royal Barbados Police, soon to be called the Barbados Police Service, want to update you on our missing person enquiry into the disappearance of Miss Vivienne Jones. Before I hand over to Inspector Ambrose who is leading the investigation, can I ask that all questions are left to the end.'

On looking across at Richard, Sandy could see that his recent confidence had drained from him, and he was slouched in his chair and his face had gone pale.

He took out his notes. 'Let me first ask that all of you stop speculating about what has happened to Miss Jones.'

He looked out at the crowd, as people were shouting out, in particular the camera crews, speak up, talk louder, sit up straight.

He lifted his voice a little louder in response. 'The last known and corroborated sighting of Miss Jones was at approximately ten-thirty p.m. last Tuesday evening, since then we have had no confirmed sightings or any sign of any activity to suggest where we can find her. We have and are carrying out various enquiries and investigations to find Miss Jones and bring her back to her family and loved ones.'

Taking no notice of the Assistant Commissioner's instructions about questions, one of the reporters asked, 'What are you doing to find her then?'

'We are doing all that we can to find her,' Richard replied, now even more ruffled.

53

'Why has it taken until today to start having boats and divers searching the marina at Speightstown? Is it because you now have specialist advice from Scotland Yard's DCI McFarlane?' another reporter asked, who Sandy recognised was from the BBC.

A reporter from Sky News asked, 'DCI McFarlane, what do you think has happened to Vivienne Jones?'

Looking around the room, Sandy caught sight of the extremely large Deputy Commissioner Bishop who must have recently arrived in the room as he was standing right at the back. He frowned at Sandy, who was now determined not to say anything which might annoy Mr Bishop.

Richard responded, 'We have been searching the water there, but it was already agreed before DCI McFarlane had arrived on the island, that if Miss Jones was not found before this weekend, we would enlist boats with sonar and divers to search more thoroughly and systematically.'

'You must then believe that Miss Jones has gone into the water and who must be, after all of this time, dead. That's what you are saying isn't it, Detective Inspector?' asked the same insistent reporter.

'Yes, that is one of my hypotheses,' Richard replied.

You just told them not to speculate, Richard, Sandy thought, *and here you are speculating!*

Looking at Seymour Garner it was clear that he was not going to intervene. Maybe he thought Richard had finished what he wanted to say?

The next question, from a different reporter, seemed to floor Richard. 'We have found out that Vivienne and Adam Scott had had a lot to drink that night and were seen to argue in public. If she has gone into the water, as you are telling us, Adam must have put her in there. Is this what you believe?'

Sandy could not hold back any longer. This media briefing had turned into a car crash. 'I would ask that you all respect Miss Jones's loved ones, respect her worldwide fans that are also so worried about her and for the media to stop any speculation that any third party, including her husband, has harmed her. There is not one shred of evidence that any criminality is the case here.'

'So, your hypothesis then, DCI McFarlane, is that Vivienne Jones has taken her own life by going into the water?' suggested a wily reporter.

Realising that they stood no chance of emerging from the briefing having got the message out for the press to keep an open mind, Sandy replied, 'There is no evidence of that either. Please stop this speculation, it is harmful and stressful to Miss Jones's family.'

Seymour Garner had had enough. 'This media briefing is now concluded. If any members of the public who are watching or listening to this briefing has any credible information, please contact the Barbados Police's switchboard.'

Sandy would have liked them to have a more personal number, but appreciated that they hadn't organised that beforehand.

After watching Deputy Commissioner Bishop storm out of the room, Assistant Commissioner Garner looked at them both and just shook his head and left without a word. Richard and Sandy exchanged a look and troubled shrug.

'That went well Mr Sandy, didn't it!' said Richard.

No actually it went as badly as it possibly could have

done, Sandy thought. But Richard didn't need him to point that out.

∞

On their way back to see how the search of the marina was progressing, Sandy's phone was almost exploding with the number of messages he was receiving. Part, or all of the media briefing must have been shown in the UK as a lot of the messages were from people there, including his family and Hannah. He had also received a message from Celia Longstaff; he couldn't remember giving her his mobile phone number, but she had somehow got it. Her message said simply, *You are all Muppets!* He had no answer to that one.

When they arrived at Speightstown Marina, Richard just dropped him off as he was playing in a Barbados Police Band concert in Holetown that afternoon and he had to get himself ready.

Walking over to the police cordon, Sandy saw Constable Paulette Weekes talking to one of the barmen from the marina clubhouse, Benjamin. They were clearly flirting with each other.

'Why did you talk to the reporters about what happened with Miss Jones and Mr Scott?' Sandy asked Benjamin. 'You should have respected their privacy, especially as Miss Jones is missing.'

Not knowing what to say other than sorry, Benjamin looked very sheepish and embarrassed.

Paulette piped up. 'You did what, Benjamin? Remove my phone number immediately from your phone now!'

'I haven't got your phone number. You haven't given it to me,' a confused Benjamin replied, holding his phone.

Paulette grabbed his phone and started typing into it, then gave it back. 'Right, my number and contact details are now in there. Remove them immediately.'

Benjamin, and in fact Sandy to a certain extent, just stood there open mouthed when Paulette grabbed the phone back again and deleted her contact details then turned on her heel and walked off. Sandy and Benjamin, after the shock had worn off, couldn't stop laughing.

The search of the beautiful turquoise blue water in the marina was going well. The team that they had got in were well on the way to completing the search of the whole open area by the end of the day.

Juliet explained to Sandy the methodology being used. 'There are two boats with sonar fitted. The sea floor, although quite deep to allow these big yachts and boats to moor here, is not too deep. If the sonar picks up anything, they have some very long poles that you can see there with cameras fitted on them. They use these to try to have a look at what it is that the sonar has picked up. If they are still unsure, or the image is not clear, one of the sets of divers will go in and have a proper look.'

'Are they confident that if Vivienne is in here, she will be found?'

'The lead guy tells me he is. Never ever been wrong before, apparently!'

'What about the shoreline around the marina, have we got anything planned to search along there?' Sandy asked, taking off his jacket and loosening his tie. He was feeling the heat already.

'Yes, Richard has organised that to start on Monday morning. They are going to start at the centre of the marina and then work outwards, and probably during the next few days get to about a mile either side of the marina. They hope to get some search dogs involved, but we have to bear in mind that they are not body detection dogs so might not be as useful as we might hope.'

There was no doubt that DI Richard Ambrose had put together an excellent search operation.

Dave Ashton arrived. He had finished at church with his family, and he was now going to take over at the marina to allow Juliet and Sandy to take the afternoon off.

Following lunch, they made their way to the Seaside Theatre in Holetown to watch Richard and his fellow police band members perform. Juliet's mum, who was going to sit with them, had replaced her jump suit with a stunning bright yellow dress and a red straw hat. Her red stilettos were possibly the highest that Sandy had ever seen. Apparently, she had been to church that morning, no doubt bringing brightness to the congregation.

The Barbados Police Band had formed over a century ago making them one of the oldest police bands in the world. The concert was excellent and the band members, including Richard, looked immaculate with the red stripe down the side of their trousers and their bright white tunic with its red sash. They not only played marching band music but also calypso and popular music. It was the popular music that Juliet's mum seemed to sing her loudest to.

Juliet told him that she had been listening to them all of her life at various times, including, if she could get back home for the February half-term holidays, as they had a festival all that week in Holetown.

As the concert was finishing Juliet took a call, following up with Sandy afterwards.

'You wanted me to check which prison the stalker, Roger Forbes, is in. Well, he is not. Forbes was released over ten days ago. This afternoon the South Wales Police visited his home address and guess what, he is not there. The neighbours say he stayed last weekend, but he has not been seen since.'

Before Sandy could ask Juliet to urgently check with the Immigration department if he was now in Barbados, she was on it and had her cousin Dave Ashton working on it too. Dave, during that conversation, had told her that he understood from the Antigua Police that the yacht *Magnificence* was either there, or shortly going to arrive. A quick visit to Antigua might be on the cards early next week to carry out a proper search. They had received no information as yet relating to the whereabouts of the Americans and their catamaran. The US coastguard was on the case though.

Spending the rest of the afternoon and evening at his hotel, on the beach, or in his room, Sandy was able to reply to all the messages he had received during the day and write a report for his boss, Jane Watson, letting her know exactly what he and Juliet had been doing so far.

Chapter Eight

The catamaran was moored in the Caribbean Sea, just off the coast of Saint Croix in the US Virgin Islands. The scene was idyllic, hardly a sound, just gentle waves splashing against the sides of the boat. The sun was in the process of rising and there was a slight early morning mist. The peaceful scene was about to be shattered. At eight a.m. that Monday morning, two US Coast Guard vessels moved forward.

Using firstly the vessels horn and then a loud hailer, one of the officers shouted out to the occupants, 'Permission to come alongside?'

After a few minutes, one of the cousins emerged, still in a state of half sleep, he waved an affirmative, so the vessels moved up, one went very close alongside and the other positioned itself in front of the catamaran.

The same officer, now not needing the loudhailer, asked, 'Permission to come aboard?'

Both Bradley and Michael Lewis were now visible on the deck.

'What is this all about?' Michael shouted out. He was in a rage. 'You scared me half to death with the loud siren! Was that really necessary?'

The officer replied, 'We have a request from the police in Barbados to search your boat.'

'I presume this is about the missing actress, Vivienne Jones, isn't it?' Michael responded. 'Well, when we were in Barbados almost a week ago, they searched this boat and I can tell you now that my cousin and I are US citizens and if you want to board and search our boat you need to go away and get yourselves a warrant from a judge.'

He stormed off, out of sight into the cabin.

'I notice that you haven't told us our Miranda rights,' Bradley noted. 'Luckily, we know them. As a US citizen, I am going to exercise my constitutional right to remain silent. Good day to you all.'

He then also disappeared out of sight.

The three officers on the US Coast Guard vessel looked at each other, totally flummoxed about what to do next.

What they did next was call DS Dave Ashton, who was sitting in the meeting room with Juliet and Sandy. Richard had gone straight to the marina to lead on the continued search of the water.

'US Coast Guard here, DS Ashton. We have a bit of a situation here in the US Virgin Islands.'

Dave placed his phone on the table and on speaker in front of the three of them. 'I have with me two detectives from London who are helping us. They are DCI McFarlane and my cousin, DS Juliet Ashton.'

'Cute,' the reply came. 'We have come alongside the catamaran of Bradley and Michael Lewis. Not so cute, as they are refusing us permission to go onboard and search and are exercising their right to silence. What do you want us to do?'

The three in Holetown looked at each other, deflated.

'Couldn't you just use the ways and means act,' asked Juliet. 'We understand there is some low-level intelligence that the two cousins are dealing in illegal drugs.'

After a short silence, whether because the coast guard officer was talking to someone else or just thinking they couldn't be sure, they replied, 'No honey, that is not going to happen. These boys know their rights. The FBI intelligence is actually better than low level, it is highly likely they are moving drugs for a couple of large-scale suppliers in Miami.'

Sandy decided to take over the conversation. 'We don't want to put you or any of your team in an impossible situation. The police here did a cursory check looking for Vivienne Jones. We wanted a much more in-depth one looking for traces of her. We don't have any information to support an application for a judge's warrant. However, what we really need is to talk to them and at least someone to take a statement. Can you give them DS Dave Ashton's contact details, please? Then I suppose let them go if they want to leave.'

'Will do. We will hang around for a while as we are enjoying unsettling them! We all love Vivienne though; she is a superstar, and her husband is not too bad an actor either.'

After he ended the call the three detectives looked at each other despondently, as the number of unresolved enquiries was mounting.

∞

At the same time as this conversation was taking place, a detective in the Royal Police Force of Antigua and Barbuda was making his way to Nelson's dockyard in the English Harbour area. He was hoping to catch *Magnificence* not long after it had docked and taken up its mooring.

A couple of days ago when he started making his enquiries on behalf of the Barbados Police, he had visited a bar in English Harbour just in time for a drink with some English ex-pats. They told him that the regular skipper of *Magnificence* was an ex-serviceman from the Royal Navy and whenever he was in Antigua, he spent time with them and took part in the six p.m. "Tot Ceremony". Apparently, in Antigua they kept on the daily tradition of partaking of a tot of rum, which the Royal Navy had stopped issuing in the early 1970s.

They told the detective, as he had his third tot and bought a fourth tot of rum for them all, that they had heard that the regular skipper was due back in Antigua from the UK at the weekend to meet *Magnificence* when it docked.

After arriving at the dock, the detective saw that there was no sign of the yacht at the mooring they had told him it usually used, which started to worry him. As he had driven there this morning, he had visions of being a hero and finding the vanished movie star Vivienne Jones, he had even told his wife that he may be on TV later that day.

On seeing no sign of the yacht, he didn't hang about but drove in panic to another place that it could be – Falmouth Harbour. There was no sign of it there either. Kicking himself that he had not come for a visit yesterday morning, as he had initially thought he would, he then convinced himself that the yacht probably hadn't arrived yet, so he went back to the original berth.

'Do you know when *Magnificence* is due back in here?' he shouted to a couple of sailors on a nearby yacht.

The yacht they were on was enormous and must have been worth an eye-watering amount of money. As he gazed around the dockyard there were a number of equally large yachts. The cost of them might have been enough for a small country to live on for a year or two.

'It will be away for several months mate, probably back early next year,' replied one of the sailors, wearing tailored shorts and a shirt with the name of the yacht on its front.

'What!' the detective exclaimed. 'Are you sure? I presume it has not been here at all then?'

'Oh yes, she arrived yesterday, and they left early this morning, heading back to the UK for a full refurbishment.'

The detective reluctantly took out his phone and dialled the contact details he had for DS Dave Ashton in Barbados, who answered straight away.

'I am sorry, but the *Magnificence* yacht was only here in Antigua for a few hours and has left for the UK.'

Dave put his phone back on the table and on speaker phone and asked, 'Why is the boat going back to the UK?'

This wasn't the question Sandy wanted to ask, that question was: how could you have missed it, or why did you miss it? He should have sent Juliet to Antigua on Saturday as he had fleetingly thought on that day.

'They told me at the Tot Club.'

'The what club?' Dave asked. 'Never mind. Go on.'

'They know the regular skipper well, but not the relief one. The skipper had gone to have a bit of a holiday at home and bring back some parts for the yacht. He was due back this weekend. A couple of sailors from a nearby yacht have told me this morning that the skipper told them yesterday that the company that owned the yacht had decided that now was a good time to get the yacht home to the UK and have a full refurbishment.'

This was a much bigger blow than not being able to search the catamaran. The three detectives were so deflated that Sandy didn't have the enthusiasm to even ask his burning question of: how come you missed the yacht and let it leave?

Sandy asked instead, 'Do you know how long it will take to get over to the UK?'

'I don't know, I haven't asked,' he replied, then shouted, presumably to the sailors on the nearby boat he had been talking to, 'How long will it take to get to the UK?'

They didn't need the answer relaying to them as they could clearly hear the response from a man with an Australian accent.

'All depends if they are going to take it in turns to pilot the yacht, and the weather is a big factor at this time of the year.'

As this hadn't answered the question, Sandy said again, 'How long?'

'At least a week,' came the reply.

∞

Before Sandy could work out what their strategy could be to meet the arrival of *Magnificence* in Guernsey, his phone rang. It was Vivienne's sister, Imogen Jones.

Kicking himself that he hadn't kept her updated on how the investigation into her missing sister was going, or in fact, not going, he reluctantly answered his phone. He didn't put it down on the table with the speaker phone on as he didn't really want the rest of the room hearing Imogen berate him.

'Miss Jones, I am so sorry that I haven't called you.'

'Don't worry. I know you haven't got anything to update me on as I have seen the news conference on too many occasions. Everyone over here in the UK seems to be showing it.'

Feeling relieved, Sandy put his phone on the table and switched the speaker on. 'The reason for me contacting you is that Celia called and asked me to check on any unusual activity on any of the social media accounts that Vivienne has. As well as a digital marketing assistant that we employ accessing them all, Vivienne herself is a great one to post photos on Instagram or videos on Tik Tok. She doesn't use Twitter at all, and we rarely do, too much trolling of her goes on there.'

The three detectives were starting to get excited with the anticipation for what they felt Imogen might tell them, and she didn't disappoint.

'Vivienne has been logging onto those three social media platforms every day since she went missing. Sorry, I am being told that is not correct, not yesterday, but back on again this morning.'

There was an audible gasp and the beginnings of more than a smile from the three detectives.

'Do your records tell you where this was happening?'

'The only information we have got…' Imogen paused, consulting with the digital marketing assistant. '… is that it is an android phone, which is what Vivienne has, but you have that in the police's possession haven't you?'

Even though they all knew that already, Dave nodded. 'One of our digital media investigators has it.'

'Good. I don't know much about these things, but I do know that you can trace phones, can't you?'

Maybe Imogen didn't know as much as she thought.

'We would need a phone number or one of the other identifying numbers that phone handsets have,' Dave explained.

'Can't help you with that. Right, I'll leave it with you. Sandy, can I talk to you privately now please?'

Picking up his phone and going out of the room, Sandy replied, 'Yes, I am private now.'

Imogen started crying. 'I'm really struggling to keep it together. I had been fine for the first few days,' she said, the the tears still flowing, 'but I am now very worried. My sister has always been a free spirit and very impulsive, so I did wonder at the start what she was up to. She contacted me most days, but I have heard nothing from her.'

There was nothing that Sandy could do to support her other than listen; the conversation was by phone and he was many thousands of miles away. He knew that he now needed to contact South Wales police to supply a local family liaison officer.

'I have got so excited and hopeful on hearing this news of Vivienne logging on, but why then has she not contacted me? She is my whole life, not just as my sister, but my working life is totally all about her. I have thought for a while that this isn't that healthy for me or her. Maybe once she is found we should try to just be sisters.'

Sandy ended the call after Imogen agreed to letting him find a local contact for her. This was, at last, a real development for the investigation. Dave Ashton was already on the phone to the DMI at his police headquarters to discuss what they could do with the information that they had received.

Chapter Nine

Juliet and Sandy decided that the best use of their time was to go to see DI Richard Ambrose at the marina, to update him personally on all of the information they had received that morning. Update him on the good news, well, possibly good news, and of course all of the bad news. On their drive there, Juliet had taken a call to say that there was no trace of a Roger Forbes arriving on any direct flight from the UK since his release from prison. That information at least helped conclude one line of enquiry.

Not immediately seeing Richard anywhere, Sandy walked over to Constables Paulette and Garry who were standing on the cordon. Sandy arrived just as Benjamin did.

'Miss Paulette.'

'Benjamin,' she replied.

'Miss Paulette.' Benjamin nodded again at her.

'Benjamin.' Paulette nodded back at him.

They were flirting again.

Garry, looking at them both, shouted, 'Garry, Garry!'

'What are you shouting about?' Paulette asked, surprised by his outburst.

'I felt I was missing out, so wanted to say my name too.'

They all couldn't stop laughing, much to Garry's angst, who kept saying, 'What, what?'

Before Sandy could ask where he could find DI Ambrose, his phone rang. He saw that it was Celia Longstaff. Preparing himself for getting called a muppet again, he answered his phone and moved away from Paulette and Garry so that they were unable to hear.

'He is here.'

'Who is there, Celia?'

'Roger Forbes. He is standing with the rest of the throng of press reporters.'

'I don't think he can be – we have no trace of him on a direct flight from the UK. I accept there are numerous other non-direct routes in, especially through the US, and we should know about them later today or tomorrow. My best guess is it is not him.'

'He now has a beard, and he is wearing a baseball cap. I am sure it is him. Adam would recognise him better than me, but he has been so down and depressed over the last couple of days, I think if he saw him he would physically assault him and let out all of his anger, sadness and frustration on him.'

'OK,' Sandy said, 'I will come to you now with a couple of uniform police officers.'

They set off at speed with Garry driving, Paulette sat in the front passenger seat and Sandy in the rear hanging on for dear life. Luckily the drive wasn't too long to the Sandy Lane Country Estate and although he wasn't going to tell Garry, he thought he was driving remarkably well.

As they arrived outside the villa and even before the car had completely stopped, Paulette was out of it and as she did so, her hat went flying off her head.

She must have spotted someone in the crowd of people

outside the villa. Paulette walked straight up to a man with a very black beard and wearing a baseball cap. How did she know that this was the person that Celia had mentioned to Sandy. The woman had a sixth sense.

As she approached the man, he was off and running down the road with Paulette in fast pursuit and Garry a short distance behind. Garry had left the police car to follow Paulette, the keys were still in the ignition and the engine was still running. This left Sandy in a bit of dilemma, whether to stay and look after the abandoned police car or join the chase. There was actually no dilemma for him as off he went joining in the chase.

The man, pursued by Paulette, ran onto the golf course avoiding and running around two golf carts, much to the amazement of the golfers in the carts who had slammed on their brakes with their golf clubs clanging in the back. The man was by now out of breath. He was not as fit as any of the three police officers and in particular the athlete, which was Paulette.

He made a decision to turn back towards the villa, where the cameras that were outside there made sure he got maximum exposure. He ran towards Paulette, who as he reached the green just below the villa, grabbed him and wrestled him to the floor. Placing him on his front they dislodged two golf balls, to the shouts of annoyance from the golfers standing on the tee box above them. Paulette in one swift movement handcuffed him behind his back.

As this happened, Garry knelt down next to them and puffing away as he got his breath back. 'Right Paulette, on my count of ten, let's get him on his feet.'

'What!' Paulette exclaimed, hardly out of breath.

'Sorry, too many, shall we say on my count of five then,' Garry said.

Not listening to another word he had to say, Paulette was on her feet lifting the man as she did so. She told him he was under arrest for a breach of the peace and harassment and cautioned him.

Sandy looked at the man. 'I presume you are Roger Forbes?'

The man, who was still so out of breath from the exertion of running, was almost bent over double, he was puffing away. He looked up at Sandy. 'That is not what my name is.'

The police car hadn't been stolen and, containing the prisoner, went off without Sandy. He wasn't sure if that had been a deliberate move or whether Paulette and Garry had just forgotten him.

Sandy weighed up his options on how to get back to Holetown police station, and also how to get away from the press throngs who were asking him for an interview or a quote. A number of them must have got both video and still footage of the arrest.

Moving away from the villa he knew that a key call he needed to make had to be to Assistant Commissioner Garner. This needed to happen before he saw the activity outside the villa on the local news. Seymour Garner answered straight away and luckily, he hadn't heard anything as yet and was grateful for the update. He wanted a proper briefing later in the day on everything that had happened so far from Sandy and DI Ambrose.

A call to Juliet told him it was actually Richard who was

going to collect him. They were going to the central station in Bridgetown to monitor the interview with the prisoner. A call with Celia confirmed that he may have moved on from her muppet description of him and Richard, as she had told him she was very impressed with the swift arrest.

∞

'What is your full name?' Paulette asked the prisoner as she and Garry sat opposite him in a small interview room.

There was a table between them which had a recording machine on it and a small video camera high up in the corner of the room. Richard and Sandy sat observing in a nearby room.

'Adam Jones.'

So, they got the right person, thought Sandy. He sent a message to Juliet asking her if she had checked both names with arrivals from the UK.

'That is not your real name, is it?' Paulette said.

'Yeah, that is not your real name,' Garry growled at him.

'Yes, it is,' Roger said, looking at both of his interviewers, not sure who to direct his answer to.

'OK. Is it fair to say that your name used to be Roger Forbes?' Paulette asked.

'Your name *is* Roger Forbes!' Garry insisted.

'My name is not Roger Forbes,' he said, looking at Garry and then at Paulette. 'Yes, I agree that it used to be, but I officially changed it to Adam Jones when Vivienne and I got together.'

'You have never been with Vivienne Jones. That is all in

your head,' Paulette stated firmly.

Growling at him, Gary said, 'Yeah, don't say that. It is all in your head, you have made it up.'

Getting fed up with Garry continually repeating things like a parrot after she had spoken, Paulette turned to him. 'Garry, stop talking now. Let me ask the questions and then you ask anything after I have finished.'

'Yes Garry, stop asking questions,' Roger or Adam or whatever his name was, said to him.

This was echoed by both Richard and Sandy.

'Why have you come to Barbados?'

'To find Vivienne. Do you know how desperately worried I am for her?'

'When did you arrive?' Paulette asked, glaring at Garry and daring him to say anything.

He made an action to her of zipping his mouth shut. Both Richard and Sandy couldn't help but laugh when they saw him do this.

'Last Friday. As soon as I heard I took the first flight here.' Roger said, just as Sandy got a message from Juliet telling him that there was an Adam Jones on the BA flight from London direct to Bridgetown.

Sandy shook his head; that was the exact flight that he and Juliet had been on.

'I have seen you at the cordon in the marina on a few occasions over the last few days. That is why I recognised you.'

'You saw me at the marina?'

'Yes, what have you been doing?'

'What have I been doing?'

Paulette was getting frustrated. 'I have already had enough of him,' she said, pointing at Garry, 'asking the same questions as me. Now you are just repeating back to me my questions. Stop it, both of you. You,' she said, again pointing at Garry, 'shut up. You,' she pointed at Roger/Adam, 'answer the questions I ask. I say again, what have you been doing?'

'I have been going between the marina and Vivienne's villa to find out any news. I then intended to be the one to find her and save her. That imposter, Mr Scott, is in her villa all of the time. Someone needs to evict him.'

'Do you agree that your actions would cause distress to members of Vivienne's family just by your presence?'

'I am the only loved one of hers here in Barbados. Her family is not here. Her sister Imogen is at our home in South Wales.'

What a sad and twisted individual, thought Sandy. Richard had to take a call and left the room. When he returned, his face was pale.

All he could say to Sandy was, 'They have found a body on the shoreline, just north of the marina.'

Chapter Ten

Sandy drove, which allowed Richard to phone the Assistant Commissioner to let him know of the latest development.

'No, sir. I am not sure it is Miss Jones,' Richard said.

'Do you even know if it is a woman?' Seymour Garner asked.

'No, sir. I do not know that either.'

'What do you know then?'

'I only know that a body has been found. I will ring you as soon as I get there and know more.'

'Yes, you do that, as at present you seem to know nothing.'

'I do know something. I know a body has been found.'

The call ended and Richard smiled at Sandy. He looked very nervous, apprehensive and unsure as to what they were likely to find themselves presented with at the scene where the body had been found.

They were stopped at the top of the road, just past the marina, that went down to the shore. A number of uniform officers were in attendance. A cordon had been erected across the road and the officers were not letting anyone pass them. As they approached one of the officers who was patrolling the cordon, they could see that there were only two or three people milling around wondering what was happening. Word had clearly not yet got out to the large number of press reporters and members of the public who were just back down the road at the marina.

The officer stood to attention and saluted Richard, his detective inspector, as they went under the police labelled tape. As they went to walk by, Sandy spoke to the officer.

'I want you to get a clipboard and make a record of everyone you let through here and the time it happens. Only let people through who are members of the Barbados Police Service.'

'Then please can you go back the other side of the tape,' the officer said, frowning at Sandy whilst he did so.

Sandy smiled. 'Good point.'

'Well done,' said Richard, also smiling. 'This is DCI McFarlane from London; he is allowed through. There may be another detective arrive, DS Juliet Ashton, she's from London too, and you can also let her through. Then as soon as he arrives you must let through the resident forensic pathologist. He is Dr Barry Braithwaite.'

'So, not just members of the Barbados Police Service, then,' the officer replied, looking straight at Sandy and then, for no apparent reason, he saluted Sandy as well.

After they walked away from the officer and the cordon and had gone about one hundred and fifty metres, they came across another officer standing at the top of a slope that led down to the water. At the bottom of the slope and peering into some bushes on the shoreline were three more people, a woman, and a man, both of them had CSI uniforms on. A uniform sergeant was also standing there talking to them.

Looking at Richard before they went down the slope, Sandy said, 'Richard, I think we need a tape across here and another officer to start a log of who goes through. We will call that first cordon, the one at the road, the outer one, and then this one, the inner cordon. We should only let through here anyone who is necessary and, in my view, only someone who is going to assist with any forensic recovery of any evidence.'

'Did you hear that, officer?' Richard said to the police officer standing nearby. 'Get on your radio and get someone to bring you police tape and a clipboard. You must then start a log and the only person, other than us, that you will let through is a Dr Braithwaite. Make a record of the time people go in and out.'

'I have some tape in my police car. I will go get it now.' The officer marched off.

This was not what Richard meant and it seemed that they might need to staff this inner cordon themselves until he returned.

It was possible from the bottom of the slope to see up to where they were now stood, as the three people below were looking up at them. So, they made their way carefully down the not too steep grassy slope and onto the muddy sand at the bottom.

After introductions, Sandy addressed them all. 'Do we think that the body has been washed up here by the tide or do we think that this is a body deposition site?'

They all looked at him with a confused and concerned manner.

Sandy continued, 'If we think it is a body deposition site, it appears that we haven't established a common approach path. I think we could recover that if we work out which way the five of us have walked down to here, as we may have ruined any forensics along those routes.'

'We also have the two volunteers who were searching and found the body,' the sergeant said.

'Where are they now?' Richard asked.

'They were standing with one of my officers at the top of the road earlier. I presume they are still there as I told them not to go anywhere.'

Sandy and Richard had missed this as they walked by, and had presumed they were just members of the public.

Richard was straight on his phone to Dave Ashton, 'Dave, can you and Juliet come to us please. There are two witnesses we need you to collect and take to the police station. When you get there make them a hot drink as they may be traumatised as it is not every day you find a dead body. Once you've done that take their statements, please.'

∞

They moved themselves into a position to see the body. The first sight that greeted them was the colour red. It was the red of the dress that they had seen Vivienne wearing on the video at the marina clubhouse on the night she had disappeared.

It was definitely her. Both Sandy and Richard's shoulders slumped and they looked at each other. They had failed to find Vivienne alive. The fact that she had died long before they had even been informed that she had gone missing, was, at that very moment, only a small comfort to them both.

The body of Vivienne Jones looked muddy and dirty. Her long, curly and beautiful dark brown almost black hair was very matted and had pieces of twigs, leaf and seaweed in it. It was not just her dress that identified Vivienne, there was no mistaking, even though decomposition was well under way and there were flies everywhere speeding up the process, that this was her.

The face that millions upon millions of people worldwide would recognise was what they were looking at. Richard moved back to call the Assistant Commissioner. He could see that the police officer was back in place and had swiftly put two sticks in the ground with police do not cross tape tied between them. He seemed very pleased with himself as he smiled and waved at Richard and lifted up a clipboard to show that he had done all that had been asked of him.

'Sir, it is DI Ambrose again. Yes, the body is definitely Vivienne Jones.'

After a slight pause as Seymour Garner processed the enormity of the information, he asked, 'Was she murdered?'

'I have no idea how she died, sir. We are waiting for the resident forensic pathologist of Barbados to arrive. He, I am sure, will need to carry out an autopsy to find out that information.'

'We should let the next of kin know and then deliver a media statement as soon as possible. Even without a cause of death,' Seymour said, thinking out loud.

'I would do nothing, sir, until I have a little bit more information. DCI McFarlane and I will come to your office as soon as we finish here. Could I ask that we try and keep this information as tight as possible for the moment.'

When he returned to the others there was a discussion in progress. They were debating about moving the body, at least further up the muddy sand and away from the water that had apparently been steadily moving closer to the body of Vivienne.

The weather had been very hot and humid all day, but the threat of thunderstorms hadn't yet materialised. Richard was unsure if it would matter if they did have a thunderstorm, as in his mind Vivienne must have spent several days in water anyway.

Sandy, on the other hand, was worried about the balance of losing evidence and retaining what they already had got.

'I don't want us to move the body until the forensic pathologist has been.' Looking directly at the crime scene manager, he said, 'Have we, or can we get as many photographs as possible and a video of the scene here and of the body whilst we wait.' Looking at the water's edge and then at the body, he continued, 'If the pathologist is not here in twenty minutes at the most, we will need to move her as the tide is coming in.'

Neither Sandy, Richard nor the sergeant had on the customary forensic boiler suits so the CSM didn't want any of them to get any closer and he told them so. The CSM and CSI were forensically dressed, and they also wore boots that had covers on them. Sandy, looking at his and Richards' shoes, now covered in sand and mud. Worriedly glancing back and forth at the tide coming in and up to the darkening sky, Sandy was beginning to get the feeling that they were not going to be able to wait the twenty minutes that he had mentioned. The dilemma was starting to eat away at him.

'Have you got a body bag in your van at the top of the road?'

'No, sorry, we rarely have call for them. I am getting one

brought up from our store in Bridgetown.'

Well, that would take at least some time, so if they moved the body in the next few moments, they would just have to carry her. Not too wise a thing to be doing with the decomposition.

∞

There was no noise that pleased them more than the whistling sound that Dr Barry Braithwaite was making as he made his way down to them.

He was an overweight, short man in his late fifties with very tightly curled black hair that was heavily flecked with grey. He had on round metal-rimmed glasses and he wore a shirt and tie, underneath the blue forensic boiler suit which he had already put on.

He was surprisingly sprightly as he came quickly down to meet them. He clearly knew the CSM and CSI well as they acknowledged each other fondly. He was introduced to Sandy and shook his hand.

He looked at Richard. 'DI Ambrose, good to see you again. You call me out to the most delightful locations.' He glanced firstly at the tide, then the sky. 'Let's get this show on the road while we can, shall we.'

He nodded at the CSI and CSM and they all moved forward into the bushes, as they did so, they all put on gloves. Sandy and Richard peered in at the activity.

Dr Braithwaite started a running commentary. 'The fishes have been busy eating away at her fingers and toes.' Vivienne had on no shoes. 'Decomposition is well on its way but no sign of any maggot infestation. Probably only been out of the water today.'

Shouting through to Dr Braithwaite, Sandy said, 'We wondered before you arrived whether this might have been a deposition site. From what you are saying, you don't think that is the case, do you?'

'I could be wrong, but highly unlikely. This body, based on the time Miss Jones was last seen, unless she had been hidden somewhere, has come out of the water today.' After moving quickly feeling all over her face and head he then turned over her body with the help of the CSM and CSI. He looked at Vivienne's back. 'No sign of bullet or knife wounds. I think this woman has drowned. However, the question I, or in fact we, might not be able to answer is whether she was pushed, fell, or jumped into the water.'

He spent several more minutes checking all over the body.

'Right, let's get her out of here and to the Queen Elizabeth Hospital mortuary in Bridgetown.'

The CSM, CSI and Dr Braithwaite gently picked Vivienne up and carried her out of the bushes and up the bank. They put her down on the ground while they awaited the arrival of the body bag and then the undertakers for the conveyance to the hospital. The CSI went back down the bank and took several more photographs of where Vivienne had lain and took a number of soil samples. He then carried out an almost fingertip search to see if anything had dropped off the body. It didn't look like that was the case as no other exhibits were taken.

Taking his gloves off and placing them on top of the body to be placed in the body bag with her, then pausing and looking at Vivienne intently, Barry said to whoever was listening, 'What a sad end to one of the world's most beautiful and talented woman. Gone from us all in her prime. One thing now though, her legend will always live on, for all eternity.'

The detectives and the sergeant who was also standing with them could only also look at Vivienne and nod in agreement.

Barry, now looking at Richard, stated, 'Gents, I will not be ready for you until late tomorrow morning as I need x-rays and possibly CT scans or MRI scans to be done first. That will take some organising for me, so I need to get on with it now. Goodbye until we rendezvous tomorrow at my luxurious home within the bowels of the Queen Elizabeth Hospital.'

Realising that there was going to be no discussion about trying to move the autopsy forward to take place that evening, Sandy just said to the quickly departing Dr Braithwaite, 'Bye, see you tomorrow.'

Chapter Eleven

The crowd at the outer cordon had grown considerably during the time that they had been down at the water's edge. On seeing the size of some of the lens on several of the cameras, Sandy glanced back to where the body was now lying. He had a sudden concern that Vivienne could be seen and photographed. With a sigh of relief, he saw that this wasn't possible.

'Richard,' he said, 'can we give instructions for the funeral director's vehicle to be taken down to that ridge there,' he pointed to the very top of the ridge, 'possibly using screens to ensure this lot,' he pointed again, this time at the photographers, 'don't get a photograph of Vivienne.'

'Good idea. I will make a call and organise this on our way to see the Assistant Commissioner.'

He told the officer on the cordon what was planned, while at the same time ignoring the shouts from the journalists for a quote.

As they got in the car with the plan for Sandy to drive to allow Richard a chance to make his calls, Sandy said, 'You go to Bridgetown. I think the most important thing I need to do now is go to the Sandy Lane Country Estate and let Adam Scott know in person what we have discovered.'

Only needing to nod in agreement, Richard took the car

keys, sat in the driver's seat and made a call to someone for them to organise the funeral director.

After being dropped down the road from the villa and away from the crowd that were waiting outside, Sandy phoned his new contact in the South Wales Police. He wanted them to go round to Imogen Jones' house and deliver what they called in policing an agony message. The time there in the UK was ten p.m. so he called the officer at home on their mobile phone.

He also wanted to phone his mum and Grandad Tom, as the message he had received earlier while he stood looking at the body of Vivienne, was that his grandma had been admitted to Addenbrookes Hospital in Cambridge. She apparently had deep-seated double pneumonia. His mum had told him not to worry as his grandma was a fighter. Rather than call, he just sent a message to both his mum and grandad. The person he did call was Hannah.

'Sorry to call so late. I am just feeling more than a bit emotional,' Sandy said, trying his best to keep his emotions in control.

'Don't be sorry, you know you can call me at any time. We might seem to be drifting apart but I will always be here for you.'

'My Grandma Margaret is in hospital with pneumonia, and I am extremely worried and feel powerless and useless as I'm thousands of miles away here in Barbados.'

'I won't tell you that it will all work out fine, but just ask that you cling to the incredible love which she has for you and your sisters. As an outsider looking in, that love was a delight for me to see. She even shows such love to me too.'

'I know you won't say anything to anyone, but I have

spent most of the afternoon with the body of Vivienne Jones. So sad. And I now have to go and let her husband know she is dead, before everyone else does that via the media.'

'How awfully distressing, Sandy. I am sure after this many days that this was the inevitable result, but that small flicker of hope has now been completely extinguished,' Hannah said softly.

They agreed to have a video call the next day.

Sandy surprised the considerable crowd outside the villa by walking up behind them. He blanked all of the questions and requests for comment and was allowed into the house by the security guard on the door.

∞

Standing in the hallway was Celia Longstaff. The confident and extremely edgy woman that she was, had gone. Celia had clearly been crying.

'Where is Adam?' Sandy asked.

Celia nodded towards the terrace and started to move with Sandy towards the open door that led outside. 'That body that they are talking about on the news, it's her, isn't it Sandy? It's Vivienne.'

After he slowly and sadly nodded, Celia cried out and started sobbing. Sandy left her in the villa and saw that Adam had jumped up on hearing Celia sob.

'What is it?' he asked. 'Vivienne?'

Without Sandy having to say anything, Adam slumped back into his seat, the one he had been sitting in the last time Sandy had been there. The gentle crying, moved to sobbing and Adam's whole body was shaking with the emotion of it all.

'We have no doubt, Adam, that it is Vivienne. I have been there and seen her. She was washed up onto the shore just north of the marina that you had been moored at last week.'

'How did she look, was she still in death…' On saying this the sobbing started again and Sandy could just make out him saying, 'beautiful.' After a long pause, he murmured, 'Where is she now? Can I go and see her, please?'

'Vivienne will be at the Queen Elizabeth Hospital in Bridgetown. We have lots of tests to carry out and then an autopsy tomorrow starting late morning. Sometime after that a visit to the chapel of rest may be possible.'

Sandy paused to ensure that Adam was taking in all that he was saying. As Celia had arrived on the terrace, he waited until she had pulled up a chair next to Adam, she held his hands.

'I would ask you to think long and hard before you decide to see her,' Sandy told them. 'The autopsy process is so very intrusive, and I need to warn you also that five days in the warm water of the Caribbean Sea and most of the day in the baking sun has speeded up the decomposition process.'

'So,' Celia said, 'the person we would see would not look like the picture of Vivienne that we remember and should retain in our memory.'

Celia nodded at Sandy for him to nod back in agreement. It was quite clear that visiting and seeing Vivienne at the hospital was something that she thought Adam wouldn't cope with.

'It is not my place to advise you about what you should

do, Adam. If you don't go and see her body, you might always regret it. If you do go and see her the results of decomposition and the impacts of a forensic autopsy might, on the other hand, haunt you for ever.' Seeing Celia nodding at him to go on, he continued, 'You might just want to remember Vivienne as you picture her now. It is your decision, and we will support you in any way we can.'

Feeling his phone buzz and looking at the caller display Sandy saw it was Imogen Jones. 'I really need to answer this. It is Vivienne's sister,' he said to them both.

Sandy answered the phone and moved to go back inside the villa. As he did so, Adam shouted out, 'I am so sorry, Imogen.'

∞

As Sandy walked to the room in the villa that Celia used as an office, he thought Adam saying sorry to his sister-in-law seemed a strange comment for him to make.

'Imogen, I am so sorry,' he said.

'DCI McFarlane, what has happened? What do you know? The officer with me is very sweet but knows no details, other than that Vivienne has died.'

'Yes, it is true that Vivienne has died. I have seen her body.' At the mention of body, there was a loud noise the other end of the phone; it sounded like Imogen had fainted. 'Miss Jones, Miss Jones?' Sandy shouted into his phone. 'Are you OK?'

After a short while she started to talk again. 'I had to sit down before I fell down,' Imogen explained. 'My sister is all

I've got.' Another loud wail. 'She is all I had, and I have got her no longer. All my family have gone, it is just me left now. What happened to my beautiful little sister?'

'We don't know exactly what has happened, but we are working on the theory that Vivienne went into the water off the yacht on the night that she was last seen by Adam and the others.' Sandy took a seat himself, overwhelmed by the emotion of the day. 'Vivienne then surfaced during last night and this morning was washed up on the shore, not that far north of the marina where the yacht had been moored.'

'I was so excited when I saw that someone was logging onto her social media accounts. I thought it must be her. Who could it be then DCI McFarlane, that was accessing her account?'

Just at that moment the doorbell rang. Celia answered it and showed Dave Ashton into the room where Sandy was sitting.

Sandy whispered to him, 'Have you got anywhere with finding out who was accessing Vivienne Jones's social media accounts?'

Making an awkward face and mouthing, 'Who is that?' he pointed at Sandy's phone.

He mouthed back, 'Imogen Jones. Why?'

'Oh dear,' Dave said.

'Why is that other person saying "oh dear", DCI McFarlane?' Imogen asked.

'Yes, DS Ashton, you had better tell us both.'

Looking very sheepish, Dave explained, 'It is us, well the digital media investigator who is logging onto the account at those times, to monitor activity. He only has Vivienne's log in detail as his access.'

'I don't know whether to laugh or cry,' Imogen said in response.

'I want to cry,' muttered Sandy. He really did want to cry, but not about this new information. This news had just made him frustrated.

'I will laugh then at the absurdity of it all,' Imogen said and gave a fake laugh.

'Sorry to butt in, sir,' Dave said to Sandy, 'but as soon as you're finished here you are required at the police HQ for a media briefing.'

'OK, Imogen, I am going to say goodbye to Adam, and I will call you tomorrow straight after the autopsy. Have you got someone to be with you tonight?'

'Yes,' Imogen replied, the mention of an autopsy clearly upset her again, 'Do you have to carry that out? Surely, she just drowned, and we can leave her alone and in peace now.'

After saying goodbye to Adam, who was just slumped in his chair and hardly acknowledged him but just stared aimlessly at the floor, Sandy and Dave were shown out by Celia, who had pulled herself together.

Chapter Twelve

With the help of one of the security guards who was positioned outside the villa, they got through the crowd which was waiting and watching for any signs of activity. Instead of increasing, it looked like the number of people had gone down considerably.

'I am surprised that the amount of people waiting has halved rather than doubled in number,' Sandy said as they got into the car.

'I'm not,' Dave shrugged. 'We have a media briefing in less than twenty minutes, and in particular those with cameras want to capture what is about to be said.'

By now this drive to Bridgetown had become so familiar to Sandy that he could have almost travelled the journey with his eyes shut, and when opening them know exactly where they were from the landmark they had reached.

On arriving at the police HQ, there was no time for Sandy to visit the Assistant Commissioner's office as he and Richard were already downstairs waiting for him.

They walked into an absolutely packed room with standing room only, and there were also a large number of people who couldn't get in. The cameras were clicking and flashing away at the three of them. The TV cameras were already filming.

Assistant Commissioner Seymour Garner looked

incredibly smart in full uniform and was proudly wearing his hat. The braid of the chief officer's insignia was impressive but not as much as his poise, presence and charisma.

'This afternoon,' he said, looking straight out at the crowd as he did so, 'the body of a woman was found by two people who were searching on behalf of the Barbados Police Service.' He paused to let the print journalists catch up, and, as the next words he was about to say he wanted there to be maximum impact. The room had gone deathly silent. 'The resident forensic pathologist for Barbados along with my officers attended the scene.' He gestured either side of him to Richard and Sandy. 'I am truly saddened to have to inform all of you, that we are as sure as we can be that this woman's body is that of Vivienne Jones.'

There were gasps and sighs in the audience. Members of the public who were also present, started crying, and the silence in the room where you could have heard a pin drop was now over. The TV news companies from all over the world now had their clip to start their news programmes with. The world would almost instantly know that the celebrity, the movie star, Vivienne Jones, had died.

Seymour Garner had not finished what he wanted to say, so after a small pause to let the emotion of what he had just said subside, about one of the world's most famous women now being no more, he continued. 'We do not at this time know what the cause of Miss Jones' death is, but we are carrying out a number of forensic tests and examinations over the next few days which will help us to establish this.'

He looked at Sandy to continue the briefing. Looking a little bit confused, as Seymour hadn't mentioned to him that he was to say anything, he made an enquiring face to him. Getting no response, Sandy looked out to the crowd of people.

'I, as some of you already know, am here in Barbados to act as support to the family of Vivienne Jones. I have personally spoken to both her husband and her sister and told them that Vivienne has died. I would ask the media to respect their privacy and for them to have this period to grieve in peace.'

A question came out of the audience. 'How did they take the news.'

'They are devastated, as you would expect them to be.'

'It is widely reported in the news that Adam Scott may have killed her. Is that a theory that you are working on as well?'

Not wanting to answer this question, as he felt it was not his place, Sandy looked across at Seymour Garner, who looked across at DI Richard Ambrose. He had no alternative but to answer the question.

'We are not ruling anything out. We intend to do everything we can to find out how Miss Jones died.'

The noise in the room erupted again and a question came out of the room, 'So, you are actively investigating Adam Scott for murdering his wife?'

Totally taken aback by this reaction and question, Richard didn't know what to say.

Sandy stepped in. 'No, that is not an active line of enquiry, we have an open mind on the cause of Miss Jones' death. That is different, don't read anything into the police doing their job correctly.'

Another question, this time aimed at the Assistant Commissioner. 'Why has it taken over five days to find her? What have the police been doing?'

'If Miss Jones had been visible during any of these five days, we would have found her. I am confident about this.' He did sound confident and portrayed that message effectively to the audience. 'I am not going to go into any detail now as to what actions have been taken by the police and will continue to be taken, but we have done all that we can, and I am proud of the actions of the Barbados Police Service.'

Not wanting the media briefing to go on any longer as the message that was intended to be delivered had been delivered, Seymour Garner told the audience that there would be no more questions. He thanked everyone for attending and turned on his heel and left the room with Richard and Sandy scuttling after him and out of the room.

∞

There were no words exchanged between any of them, so Richard and Sandy walked out of the police HQ and set off walking at speed to Bridgetown Central Police station. They kept glancing around to see if they were being followed but they weren't. All the journalists were either phoning in their copy of the media briefing or filming themselves to camera to give their views on what they had just been told.

They walked into some gardens that surrounded a pink rendered stone building that was an Israeli synagogue. They walked on further, coming across a monument to the emancipation and then the Montefiore Fountain. It was erected over one hundred and fifty years ago in memory of a local businessman who had died of cholera, at one time it had sprouted clean water, but no water was coming out of it at the moment.

The library was opposite them and then they headed past the law courts, an incredibly impressive array of buildings and then entered the almost adjoining central police station.

They found the rest of the team were all present in a fairly large office. Juliet was just about to say something to Paulette and Garry. Her cousin was on his phone, she stood up and gave first Sandy and then Richard a hug.

'Hey guys.' She had definitely reverted to talking like she was a Bajan from Holetown, which of course she technically was. 'I hope you are both OK after seeing the body of Vivienne. I am sure it wasn't a great experience. I am here for you both if you need me.'

The welfare-minded and the big heart of Juliet had always been an inspiration to Sandy since he had started working with her. Sandy and Richard both nodded in appreciation.

'Paulette has just asked me what I know about stalking,' Juliet continued. 'I used to investigate lots of domestic abuse in my last role before I went to work at the FCDO.'

'When I told Roger Forbes, which is what I am calling him,' Paulette said, 'that Vivienne had died, he threw himself on the floor in his cell and is sobbing like a baby. I asked DS Juliet Ashton if stalkers suffer from mental illness. He most certainly does!'

'Stalking,' Juliet explained, 'is the unwanted behaviour by an individual who is fixated or obsessed with someone and is repeated continuously, as has been the case suffered by

Vivienne Jones from the actions of Roger Forbes.'

Making sure that everyone was listening, including her cousin Dave who was now off his phone, Juliet was about to continue when Dave spoke up.

'Sorry to butt in, Juliet, but I have just had it confirmed from the border police who have checked their records and the CCTV shows that the person who entered on the BA flight on the Friday after Miss Jones went missing, was definitely our boy in the cells here, Roger Forbes.'

There were visible and loud sighs around the room as everyone had been hoping that if anything untoward had happened to Vivienne, it would have been Roger Forbes who was the culprit.

Juliet, not knowing whether it was worth her while to continue, decided to anyway. 'There are a number of types of stalkers, the most common one, which doesn't seem to fit here, is the rejected stalker. They are normally a former partner of some description, even after just a few dates. They can become fixated and obsessive.'

'It can happen with celebrities though who live their lives on social media,' Sandy said. 'The stalker feels they know them and are in a relationship with them. In the case of Vivienne though, he did know her when she was younger. He dated her sister Imogen for a short while, but then became fixated on Vivienne as he mistakenly thought her friendliness and charisma was because she was interested in him. How wrong could he be.'

'He is a sicko!' shouted Paulette.

'This type of stalker can suffer from mental health problems and needs clinical help,' Juliet continued. 'Of the other types of stalker, he fits to a certain extent the intimacy-seeking stalker as they are delusional, as he is, convinced they are in some sort of relationship with the victim.'

Richard stood up. 'I think he is a distraction to our investigation that we don't need. Paulette can you and Garry go down and speak to him and convince him that he needs to leave on the next flight to London. The one that is going this evening.'

'Inspector, surely we are going to charge him with something?' Paulette demanded.

'What, and for what purpose? No, let's get him gone, and I don't want him on the island as he will be a nuisance to Adam Scott and then to us.'

Following that very clear instruction from DI Ambrose, Paulette and Garry went off to speak firstly to Roger Forbes and then the sergeant in charge.

Richard turned to Juliet, Sandy and Dave. 'I suggest we all head back home now. It has been an exhausting and emotional day, and we have a longer day to come tomorrow.' They all nodded at him, looking tired and drained. 'In fact, Sandy and Juliet don't come in first thing tomorrow.' Looking at Juliet he said, 'Take him out for a little sightseeing before bringing him to the Queen Elizabeth Hospital for midday.'

When Dave dropped Sandy off at his hotel, Juliet, who was also in the car, asked him if he wanted to join them for dinner, but he declined. A short time on the beach before the sun went down and then a swim in the hotel pool is what he fancied more than anything.

Chapter Thirteen

The next morning, the first calls Sandy made were to his mum and grandad. They were both saying that his grandma was doing better and was on a machine that was supporting her breathing, and it was helping.

He didn't call Hannah as he knew that as it was the afternoon in the UK, that she had a conference with a police team in relation to a future case that she was going to be prosecuting in the next few weeks. He just sent her a message hoping that it all went well. For such a young barrister her career was going extremely well.

He was dressed in his work suit when Juliet arrived at his hotel to collect him. He was starting to realise that being in a hotel by himself was actually quite lonely. Although the hotel he was staying in was beautiful, on a gorgeous beach and on the incredibly lovely island of Barbados and he was also inextricably involved in a case that the whole world was watching with interest, he was missing home. He was missing his girlfriend, if Hannah was still his girlfriend, and his family greatly.

Sandy was pleased to see Juliet as not only was she a work colleague, but also a friend. They headed off and drove the short distance to St. Nicholas Abbey, which was a historical plantation house and was quite stunning set in an equally beautiful location of rolling hills and the landscape was lovely countryside. On arriving there Sandy was surprised to see Lord Andrew Lloyd-Weber walking around. Juliet thought that he must have a home on the island.

They took a tour of the seventeenth century house and heard about the history and the architecture. Juliet looked bored, having heard it all a number of times before.

While they were walking around the beautiful grounds and having had a quick look in the museum, Juliet told him, 'Roger Forbes has willingly gone back to the UK as he wants to erect a memorial to Vivienne outside her house in her home village in South Wales.'

'Won't that breach the terms of his licence?' Sandy asked. 'That condition probably won't apply now as Vivienne is dead, will it?'

'I contacted his probation officer this morning and told them that he is probably on his way home now. They say he had a licence condition that he is not to contact any member of Vivienne's family and as Imogen lives there as well, that would count.'

Deciding to contact Imogen straight away, he sent her a message to contact the local police as soon as she caught sight of Roger Forbes. The last thing Imogen needed was Roger Forbes adding to her grief.

There was no time for a visit to the rum distillery, but Juliet told him that it would be worth their time to visit if they could, depending on how long they ended up staying in Barbados.

As they drove to the Queen Elizabeth Hospital, Sandy took a call from Richard. He told him that they had found nothing else at the place where Vivienne had been washed up, so he was releasing the scene and opening it up to the public.

It was a pleasant surprise for Sandy to travel a different way into Bridgetown from the Abbey and see other views of Barbados. The weather had been glorious sunshine so far that day and the threatened rain had not yet arrived. What a contrast it was to the dreary English late autumn that Sandy's family were experiencing at home. Still, he would have loved to have been with them and be of support while his grandma was so ill.

∞

Juliet left him and went firstly to the British High Commission to brief them, then onto the police station in Holetown. Sandy wandered through the corridors of the hospital and at the rear he found the entrance to the mortuary. Waiting in a little office beside the doors to the examination room where the autopsy was going to take place, was Richard. It appeared that Dr Braithwaite had delayed the start time as he wanted some more tests carried out on Vivienne before he started. The two CSIs had been in the room helping take photographs for a while now with Dr Braithwaite organising proceedings.

After a short period of time, they were called in by one of the CSIs. Sandy could see that Richard was very apprehensive and it appeared that he had only attended a couple of autopsies in the past. Sandy patted him on the back and shoulder to emphasise that he was there with him and would support him. It was only bravado as Sandy himself was not particularly comfortable being present at an autopsy.

Barry Braithwaite greeted them as they entered and they took up a position overlooking the examination table through a Perspex screen. 'Gentlemen, welcome to my humble abode.' He laughed at his comment, which both Richard and Sandy also did out of politeness, rather than finding it humorous. 'Sorry for the delay,' said Dr Braithwaite, indicating to Vivienne's body now lying on a stainless-steel examination table.

She was face down and her hair had been shaved off. There were it seemed lots of other people present in the room: two CSIs and two others, who were probably mortuary technicians, and another woman who was busy taking down some floor spotlights and putting away a camera. They were all dressed in scrubs and had hair coverings and masks on.

'The x-ray,' Dr Braithwaite explained, 'showed a sharp fracture to the neck, very high up, just below the skull.'

The two detectives were now totally enthralled and listening intently.

'I believe this alone could have caused death, but what I don't know is when this happened. It could have been that the fall from the yacht was at an angle to cause it, or it could have happened on the yacht and she went into the water afterwards.'

'Could it have been inflicted by a third party?' Sandy asked, intrigued.

'Who knows. Yes, could have been. I have had a CT scan done as well and will get the results in the next day or so. I couldn't get an MRI scan done at this hospital at the moment.'

Just as the person with the camera and lights was about

to leave, Dr Braithwaite pointed to her and said, 'This kind lady is from our Barbados Forensic Science Centre and has just taken photographs using an alternative light source and also ultra violet photographs of the area that will show, well hopefully show, any marks in the soft tissue that are not clearly seen by the human eye on the surface of the skin.'

'Have you seen something then that makes you hopeful of finding something?' Sandy asked.

'My mind might be playing tricks, but it looks to me ,' he pointed directly at the area on the neck, 'like there are two horizontal linear tracks across here.'

He then picked up a scalpel and went straight to the neck area and using a very swift and deliberate motion sliced open the skin and after peeling it back, then pointed to the CSI who was going to take the photographs.

'As I thought, the fracture is very visible and the spinal cord has been severed. This took some force.'

Sandy looked at Richard who was looking more than a bit pale as soon as the skin was first cut.

'Just one motion or more than one?' Sandy asked.

'Just one. It could have happened hitting the water, but I wouldn't think so, albeit compounding the problem even more is that the trauma experienced by the body from ocean exposure is hard to differentiate from the trauma that occurs from foul play. Helpful...' He looked at them. 'I think not!'

'What about a stationary propeller blade like the yacht has?' Sandy asked, thinking aloud. 'If a current had pushed her back at force into it.'

'Good thinking,' Dr Braithwaite said, while looking at Richard and pointing at Sandy with his scalpel in hand. 'I can see why you brought this one in to help!'

The pathologist then continued his examination of the whole back area of Vivienne. Her feet were quite badly bitten by the fishes and were almost detached.

'I don't normally start on the back, but as we are here it makes more sense to do it this way,' Dr Braithwaite said.

When he had finished, he, with the help of the mortuary technicians, carefully turned the body over.

∞

Seeing Vivienne Jones with a fully shaved head was more than a bit unnerving, not just for the detectives, but, it seemed, for all present. An audible sigh was heard from them all. The face of the woman who had graced cinema and TV screens and giant billboards around the world still looked extremely beautiful but without her trademark long dark curly hair she looked different, very different. Surprisingly so, this was the main reason, rather than the fact she was lying on a metal table naked and dead.

Dr Braithwaite carefully examined the whole body. The moving of her body had made the smell much worse.

'Drowning almost always occurs due to the fact that people can't swim. Could Miss Jones swim?'

Richard answered, 'We presume so, because on the trip over from Antigua they often stopped to swim and snorkel.'

'I saw her swimming in that film *The Pacific*,' one of the technicians commented, 'so, she must be able to swim.'

'Not necessarily, as it could have been a body double.' the other one said, and they all laughed.

'I think I will take it that Miss Jones was able to swim,' Dr Braithwaite said, as he opened up the chest. After examining the heart macroscopically, he remarked, 'Looks a young healthy heart. I will have a look at a few tissues under the microscope though.'

Then he moved to the lungs.

'As an individual drowns, their lungs will fill with water and the ability to transfer oxygen into the bloodstream fails and as the person struggles to breathe, water is forced in. Losing your ability to breathe will lead to the oxygen in your blood falling rapidly, as a result of this the individual will lose consciousness in a very short space of time.' After a short while looking in the lungs and taking syringes of fluid for examination, he said, 'I think it is safe to say that Miss Jones had been in the water for over five days. There are occasions when it proves difficult to establish whether or not the person was alive when they entered the water; this is because that even if they were dead when they entered the water, providing the body remains submerged for a period of time, which is what we presume happened here, then the lungs will fill up anyway. I will just check this fluid is salt water not fresh water.'

'There was no bath on board the yacht, so it couldn't be a fresh water drowning then thrown into the sea,' Richard said.

Stopping and looking through his round rimmed metal glasses at Richard, the pathologist replied, 'You might think I am wasting my time but better safe than sorry with a high-profile case as this.' Having firmly established he was in charge, Dr Braithwaite continued, 'I know you detectives always want me to come up with a time of death, However, in cases like this where the body has been in the ocean, the body will have been exposed to many changes in the surrounding temperature, pH and salt content. This makes the determination of the time of death difficult. In fact, it will be impossible to establish.' Looking back at Richard, he asked, 'What was Miss Jones last meal, that might help?'

'I don't think we know, do we?' Richard said, looking at Sandy. 'Oh wait, the waiters at the restaurant told us she had fish tacos and lots of alcohol.'

'I will take stomach contents, blood and urine and let you know. Alcohol levels are moderately elevated in cases of drowning, but if it is a high figure we can make an estimate of intoxication.'

'From the information we have so far, we believe that Vivienne had a lot to drink on the evening before she went missing.'

After spending a considerable time examining every inch of the body, Dr Braithwaite came to a stop.

'The cause of death was possibly from drowning. However, also possibly from being struck on the neck by a blunt instrument and then going into the water.'

Before Richard or Sandy could ask the inevitable question, he continued.

Give me a few days to look at the marks on the neck and toxicology.' With that he left the room for the technicians to clear everything up.

One thing that Sandy was sure of was that after this very intrusive autopsy, Adam coming to see Vivienne's body was not, in his view, advisable.

Chapter Fourteen

After a leisurely walk on the beach and a quick breakfast, Sandy set off to the police station. They were that morning having a briefing, which was going to be a complete review of the investigation and devise a plan for what to do next.

The previous evening, as he hadn't wanted to eat alone in the hotel for the third night running, Juliet came and joined him at the Surfside Restaurant and bar, a place where he had either run or walked past on the beach since he had been there. It turned out to be as enticing and entertaining as he had thought and hoped for. As was, as always, Juliet's company.

Everyone in the team were arriving at the same time, and were also joined by the Crime Scene Manager, Crime Scene Investigator and, sitting ominously in the corner, was the Assistant Commissioner, Seymour Garner.

'What is he doing here?' Richard whispered to Sandy as they took up their positions at the front of the room.

The last thing any senior investigating officer enjoyed was one of their senior officers interfering with their investigation.

Richard outlined to the group what Dr Braithwaite had found out so far at the autopsy. The CSI contributed with what had happened to the samples that were now exhibits. Sandy was really impressed with Richard's comprehensive notes. Note taking was something he prided himself on, and had to admit Richard had done a good job.

'Is it a murder enquiry now?' asked Paulette.

'Not sure. Yes and no,' Richard replied.

Seymour Garner added his thoughts, 'What does your detective training, in fact your police training, tell you to do in these situations?' He looked around the room and then answered the question himself, 'To investigate with criminality in mind but do it sensitively in case it turns out not to be the case.'

'OK then, we are investigating the murder of Vivienne Jones,' Richard firmly stated.

'I don't want that terminology used outside this room,' Seymour said, backtracking, 'The media circus would be overwhelming if we do that. We should stick with the line; we have an open mind and are exploring all possibilities. I hate having to label a crime before we know if it is a crime or not.'

The CSM talked about the tests that Dr Braithwaite and the Forensic Science Centre were carrying out and warned of probable delays in timescales.

'Who are our suspects?' Richard asked as he picked up a pen and walked over to the flip chart that was behind him in the room. 'Obviously, one is the husband, Adam Scott.' He looked around and everyone nodded.

This nodding included Sandy, though reluctantly. He was compromised as he was here in Barbados in support of the family, especially Adam, and he had warmed to him greatly. When he had rung him last night and then Imogen this morning, he had just told them that the autopsy had finished and there were a number more tests that needed to be done to try and identify the exact cause of death. Neither of them queried this any further.

Richard then wrote down the name Roger Forbes. 'Not a suspect any longer is he. He wasn't on the island at the time.' Not even looking for an answer, he put a line through the name.

'The Americans, Bradley and Michael Lewis, have got to be suspects. Must be,' Juliet said, 'their whole actions were, and are, highly suspicious.'

'Yes,' Richard said writing their names down. Then he said, 'Theo Le Tissier, the yacht skipper, was there at the time, but he is an unlikely suspect, isn't he?' He looked around the room. 'Not sure what his motive could be though.'

'We will know more when we get a chance to properly speak to him and search the yacht,' Sandy said. 'What is our plan for Guernsey?'

Garry, who was sitting at the back of the room, shouted out, 'Guernsey, is that a country?'

Ignoring him, Richard said, 'I haven't thought too much about that. Sandy, is it possible to get someone from your offices in London to liaise with them and attend if necessary?'

Answering for Sandy, Juliet said, 'Leave it with me. If we are home this weekend we can do it, if not I know others in the office will happily get involved.'

'Right, we now need to think about our arrest strategy,' Sandy stated.

'Arrest!' said a startled Richard. 'Can't we just invite Adam Scott in for an interview?'

'What about the Lewis cousins?' Juliet queried. 'Surely we will have to get international arrest warrants for them?'

'Let me sort those arrest warrants out,' Seymour Garner said, wanting to be helpful. 'Dave, I will get you to give us all of their details.'

'In England, the decision to arrest,' Sandy said, 'is a two-stage one. Firstly suspicion.' He looked at Richard and Seymour. 'We have this; hence we are calling them suspects.' After seeing them nod, he said, 'The second stage is what you are talking about, and whether the arrest is necessary. We call it the necessity test.'

'I don't now remember all of the criteria fully, but I'm not sure that Adam Scott, for example, fits any of the necessity test reasons,' Juliet said. 'We could offer him the option to come in and be interviewed voluntarily. It is,' she looked at Richard, 'your discretion that counts, as the person leading this investigation.'

'As long as we are protecting both the criminal justice process and Mr Scott's legal rights, it works for me regarding him,' Sandy added. 'The criteria for a necessity to arrest is met many times over for the American cousins. Just two examples: one is, preventing any prosecution being hindered, this fits due to their disappearance; two, we need to search their catamaran.'

Everyone in the room looked at Richard Ambrose, who had slumped down onto his chair. 'Look, we have nothing in writing as yet from Dr Braithwaite, let's go round now and collect Adam Scott, not to arrest him but take him to the central police station in Bridgetown.'

∞

110

Remaining at the police station while everyone else went off were Juliet and Sandy, whose job was to research and then contact the owner in Guernsey of the *Magnificence* yacht and to contact the police there to assist. Dave Ashton was to concentrate on the Lewis cousins, and Richard with the two uniformed officers had gone off to pick up Adam.

Less than thirty minutes had passed when Sandy's phone buzzed; it was Celia Longstaff.

'It's Celia, no doubt calling to moan about Adam being carted off to Bridgetown.' He and Juliet both smiled as he answered the phone. 'Celia, what can I do for you?' he asked, trying to feign surprise that she had called.

All Celia said was, 'Get yourself round here now. Make it snappy!'

Not knowing what to think, other than to do as he was being told by Celia, Sandy stood up, encouraging Juliet to do so as well. His phone rang again. This time it was Richard.

'Mr Sandy, we have a bit of a standoff here.' The confusion in his voice was evident. 'Miss Longstaff won't let us past her to talk to Mr Scott. She wants you to come and explain things to them. Can you come here please?'

'On our way.'

The media and public had been moved much further down the road and their numbers had diminished somewhat, unlike the bunches of flowers which had not diminished, in fact these were growing into a large pile. Sitting outside the villa in the driver's seat of the marked police car was Paulette.

As they approached, she wound her window down. 'I would arrest everyone. You don't get this sort of situation happening if you do that.' Before Sandy could answer,

Paulette went on, 'What will the public think? Inviting someone who is suspected of murder in for a cosy chat. What will the man or woman on the street think? It is a murder we are investigating. I arrest for everything anyway.'

There was no answer to Paulette ranting away and Sandy understood her point but could also understand Richard's. It was really not as clear cut as how Paulette's mind worked. There was still a realistic possibility that Vivienne Jones had just drowned.

As he walked up to the front door it was opened immediately by Garry. Standing there was Celia Longstaff, only five foot tall and possibly only eight stone in weight, she was stood firmly in the way of Garry, who was almost twice her size, with huge muscles, alongside him was Richard Ambrose. It was quite, no not quite, it was a very comical sight.

'This gentleman,' Celia said, pointing at Richard, 'has come round here talking about murder and wanting to talk to Adam about it at a police station in Bridgetown.'

'Please can we at least move out of this hallway,' Sandy said, slowly moving them all forward. He could see Adam standing at the doors to the terrace, 'Mr Scott, let us in so we can explain what we need to do?'

Looking totally dishevelled and wearing the same clothes that he had had on for the last few days and unshaven, Adam Scott shouted back, 'It is not me. It's that mini stick of dynamite that is not letting them in.' He pointed to Celia. 'Celia, stop it now. You will end up getting arrested as well.'

'Don't care. Don't care at all,' she shouted back but at the same time letting Richard and Sandy past, then just stood there glaring at Garry, daring him to go past as well.

They entered the terrace and Adam slumped into his usual chair. He really did look a mess and in a state of distress.

'You are not going to be arrested,' Sandy reassured him, 'but DI Ambrose here is going to caution you.'

Adam looked up from the spot on the tiled floor that he was staring at when Sandy said the word caution.

'Richard, can you do this now? It is safer for all of us.'

There was a loud noise coming from the entrance hall along with shouting then the front door opened and slammed.

Celia walked out onto the terrace. 'Just evicted that musclebound young copper. Now let me tell you how this deal is going to work out.'

'This is not a business deal, Celia,' Sandy said.

But Celia was not listening. 'Listen to me, sonny boy. You might be the great British detective that Viscount Peveril and his sister Arabella Montague rave about, but you are going to do what I say here. Let this lump of current uselessness,' she pointed to Adam, 'get shaved, showered and changed. Then you two,' she pointed now at Richard and Sandy, 'can take him with you in an unmarked car, and return him to me as soon as possible.'

Richard looked at her sheepishly, and asked, 'Am I able to caution him now?'

'Yes, get on with it. I will get a lawyer to meet you, I presume at Bridgetown police station.'

∞

Everybody did exactly as Celia had instructed. Juliet had

gone back to Holetown police station with Paulette and Garry, which meant that Richard and Sandy could take Adam to the police station in Bridgetown.

Sitting in a chair in the interview room with a local lawyer, Adam again looked every bit the movie star that he was. Richard and Sandy sat comfortably in a side room watching the screen, ready for the interview to start.

Two local detectives walked in and introduced themselves, then one of them read out a caution.

'You have just told me your names,' Adam said, 'but who are you and where are DCI McFarlane and DI Ambrose?'

On the journey to the police station Sandy had explained to Adam that two trained specialist interviewers would carry out the interview, not them, and this was usual procedure, so he was a bit surprised that Adam was asking this.

'Well,' one of the interviewers said, 'DCI McFarlane is only a guest police officer on the Island and DI Ambrose does not normally carry out suspect interviews, but we do. So, I am afraid you are stuck with us.' He laughed, but no one else other than his colleague did.

'Suspect, am I?'

'Yes, that is why you are here. You know that don't you?'

'I don't know anything anymore really. I saw a doctor yesterday and he thinks I am suffering from Post Traumatic Stress Disorder,' Adam replied, shrugging his shoulder and shaking his head.

'We will keep this as straightforward for you as possible,' the lead interviewer said, nodding his head at Adam sympathetically, 'We have two topics to cover. Firstly, is there any past history of abuse between you and Miss Jones?'

'No, none at all!' Adam, suddenly alert, said in an indignant voice.

The second interviewer got out of a folder that he had on the table with him, a photograph of Vivienne Jones with a bruise to her face, the one that Sandy had seen online.

'Did you cause this injury to Miss Jones' face?'

'No,' even more indignant now. 'Of course not. That happened on a film set. I was not even there, and I am sure there must have been dozens of witnesses from the film crew.'

'What about verbally and also grabbing Miss Jones and pulling her?' The second interviewer handed the lead a sheet of paper with names and places. 'We have a small list of people who have witnessed numerous instances of this happening, and we haven't even started to look yet in any depth.'

'We are as bad as each other. Hot headed and emotional,' Adam replied.

'You admit to having a temper then?'

'What?' Adam shouted.

'Yes. We see you do have a very short and sharp fuse. I also need to challenge your comment about being as bad as each other. Can't you see there is a power imbalance between the two of you? Just look at your size and strength compared to Miss Jones. There is no such thing as mutual abuse.'

The lawyer gently put his hand on Adam's arm which settled him and caused him not to respond to the question and challenge.

'Tell us about the evening that Miss Jones went missing?' asked the interviewer, undeterred by the previous silence.

'I have already made a statement about that, and DS

Ashton recorded it,' Adam said quietly. He was now troubled, subdued and looked emotionally exhausted.

'We,' the lead interviewer said, nodding at his colleague, 'have both read your statement, the transcript and have seen the video.' *Very impressive*, thought Sandy. 'We have also seen the statements from the waiters and barmen at the marina club. You lost your temper with Miss Jones, didn't you? And you were seen to grab her.'

'I didn't, did I?' Adam said, looking at them both and then at his lawyer. He looked totally lost.

They showed him a still photograph from the CCTV of him grabbing Vivienne, at which point he put his head in his hands and started sobbing. Was the movie star playing his greatest role or was he genuinely upset? Hopefully, time would tell.

After giving him a little time to recover, the lead interviewer said, 'Following the autopsy the pathologist states that Miss Jones' neck had been broken.'

'What!' Adam shrieked. 'Would she have been in pain?'

'Do you know how this could have occurred? Is there a plausible explanation for this injury?'

'Not that I can think of. I was drunk I went to bed and my memory, because of this PTSD, is getting hazier about that night with each day that passes.'

Undeterred, the interviewer went on, 'Dr Braithwaite the pathologist says this was possibly caused by her having been struck on the neck by a third party. Was that third party you, Mr Scott? In a fit of temper?'

The lawyer intervened, '*Possibly* seems a bit of a loose term to bring in Mr Scott to be interviewed, doesn't it?'

'We felt that it was only fair to Mr Scott to put the emerging allegations and circumstances to him at the earliest stage. Did you cause this injury, that might have killed her, Mr Scott?'

There was no answer as Adam had his elbows on the table, head in hands and was crying.

His lawyer said, 'Come on officers, this is pointless, using terms like "possibly" and "might". I suggest that we call this interview to a halt until you have something more definite.'

Chapter Fifteen

The lawyer had agreed to take Adam back to his villa, which allowed Richard and Sandy, following a quick debrief of the interviewers, to head straight to the police station in Holetown. They were probably more than half-way there when Sandy's phone started buzzing. On looking at the caller ID he saw it was Celia. The last thing he wanted to do was answer it and listen to her berating him. But he knew he had to, and did.

'There are videos and pictures online of Vivienne's body. A police officer must have leaked them,' Celia shouted; she was furious, but at the same time had a sadness to her voice. 'This is outrageous! Someone is going to pay for this. Do you know how distressing this is. Adam has come home in a heap. I can't let him see these images; it will finish him off. It will destroy him.'

Both Richard and Sandy's phones seemed to be on overload. Richard had a call coming in from Seymour Garner and at the same time one from Dave Ashton. Sandy had a call from Imogen Jones and then from Dave Ashton and Seymour Garner, both of whom had clearly given up calling Richard. He was driving and not answering the phone to anyone, not that he wanted to anyway when Sandy told him what Celia had said.

What a mess, Sandy thought. *Now pause and breathe*, he said to himself. Who should he speak to first? It had to be Imogen. Richard turned the car around to head back to Bridgetown and Sandy rang Imogen.

'Imogen, if you have been calling me about the photos and videos, we are onto to it now and we will get them stopped as soon as we can.'

Imogen could hardly speak, she was so upset. 'It is vile,' were the only words that she could mutter.

On reaching the police headquarters, Dave Ashton was waiting for them.

'Boss,' he said to both Richard and Sandy, addressing them as one. 'We have established the images are on Facebook. The videos are on TikTok and YouTube.'

'Who has posted them? Which police officer? I will do them. I really will!' Richard said furiously.

Both Sandy and Dave looked at him, they had never seen him anything but mild mannered even when extremely stressed. He really was hopping mad.

'We need to go and see the Assistant Commissioner now!'

They went into the building and almost ran up the stairs into Seymour Garner's office, who was sitting at his desk waiting for them.

Everyone in the office looked at Dave Ashton to continue his update.

'YouTube have taken the video down immediately on us asking. They did say they had done it on finding it themselves anyway. Tik Tok have it in hand and will do so worldwide in the next hour. Facebook are playing a bit slower as the image is not clear and is of a body bag being carried rather than a body and the hits on the post are going viral, but they do say it will be off their site as soon as they can.'

Everyone in the room breathed a sigh of relief.

'I have seen the video,' said Seymour, 'and it is from a little distance away, clearly on a camera phone. Although you can make out it's a body, you would have no idea it is Miss Jones. We know it is her due to where the image is from, and the body being placed in the body bag and taken away up an incline to the funeral directors' vehicle. Could it have been one of them, rather than a member of the Barbados Police?'

'You know we have been plagued by social media investigators, sending images from all over the island showing them investigating the disappearance. This is one of them that has been posting,' Dave said. He looked around and seeing everyone was following his every word, he then continued, 'It is one of our search volunteers, he must have been in the area as well as the two that found her. He goes by the name of Justice-Marlon.'

Banging his fist on his desk, Seymour stood. 'Thank goodness it is not a police officer.'

Looking firstly at Seymour but also then at Richard and Dave, Sandy added, 'You did though state at the media briefing that the search volunteers were part of the Barbados police, and as a result you had found her body.'

Seymour sat down again in a heap. 'Damn! Oh dear! I did say that didn't I? Who vetted them?' He looked straight at Richard who just shrugged his shoulders as he had no idea, he just accepted all the help he could get. 'Where is this Justice-Marlon, now?'

'His name is Marlon Rochford, and he lives in St Lawrence

Gap,' Dave said.

'Why are you still here then?' Seymour asked all of them, while ushering them out of his office as he no doubt had to brief his bosses. 'I want him arrested within the hour.'

∞

St Lawrence Gap, just known as "The Gap" by locals, was a short drive onto the south coast from Bridgetown. They parked at the St Lawrence Church and waited for the others in the team to arrive from Holetown. The church was a pretty, white-washed building, built in 1837, and was in the centre of St. Lawrence Gap. It seemed to Sandy an odd place for it to be situated, surrounded by dozens of bars and restaurants. The location though was in fact stunning. The sound of the sea crashing on the rocks below added to the effect and gave it a peaceful feel while at the same time, because of the church being there, a spiritual feeling.

"The Gap" itself was a small street, but the area was known for its 1.3 km length, that was a combination of million-dollar apartments, which were on the coast side, opposite low budget accommodation on the inland side of the highway, which is where Marlon Rochford lived.

Following a briefing from Richard, the team separated and walked across Highway Seven to the block of apartments where Marlon was believed to be living. Paulette and Garry went to the first floor and up to the front door. Around the back of the block went Juliet and Dave. Standing further back taking in the whole scene were Richard and Sandy. Apparently, according to Richard, the troops should do the work and the senior officers should supervise. Not quite Sandy's style, but it was not his show.

As they watched the officers approach the door, the butterflies started to build and the tension began to rise. Bang, bang! The glass on the door reverberated as Paulette not very subtly knocked. The plastic blinds on the window twitched.

'He is home,' Garry said so loudly that everyone could hear, 'I saw someone inside.'

The children and local people hanging around outside had already stopped to stare at the uniform cops as they walked by. They went totally quiet hearing the door being banged so loudly. They too like Richard and Sandy were witnessing the scene.

The door was banged again, and Paulette shouted, 'Open up Marlon, it's the police.'

The door did open and standing there was not Marlon but a grey-haired older woman wearing a short skirt with an apron tied around it and a red coloured top. She was most probably Marlon's mother.

'He's not here. Why do you want him? Is it because he is a hero, having helped to find that movie star?' the woman said.

Not waiting for a reply, Paulette barged past her followed by Garry and they went quickly into the apartment leaving the woman to close the door behind them.

After a few moments a man cycled up on a new mountain type cycle. He had shoulder length tight dreadlocks; he wore long white shorts and a colourful shirt.

'That's him,' Richard said. 'He was one of the search volunteers that I briefed the first day.'

Not waiting for any more comment from Richard and

needing no more invitation, Sandy was off running from where they were standing across the street up to the man as he alighted his bike. The small crowd turned from looking at the now closed door to the white man in a suit running towards the man and his bike. On seeing him approach, the man with dreadlocks got back on his bike and swung around the flaying and failing arms of Sandy who tried to grab him.

There were shouts of, 'Go on, Marlon!' from an onlooker.

Sandy hoped Richard who was following behind had a better chance to grab him, but with the smallest of swerves Marlon was past him as well.

The chase was on, and in normal circumstances they wouldn't have stood a chance, but it appeared Marlon had decided to cross Highway Seven to get to the beach, where cars were steadily going by in both directions. It seemed that using the cycle to cross was slowing him down as Sandy made good progress and was catching up with him. The scene behind him involved a fast-moving Paulette and Garry catching them up but a slower Richard was still some distance behind.

Marlon turned around and dismounted his bike, he put on a Gro Pro camera that he had fixed to the headband he was wearing.

Looking straight at Sandy, he said loudly, 'Police oppression,' then picked up and threw his bike at Sandy, clattering into him and almost knocking him to the floor.

With that he was gone, across the highway with car horns blaring as he ran across the road. Pushing the bike out of the way and being now caught up by Paulette, they crossed the road, cars stopping at the sight of the police uniform.

On reaching the beach area they found it extremely busy. The beautiful white sand beach was not quite full of people, but plenty were there, making finding Marlon harder as he was nowhere to be seen.

An out of breath Richard had also arrived and he told Paulette and Garry to head west towards Dover Beach. He and Sandy would look around where they were now. Richard told them to look in all the bars and restaurants dotted about. When Dave and Juliet arrived, he got them to head east along the beach front towards Bridgetown.

Taking a methodical approach and dividing up each section of the beach into rectangles, which included any bar or restaurant areas, they scanned each section. It became obvious after completing the first section that Marlon could just go out of the bar or restaurant and onto the road, so Richard moved Juliet and Dave to just stay the roadside and scan the crowds for anyone fitting Marlon's description.

They completed section after section, getting more despondent that they weren't finding him as they moved through the beach. Richard had a growing fear racking his whole body of returning to Police HQ, without the prisoner and facing the wrath of the Assistant Commissioner.

Suddenly, along the way to the west of them were shouts coming from a bar and Marlon came hurtling out followed at speed by Paulette with Garry only metres behind. People who had been lying peacefully on sun loungers or towels were shrieking as there was sand flying everywhere and they were worried about being stood on.

He had almost reached the sea when Paulette grabbed Marlon and pulled him to the floor giving both of them a mouthful of sand. In one swift movement Garry was also on him and they pulled Marlon to his feet and handcuffed him behind his back.

'Police brutality,' Marlon was shouting, 'I have got it all on film.'

As he said this Paulette ripped the headband off him and shoved it in her pocket and they unceremoniously marched Marlon off the beach onto the road.

The Ashtons had gone off to collect the two police cars. Dave then took the prisoner and the two uniformed officers to Bridgetown Central Police Station, and Juliet took Richard and Sandy to see the Assistant Commissioner who wanted to see them again.

Sitting opposite each other in the interview room were Marlon and Garry. Paulette sat to one side and had decided to let Garry lead the interview. Marlon had declined having a lawyer, so it was just the three of them.

After the formalities of introductions and cautions had been completed, Garry said in an almost threatening way, 'I can't believe that you would post online photographs and videos of a dead body and of that beautiful woman Vivienne Jones.'

Looking straight at Garry and in exasperation, Paulette said, 'We went through this when we planned the interview, Garry. Open question like, How, where, why, when. Not I can't believe.'

'Well, I can't believe him,' Garry said, pointing at Marlon. 'Who would do that sort of thing?'

'I am right here,' Marlon huffed. 'Shouldn't you two be

talking to me not each other?'

'Why did you do it?' Garry asked, nodding at Paulette while he said it.

'I am a social media sleuth. I fight for justice. I felt my public needed to know what actions the police were taking. It was in the public interest.'

'No, it is not. It is not in anyone's public interest and definitely not in Miss Jones' family's interest.' Seeing Paulette glare at him again, Garry then said, using an open question, 'How do you think the family feel about these images being broadcast all over the world?'

For the first time, Marlon looked subdued. 'I am sorry, I didn't think about them. Maybe I should have.'

'Yes, you should have,' said Garry. Then remembering that he needed to ask open questions, he added, 'When did you go inside the cordon to take the videos?'

'I didn't. I was the next one along from the other two searching, when they found the body. I just hung around to try and take a video of the examination of the body. I couldn't get close enough without being seen until the body was moved for the undertaker to take her away.'

'Have you made any more copies other than the one you have taken on your phone and posted online?'

'No. You have my phone and I saw that my posts had been taken down.'

'You do realise that you are in lots of trouble now, don't you?' Garry asked.

'Yes, but it might have been worth it as my Tik Tok post made over one hundred thousand views in the few hours it was a live feed.'

Chapter Sixteen

No sooner had they arrived in Seymour Garners office he took them off to the Deputy Commissioners office. The look between Richard and Sandy as they followed along the corridor was one of apprehension. This was not going to be a nice experience. Juliet Ashton was nowhere to be seen, probably hiding out of the way.

Standing behind his desk was the immensely tall Carlos Bishop. He was in full uniform and the atmosphere in the room was as intense as his angry face. Carlos motioned for the two of them to sit. Seymour Garner had opened the door for them and had almost pushed them inside. He must have made a hasty retreat as he was now nowhere to be seen.

Making no attempt to sit, Carlos started not by shouting but spitting out his comments staccato style, 'What a total debacle! That first media briefing was awful – no, horrendous. Your idea, I presume?' He thrust his thick index finger at Sandy.

Careful not to say anything so as not to aggravate the man anymore, Sandy just nodded, it didn't matter if it was his idea or not.

Then, thrusting the same finger forwards at Richard, he snarled, 'And you made out that the incredible and well-loved Vivienne Jones was an alcoholic and had fallen in the water.'

'I didn't exactly say that, did I?' Richard was not as politically smart as Sandy.

This comment made Carlos Bishop erupt. 'Might as well have done. The idiot at the marina had already told the media she had been drinking. You should have been alert to that. Look you two, stop talking, I need you to just listen.'

He paused momentarily to see that both Richard and Sandy understood. They both nodded sheepishly.

'Then her body is found by some volunteers, they are not Barbados Police officers. How embarrassing. We then try to claim it was us that found her.'

Richard wanted to interrupt, but it was best not to prod the beast now shouting at them.

'Then another of these so-called volunteers films and broadcasts everything.'

'We have caught him, and he is currently in custody,' Richard said, bringing about a slight abatement of the rage. This seemed new information to him.

'Then you let the prime suspect for Miss Jones' murder go. Why haven't you charged Adam Scott with her murder. It is obvious to everyone, including the worlds media, that it is him that has done this, and we had him in our grasp.'

Was this a question? Richard and Sandy looked at each other as to who should answer it.

It wasn't a question, as Carlos continued, pointing at Sandy. 'You need to now leave Barbados and take your sergeant with you and we will say thanks for nothing.' He then pointed at Richard and said, 'You need to get on and solve this murder and put Adam Scott behind bars before I have you walking the beat here in Bridgetown as a constable.'

The two of them got out of the office as fast as they could, practically running out of the door and down the corridor.

'I wonder what he does all day?' Sandy mused. 'He has no computer or paperwork on his desk.'

'He pokes pins into an effigy of you,' Richard replied, making them both laugh loudly.

Seymour Garner was waiting for them. 'How did that go boys?' he asked.

'He has told me to leave and go back to England,' Sandy said.

'Maybe for the best. Don't you think? You have been incredibly helpful but not much more to do here at the moment is there?'

Richard, on the other hand, did not think this was a good idea. 'I think he should stay for at least another few days. It would be incredibly useful to us. Well to me.'

'I am happy to leave. I can still be involved in the investigation and the yacht will be back in Guernsey next week, so I can lead on that, and we can have video conferences,' Sandy said, actually quite keen to grab the opportunity to get home to his family.

'That is decided then,' Seymour said. 'Book your flights for tomorrow and thank you so much for everything. I am sure you will be back as and when needed.' With that he went back into his office and closed the door behind him.

They walked back down the stairs to look for Juliet and give her the news that they were going home. Although she regarded Barbados as her home, Juliet had seemed in the last few days or so to be pining for her husband and children, so the news would be welcome. Sandy put his arm around

Richard and comforted him as he was looking very forlorn and quite alone.

∞

The next morning when Sandy awoke, he saw that he had received a message from his mum that only said one word, *Good*.

He had sent a message to her telling her that he was coming back to England and would land early Friday morning. He had sent a similar message to Hannah who had sent a slightly longer reply but not much, *Let's meet up Saturday. Either in Ely or Cambridge. You choose*.

He checked out of the hotel after having one last lingering look at the beach and the Caribbean Sea, and went with his bags to Holetown police station. This was another place he would miss. The police station was and had been a lovely place to work.

The first topic on the briefing was the outcome of the interview with Marlon Rochford.

Standing up and looking pleased with himself was Garry. 'Following a confession…'

Paulette could be seen rolling her eyes.

'… Marlon was charged with a public nuisance offence and will appear in court in a month's time.'

As Garry sat down there was a murmur in the room of "well done", not just to Garry but also Paulette whose athletic prowess had again contributed to the arrest of this offender.

Last night Sandy had notified Imogen of the arrest and the taking down of the post. He was fully aware that it was

130

the middle of the night in Wales, but he had sent a message anyway and had a reply waiting for him this morning just saying thank you. He would call later to tell her of the charge and court date. At the same time, he had let Celia know; no message of thanks from her, she just messaged the word, *Good.*

The team went through the outstanding tasks and actions that needed doing. Firstly, they had found out that *Magnificence* was still a long way off Guernsey, the weather in the Atlantic had not been kind to it. When Sandy had contacted the investment bank that owned this yacht and two other similar yachts, they had been very obliging and had given him full written permission to have the yacht completely searched on its arrival into St Peter Port. The current prediction of arrival was not until the following Wednesday or Thursday. Juliet and Sandy had agreed with Richard that they would lead on this part of the investigation.

The catamaran had been sighted a few times in the last few days, but the international arrest warrant had not been granted as yet for its search and the apprehension of Bradley and Michael Lewis. There was something just not right about them, everyone in the room had that feeling, but did that feeling amount to them being the ones that had harmed Vivienne? Maybe yes, maybe no. Dave Ashton was going to lead on this part of the investigation.

Richard was going to wait until Monday before he started troubling Dr Braithwaite for an update, he told Sandy that he would inform him as soon as he heard anything. The CSI had sent everything in for analysis and they knew that the Barbados Forensic Science Centre was helping with the possibility of there being a mark on the back of Vivienne's neck.

After a long and involved discussion, it was decided that there was nothing else that could be done with Adam Scott at the present time. This was despite the deputy commissioner telling Richard and Sandy that Adam was the murderer. What did he know, Richard and Sandy laughed together.

Richard was even able to mimic Carlos Bishop. 'That first media interview was horrendous.'

They and the others all laughed together, brave now that they were not sitting in his presence.

As there was still a couple of hours before Juliet and Sandy needed to leave for the airport, Sandy sat with Richard and the two of them went through the case to date, meticulously ensuring everything that had been done was written up accurately in both notebooks and a key decision log. This was a strength of Sandy's that had stood him in good stead in the past and he could see that Richard understood how important it was too.

∞

As Juliet and Sandy arrived in the departure terminal after having been dropped off by Paulette and Garry, waiting for them were Juliet's mum and dad. They had been given strict instructions not to be there by Juliet, but clearly they had taken no notice. Juliet's mum, for a change, while still dressed beautifully, was not wearing any vibrant clothing, just jeans and a blouse.

The tears were flowing from all three of them as they

hugged, Sandy was sorely tempted to go in for a group hug, but he just shook hands and proceeded to join the busy British Airways check-in queue for the flight to London.

After they had made their way through security, they wandered round the few shops offering duty free and other souvenir goods. Although the boarding gate wasn't showing on the overhead display boards yet, the British Airways aircraft was in position, so Sandy made himself comfortable, sitting in a row at the front by the desk. He put his earbuds in and listened to music while reading a book that he had with him. He had saved a place for Juliet beside him.

A commotion, unrest and noise was building all around the boarding gate, so much so that Sandy could hear it over the music playing in his ears. He looked up from his book to see what was going on. Standing at the priority desk in front of him talking to a member of staff, was Adam Scott, and standing a little way back from him was Celia Longstaff.

Jumping up in surprise, Sandy walked over to the two of them. A number of people were asking Sandy to get out of the way, as they were trying to get a better view of the movie star or take a photograph of him on their phone.

Showing equal surprise, Adam and Celia looked at Sandy walking towards them.

'What are you both doing here?' Sandy asked.

'We could ask you the same thing, DCI McFarlane,' Adam said, smiling and taking his sunglasses off, which seemed to trigger more photographs being taken. 'I am going home. I need to see my two daughters.'

'Does DI Ambrose know that you are leaving Barbados? Are you allowed to leave?'

Celia pushed her way forward. 'How are you going to stop him? He is not under arrest, not out on bail and has no conditions to remain here.'

'Just wait there a moment. Let me call DI Ambrose,' Sandy said, as Juliet arrived.

Luckily, Richard answered straight away. 'Missing me already, Sandy? Has your flight been delayed or cancelled, and you want me to arrange a pick-up?'

'No, just listen a minute. I am at the gate ready to board the plane and standing with me is Adam Scott.' He waited for this information to register. 'Did you know he is leaving the country and what do you want me to do?'

The silence was so long that the feeling of panic and indecision from Richard was palatable.

'I don't think we can stop him. Can we?' Richard eventually replied.

Not really needing to think about it, Sandy said, 'Yes, we can if you want me to arrest him.'

He had the sinking feeling that he might not be going to be going home after all.

The wait was even longer for a response this time.

'What else would we talk to him about?'

'We could bail him with a condition to remain here until after we get the autopsy report. We would then have something else to talk to him about. That should be next week. Possibly even early next week.' Sandy was aware that he needed a decision fairly quickly, as Adam and Celia were getting restless. No doubt first class passengers would be boarding at any time.

'Let him go,' Richard said. 'I don't want to cause an

134

international incident. You do support me on this, don't you Sandy?'

'Yes, of course,' Sandy said. 'Write down your decision now and why you are making it in case someone questions you about it.'

Sandy did absolutely support him, but wondered whether they were letting their prime suspect for the murder of his wife slip out of the country.

Walking back to Adam, who was flirting unmercifully with Juliet and the female member of staff, Sandy said, 'Mr Scott, where will you be staying in England? Eaton Square, I presume?'

'No. I have a home in Sussex near where my daughters live, and I intend to go there. I will occasionally go to Eaton Square for a few days. I may visit Swansea in South Wales to see Imogen and to discuss a memorial service and eventually a funeral.'

'Can you always ring me or message me to say where you are residing, when you move about?' Sandy asked.

Jumping in and answering for Adam, Celia said, 'Yes, of course, and can you always ring us or message us to keep us up to date on what is happening in the case.'

Knowing that he was playing with someone who was a formidable chess player, Sandy just nodded and pulled Celia to one side.

'I presume you persuaded him,' he whispered, pointing to Adam, 'to not go and see Vivienne's body.'

'Yes, it is for the best, isn't it?' Celia, for once, sounded unsure.

'In my opinion, yes,' Sandy confirmed. 'However, when

Vivienne's body is repatriated, you might need to think about it again.'

The first-class passengers, including Adam and Celia, were then called forward and they went off to board the plane. When Sandy turned right on boarding the airplane, he did wistfully think what it might be like to turn left once in a while.

Chapter Seventeen

The whole world seemed to have landed at London Heathrow at the same time the next morning. After having a fairly sleepless night, a very bleary-eyed Juliet and Sandy made their way to the baggage belt just as they could see in the distance Adam and Celia making their way to the exit. Clearly the bags had arrived for them to collect.

As soon as Sandy had switched his phone back on, he felt it buzzing, he had missed calls from his mum. *So early,* he thought, *what's going on?* He didn't have long to wait before his phone rang again.

'I presume you have landed. Please come straight to Addenbrookes hospital to see your grandma.'

'Is she bad?'

'Yes, very bad. See you as soon as you can get here.'

Letting Juliet know what was happening, and accepting her brief, wordless hug of support, he ran out of the exit and the terminal. He was beyond pleased to see waiting the two cars that the Foreign, Commonwealth and Development office had sent for him and Juliet. He jumped into his car and asked the driver to please take him as quick as he could to Addenbrookes hospital in Cambridge, rather than his home in Ely.

The M25 motorway around London was an absolute

nightmare and the journey was very slow. Sandy kept looking at his phone waiting for an update, but none came.

Getting out of the car directly in the entrance way to the hospital, Sandy had a foreboding feeling. Even though he was carrying his bags, he leapt up the stairs towards the ward where his grandma was.

Waiting outside the side room which must have been his grandma's room, were his mum and grandad. He looked at them and knew, he just knew, that his grandma had gone, she had died. Sandy burst into tears and started sobbing, as did his mum and grandad, hugging each other in that lonely, empty and silent hospital corridor.

'I should have gone and seen her before I went. I should have come home sooner,' Sandy wailed. 'I am so sorry. I am so very sorry.'

'Don't be sorry. Your grandma was so very proud of you and she would have wanted you to be doing exactly what you were doing,' his grandad said. 'When she saw you on TV at that press conference last week, she was so proud, saying "look at our boy Alexander".'

She was the only family member who ever occasionally called him by his real first name. Now, never to happen for him again.

'Can I go in and say goodbye and spend a little time with her please?' Sandy asked, looking at them both for permission.

'Yes, the nursing staff have left everything until you got here,' his mum reassured him. 'Your dad has just taken your sisters home and I will take you and Grandad Tom back when you are ready, son.'

As he walked into the small room that had a bed in the middle of it, he saw two machines one that was a monitor that was switched off and the other must have been the machine that had done the breathing for her in the last few days. The room was quiet, in total eery silence.

Pulling up the chair a bit closer to his grandma, Sandy looked at her and although dead, she looked just as he pictured her and always would. He kissed her lightly on her cheek and sat down holding her hand. Sandy came to the realisation that he didn't want to say goodbye to his grandma because he never would; she, like his other grandma who had died a few years earlier would always be with him, there was no goodbye required.

He just sat there holding her hand and telling her how much he loved her and how lucky he had been to have her play such an active part of his life and he would always do all that he could to make her proud of him. The tears just rolled and rolled down Sandy's face.

Saying a final prayer, giving her a final kiss and smiling ruefully at his grandma, he got up and walked out of the room, resolutely knowing that he now needed to be strong for the rest of his family.

∞

The journey home was not subdued because each of them told amusing or fond memories of Margaret, their wife, mother and grandmother. Sandy told them of the time he had bunked off school (he had gone to the King's school in Ely) and was sitting in a café in the high street, when, his grandma had walked by. They both looked squarely at each other and after she had winked at him, she had walked on by, and never told anyone, even his mum.

On arrival at the family home on the riverside of the Great River Ouse, both of Sandy's sisters were there, but neither of their husbands were. He presumed that his youngest sister, Isla, was having marriage problems, as the last time he had seen her she had also been there without him and had been very upset. He also presumed that his sister Aileen's husband was looking after their two boys. Those two boys would really miss their great-grandma as she often helped out by looking after them and they had formed a loving bond.

Within a few moments of getting in the house the wave of grief hit them all again and they started crying almost in unison. Sandy knew the waves of grief and loss would hit them all differently and at various times, but with his grandma only dying that morning their loss felt extremely raw and the pain of it hurt incredibly.

Retreating to the privacy of his bedroom, Sandy got changed and sorted out his clothes for the washing that his mum wanted to get on and do. The normality of mundane daily life seemed a bit strange after what they had and were experiencing.

After letting Juliet know what had happened, Sandy phoned his boss D/Supt Jane Watson, who had just listened and told him to take as much time as he needed and to not come into London and the office at the beginning of next week, but to take it as compassionate leave. Jane was a great boss to work for. What Sandy did do though, was send her an email update on exactly where they were up to on the death of Vivienne Jones enquiry. Also, the Guernsey part of it that he may or may not need someone else to help Juliet out with.

When Sandy got downstairs, he saw that his other grandad, John McFarlane, had arrived. He did know that anyway as he heard his old diesel Mercedes car pull up at the rear of the house.

Looking at his two grandfathers sitting morose on the sofa, Sandy said, with the encouragement of his mum, 'Why don't the three of us go out and get some fresh air and have a walk around the block.'

'Far too cold,' Tom said, and he was right – the difference in temperature to Barbados was striking.

'Not sure if my knee will be up to walking that far,' murmured John.

'I will tell you both all about my case in Barbados and the death of Vivienne Jones as we walk around,' Sandy offered.

That was all the encouragement they needed, the retired senior detective and retired family court judge were always fascinated by Sandy's cases, and in particular a high-profile case like this.

They walked through Jubilee Gardens and across the road and along to Cherry Hill Park. This was the route that Sandy had always taken to walk to school, and it had a stunning side view of Ely Cathedral. They stopped and looked across the meadow to the cathedral and pulling his coat tighter and his hat down to keep the cold of the late English autumn out, Sandy told them what had happened in Barbados.

'That first media briefing wasn't brilliant, was it?' Tom said laughing.

This walk out is doing him some good, Sandy thought.

'Not your finest hour, my boy,' John added.

Sandy wanted to protest that he actually hadn't done too badly, it was the other two, but he knew from experience that was pointless with his grandfathers, who both had incredibly quick intellect and wit.

'So it looks like murder then, Sandy?' Tom asked.

'Not definitely at the moment,' John, always the barrister, argued, 'I mean based on what is currently known, it is going to be hard to prove murder.'

'I am hoping we will get some more autopsy results back early next week that might help.'

'If it is murder, it will be Adam Scott,' Tom said. 'The vast majority of women that are murdered are killed by their current or ex-partner. That is where you must concentrate your efforts.'

'I know that when I was sitting in the family court, we were very aware that two to three women every week were being killed at the hands of their partners or ex-partners,' John said. 'It used to amaze me in custody disputes the bitterness to each other, and I was very aware of the risks posed to mostly women, but not always, by the men involved.'

∞

The walk around the block as Sandy called it, didn't take place, as his mum had called and said that lunch was almost ready. As they walked home back the way they had come, Sandy told them about the other suspects, the American cousins and then the skipper of the yacht Theo Le Tissier.

'If she had gone to their boat or been picked up by them,'

142

Tom said, 'they are also clearly suspects,'

'You can't prove that happened though, can you?' John argued.

'Only what Theo said about hearing a small boat engine and then the yacht's small boat being found having gone adrift,' Sandy said.

'What motive, then?' John asked.

'Vivienne found out that they were dealing in drugs, or they tried to have sex with her and she turned them down?' Sandy offered.

'Any sign on the autopsy of sexual molestation?' John enquired.

'Dr Braithwaite took swabs but what with being in the water all those days and the decomposition, he holds out little or no hope,' Sandy said. 'Their actions towards the police were extremely suspicious though.'

'What do you know about the skipper of the boat?' Tom asked. 'Did you say his name was Theo Le Tissier?'

'Very little,' Sandy replied, 'other than he was a relief skipper for the yacht but had worked on the yacht from time to time. We will hopefully learn a lot more next week.'

On entering the house, they found that Isla had gone off with Aileen to her house for the afternoon. Leaving Sandy with his mum, dad, and grandfathers.

Following lunch, Sandy sent a message to Celia asking if they had got home safely and, presumably, they were at the address in Sussex. The reply he got was typical cryptic Celia, *Yes, home safely to my address in London.* Sandy didn't know what her address in London was, so felt a bit stumped. Then only a couple of minutes later, Celia sent another message, saying, *Sadly, I know it isn't me darling that you are interested in. Adam is at his home address in Sussex. Happy now?* Yes, he was happy and sent a message to Richard letting him know where their prime suspect was now.

Sandy declined the offer to go with his mum and grandad to get some change of clothing, as Tom was going to stay with them for a few days. They were also going to think about how best in the coming days to deal with Margaret's clothes. Visiting the house without his grandma present was something he knew he would have to face at some time, but not so early on. He also declined the offer to go food shopping with his dad as the house had a lot more people in than it normally did, and extra food stocks were needed.

As it turned out, not going out, was a very good move for Sandy, because when he opened the door following a knock, he found that Hannah had turned up. They fell into each other's arms and Sandy found himself again crying, while they embraced.

'I came as soon as I could get away from court,' Hannah said. 'I am so sorry for all of you. What an incredible woman your grandma was.'

'Hearing my grandma spoken about in the past tense, is going to take some getting used to,' Sandy said, pulling himself together and moving to put the kettle on for a cup of tea. He looked at Hannah expectantly. 'Are you going to stay with me— us for the weekend?'

'I would like to but only if you want me to. Your mum sent me a message this morning, telling me how sad she was that you had not made it to the hospital to see your grandma before she died. Let's just get through the next few weeks until after the funeral before we sit down and work out what the future looks like for the both of us. Shall we?'

He was not able to answer and only had time to nod, before their peace was shattered, as in walked both of his sisters, Aileen's husband, and his two nephews who had just been collected from school.

Chapter Eighteen

The weekend could best be summed up as full of people, this was not just family members in and out of the house but also so many visitors calling or messaging. Sandy's grandma had been incredibly well loved by all.

Hannah and Sandy shared a long walk on the Saturday. They had walked from Sandy's home, travelling the same route up through Cherry Hill Park that Sandy had taken with his grandfathers, gazing over for a lingering view at the cathedral then on past his grandparents' house which Sandy found not as unsettling as he thought it would be, in fact it was comforting to see their home. Hannah and Sandy spoke incessantly about their work, but not about their relationship as they went along ancient droves and tracks to the village of Little Downham, which had an interesting church, St Leonard's. They then continued in a circular route back to Ely eventually reaching the meadows along the River Great Ouse, and then back to the madness and busyness that was the McFarlane home at that time.

On the Sunday, although originally saying he would go, Sandy eventually decided he wouldn't be able to cope with going to the service in the cathedral that morning and everyone telling him what a wonderful person his grandma was. He knew that anyway.

His youngest sister Isla's husband had turned up late on the Friday evening with their lovely dog and they seemed to be happy together, so Sandy was unsure what had been the problem with his sister, obviously it was not something to do with her husband. Maybe the problem with his own relationship with Hannah had caused Sandy to jump to a wrong conclusion. They had left early Sunday morning and headed home to Durham.

Everyone had left Hannah and Sandy alone in the house that Sunday morning, the peace and the chance to be alone they found lovely, even if it was only for a short time. Very much enjoying being together, they both came to the conclusion that they were most probably going to be OK after all. Even when his phone buzzed telling him he had a call coming in, Sandy didn't leap up and answer it.

As it turned out, maybe he should have done. When the caller rang back, Sandy saw it was Imogen Jones.

'I am sorry I didn't answer earlier, Imogen. What can I do for you on this Sunday morning?'

'He is here again. He is driving me crazy.'

'Who is there?' Sandy asked, having no idea who she was on about. Surely Imogen was not talking about Adam?

'Roger Forbes, or whatever he calls himself. We have thousands, and I mean literally thousands of flowers that have been laid on the floor by the front garden wall. He is standing out there as if he is in charge of everything.'

'Have you called the police?'

'Yes. Yesterday one of them chased after him but couldn't catch him.'

They need a Constable Paulette Weekes to catch him,

thought Sandy.

Imogen continued, 'I am starting to feel trapped in the house because I don't want to meet up with him.'

'Take pictures of him there and I will get the local police and his probation officer to try and stop him.'

'No need for pictures, I have him on the CCTV that we installed a few years ago because of him.'

'OK, I will call the South Wales Police in the morning, but if he comes into the garden call the police straight away.'

'He won't do that. It is me that feels trapped in here and not able to even go into the front garden because of him,' Imogen said. 'When will we get my sister's body released so I can get her home and think about a funeral? We will need to use the cathedral in Swansea for the service and then I am going to have her buried next to our mum and dad in the local churchyard.'

The thought of funerals was something very much on Sandy's mind with all of the planning going on in his house for his grandma's.

'We are hoping to speak to the forensic pathologist from Barbados early next week. I will try and push him for an update on the release of Vivienne then and let you know.'

∞

The priority for Sandy on Monday morning was that he had been asked to help with the registration of the death of his grandma. His grandpa John had taken Hannah home to Cambridge after lunch on the Sunday, and due to her having some spare time on Monday morning they were going to meet up after he had been to see the registrar.

The coroner's office had called late on Friday to say that they had a cause of death from the hospital of double pneumonia, so they were now able to release the body to an undertaker of their choice. The registry office in Ely was only open for appointments and although they had space later in the week, the office in Cambridge allowed people to visit, so they decided to go there.

The registry office in Cambridge was at that time still opposite Castle Hill car park and next to Shire Hall, the home of the County Council.

Driving there in his Morgan roadster and separate from his mum, Sandy was enjoying his driving experience. It felt like he hadn't driven his car for a number of weeks. Due to traffic, the journey to Cambridge was slow on that Monday morning, so he rang Juliet and asked her to call the contacts in the South Wales Police to deal with Roger Forbes harassing Imogen, and also to call Roger's probation officer. Juliet was in the office at the FCDO and he could hear Clare Symonds the CSI saying to Juliet to pass on her condolences.

The registration of his grandma's death turned out to be a lot more emotional than Sandy or his mum had expected, they couldn't help but cry at certain moments of the questioning to complete the forms. The registrar turned out to be a Cruse bereavement counsellor and handed a leaflet for them and Sandy's grandad to think about making use of a counselling service.

Waiting outside in the car park was Hannah. After saying goodbye to his mum, Sandy and Hannah walked up Castle Mound which was at the other end of the car park. Castle

Mound is a grassy hill and an historical mound, situated on the site of what was believed to be a castle. The view across the city of Cambridge was well worth the short climb up the mound.

Although extremely proud of Cambridge, he was more so of his home city of Ely. He realised that he had possibly never told Hannah of the mound in Cherry Hill Park that was also most probably the site of Ely Castle. As he did so, Hannah laughed, and their easy-going relationship was returning.

With Hannah only having time for a snack and a coffee before going into her chambers which were the other side of the River Cam, they went to Fitzbillies Café, an artisan bakery in Bridge Street. This was not the original one in Trumpington Street which had been there for almost one hundred years, but it was the nearest. They both had one of the bakery's fabled Chelsea buns and a coffee.

After Hannah had left, Sandy walked past the Great Gate entrance to St John's, his old Cambridge college, and down the road to Heffers bookshop. Although he liked Toppings bookshop in Ely, this was his favourite bookshop which he had spent many hours, if not weeks, during his three years at St John's college. Sandy picked up a couple of guidebooks to Guernsey so he could learn a bit more about the place.

Thinking about the yacht *Magnificence* and wondering where it was on its route to St Peter Port, Sandy called his contact in the leisure office of the investment bank that owned the yacht. Although he knew that his boss Jane Watson had wanted him to take a couple of days as compassionate leave, having some sort of normality was helping him.

The *Magnificence* had apparently stayed in port in the

Azores for a day longer than planned, so would be in St Peter Port late on the Wednesday or early Thursday of that week.

A further call to Juliet found that she was already in contact with a Detective Sergeant in the Guernsey Police who was going to look after them and help facilitate everything. The plan was to fly there on Wednesday morning, and the key question Juliet wanted to know was whether Sandy wanted to go or not. If he didn't feel up to it, she was going to ask the other DCI in the office if he could free up a couple of days. Without even thinking about it, Sandy told her to book him on the flight and into the planned accommodation.

∞

When Sandy woke up the next day, he saw that he had a message from Richard asking him to be available at ten a.m. Barbados time for a Zoom call with Dr Braithwaite. That would be three p.m. for him, so Sandy set about that morning doing as many household jobs as he possibly could to help out his family. He also did a couple of charity shop drop-offs of his grandma's clothes, which didn't feel weird because they were all in black bin liners rather than him looking at the clothes she used to wear.

When he had finished his last drop, Sandy received a call from Juliet telling him that the South Wales Police and the probation officer were already onto Roger Forbes and that that morning he was going to be arrested as he had breached his probation order. *Good news*, Sandy thought. He hoped they had with them someone who was quick on their feet because Roger Forbes was a runner. Sandy also roped Juliet in for the meeting with the forensic pathologist, just as a precaution as he was feeling a little bit out of his normal stride and didn't want to miss anything.

The first one to log into the meeting was Sandy and he wondered for a few moments if he had logged into the correct meeting as no-one else seemed to be appearing. He checked his code again and it was the right one. Yes, it definitely was, as Richard, Juliet, and then lastly Dr Braithwaite joined them, who was introduced to Juliet as he hadn't met her before.

'The water in Miss Jones' lungs,' Dr Braithwaite began, 'was seawater. So, we can rule out any forced drowning in freshwater.' Not allowing time for anyone to comment, he continued, 'The examination of her stomach contents fits with fish, so fish tacos as reported matches, I would say.'

Before he could say any more, Juliet asked, 'Does the digestion stage of the food help with a time of death?'

'What is it with you detectives? You are obsessed with a time of death,' Dr Braithwaite laughed in his deep baritone voice.

I wonder if he can sing? thought Sandy.

'I can only say it fits with her having eaten within a couple of hours or so of death,' Dr Braithwaite informed them.

That didn't rule out any of their scenarios. It could still fit murder by any of the suspects.

'Are you in a bedroom?' Dr Braithwaite suddenly asked Sandy.

'Yes, I am at my parents' house, well my home as well. My grandma died a few days ago and there is too much activity in the house, so I have retreated in here.'

'DCI McFarlane, I am sorry to hear about your loss,' he

said. Then looking down at his notes, he carried on, 'I have another autopsy in half an hour so I will continue if I may.' He looked up at his screen and, seeing everyone nodding, said, 'I, as you know, took blood, urine and vitreous fluid from the eyes. The alcohol level was extremely high. It was 165 milligrams of alcohol per 100 millilitres of blood.'

Sandy whistled. Even allowing for a moderate elevation due to being in the water, it was over twice the drink drive limit in the UK.

'Now we come to the interesting part. Let me share some pictures on my screen,' Dr Braithwaite continued, staring intently at the icons on his screen.

There appeared on screen an image of the back of Vivienne Jones' neck. Clearly seen were what was best described as two deep red marks that looked like tramlines, spreading horizontal across her neck. They were about one point five centimetres in width apart, and went almost the entire distance of her slim neck. Also, in the centre of the tramlines were two or three circular holes evenly spaced.

'What is that?' Richard asked, before Juliet or Sandy could ask the same question.

'This is what killed Miss Jones,' Dr Braithwaite said. He was enjoying the moment. 'She must have been struck on the back of her neck here, with such force that her cervical spine was fractured and the carotid artery ruptured. She may have even been dead, or just about dead, before she hit the floor.'

There was stunned silence before Richard ventured, 'So, you are saying that Miss Vivienne Jones was, in your opinion, murdered?'

'Yes.'

Chapter Nineteen

The first person to speak was Sandy.

'What do you think could have been used to cause that injury?' He was staring intently at the photograph on the screen. 'Could it be something like a metal bar?'

'The only thing I can say at the moment, in fact all I will be able to say, is that it must be a blunt instrument of some description,' Dr Braithwaite said. 'This is blunt trauma that you can see. Good job we used all those various types of photography because at the autopsy this injury was pretty much diffused, so much so that I could hardly see it.' He then stopped sharing the pictures. 'Didn't miss it though, did I!'

He grinned widely at them, clearly very pleased with himself, as they all were of him.

Looking back at his notes, he said, 'Is there anything else that you wanted to know?'

'Anything on the swabs that you took for possible sexual contact?' Juliet asked.

'Yes, only on the high vaginal swab where we have found semen. This needs checking as to who it might be,' Dr Braithwaite said. 'I wouldn't though rule out the fact that there was nothing on the other swabs, as Miss Jones was in salt water for over five days so that might have diffused any samples out.'

There appeared to be no more information that Dr Braithwaite was in a position to impart at that moment in time.

Sandy asked, 'I have been asked by the family when you might be able to release her body for repatriation to the UK?'

'I am happy to release her, but the family need to know that we have a number of samples of her organs and cell tissues that will not be so easy to return. I would want us to retain all of them for any future examinations, especially if you are ever in a position where you have a court case, the defence would want the opportunity to carry out examinations themselves.'

Looking around the bedroom that he had had since he was a little boy, Sandy found it all a bit surreal being in there and talking about body parts and human tissues.

'I can understand why Mr Scott is keen to get her home and buried or cremated as quickly as possible,' said Dr Braithwaite.

There was no doubt who he thought was the person responsible for this murder.

'He is not actually her next of kin. It is her sister Imogen Jones who is, and it is her that asked me,' Sandy corrected.

An only slightly embarrassed Dr Braithwaite replied, 'Sorry. I jumped to a conclusion.'

You and the rest of the world too, thought Sandy.

Dr Braithwaite continued, 'I was always told in my profession to never presume. But test and then test some more. Same for you detectives as well, I presume. Keep an open mind. Hard in this sort of case though.'

Dr Braithwaite could be seen on the screen putting all his

papers together, he was clearly now ready to move on to his next appointment.

'What are your timescales for getting a report to us, please?' Sandy asked.

Looking flustered for the first time in the meeting – clearly putting pen to paper was something he didn't enjoy – Dr Braithwaite replied, 'Putting timescale pressure on me, that must be a British thing. DI Ambrose knows better than to ask me that.'

Realising that he was evading answering the question and knowing the value of having what Dr Braithwaite said in writing, Sandy pushed a little harder. 'An early estimate would be so useful to us. Even if it was only an interim report, that would also be extremely helpful.'

'I will send you and DI Ambrose the photographs of the injury to the back of the neck now.' He fiddled about with his keyboard whilst he was talking. 'I realise this is a high-profile international case, so I will spend this evening putting down all my information on a recording and let my secretary sort out a report for you by early next week.' He then looked up at them. 'There, you should have the photographs now.'

Richard nodded as he had his emails open on his computer. Quickly saying goodbye to everybody, Dr Braithwaite was gone and had left their screens.

∞

'Are you both able to stay on the call for a few more minutes?' Richard asked Juliet and Sandy.

Before they could reply, he shouted out to Dave Ashton

to join him.

'Dr Braithwaite has just told us that Vivienne Jones was murdered by being struck by a blunt instrument to her neck,' Richard said, looking at Dave.

Still looking at each other, rather than Juliet and Sandy on the screen, Dave replied, 'Not really surprised after what was being discussed at the autopsy.'

'This means, Richard, that your possible hypothesis of Vivienne falling overboard and drowning is no longer feasible, and you, we, need to change it.' Seeing that he had got everyone's attention looking at him on his laptop screen, Sandy added, 'We now have the clear hypothesis that we are investigating the murder of Vivienne and must decide and firmly declare who our suspects are.'

'Why does it always happen to me,' Richard wailed. 'There can only be one suspect and I have let him go. The deputy commissioner is going to kill me, and you Sandy, had better not set foot on Barbados ever again.'

'Richard, don't worry, we know exactly where Adam Scott is. He is at his home in Sussex. I will ask Viscount James Peveril and his sister, Arabella Montague to let me know if he turns up in London at the Eaton Square house and I can ask the same of Imogen if he turns up at her home near Swansea,' Sandy said, trying to reassure Richard. 'He is so high profile, I can guarantee we will be able to arrest him whenever you want us to, if and when you send over an international arrest warrant.'

'He is not our only suspect though, is he?' Juliet said. 'Let's not lose sight of Michael and Bradley Lewis and Theo Le Tissier.'

'What can any of those three's motives to murder her be though?' Richard asked.

'OK, so for me the motive that best fits Adam is one of murder to control someone or get them to do what you want and not what they might want. This is the key motive in most domestic homicides.'

'This would also fit Michael and Bradley Lewis,' Juliet said. 'If Vivienne did go across and visit them and she didn't, for example, want to stay any longer or she wouldn't let them have sex with her. Wouldn't it?'

Nobody said anything but all were furiously nodding.

'We have the international arrest and search warrants in place for them,' Dave said. 'I have notified all Caribbean islands about it and also the FBI in Miami.'

'There are a couple of other motives,' Sandy added. 'Not sure they fit at all, for example carrying out a murder to gain something, like in a robbery.'

'No evidence of that in this case. Miss Jones wasn't robbed,' Richard offered.

'Finally, there is the motive of anger, or loss of face,' Sandy said. 'This happens where someone has been, say, punched in a pub brawl and they lash out. In the case of the loss of face motive, Grandad Tom talked about this in cases he had within the Eastern European community, where loss of face mattered so much to them that they wouldn't step back from gaining revenge through murder.'

'That doesn't fit here, and I'm not sure where Theo fits in, other than he was there at the right times. Everything must point to it being Adam Scott.'

'Juliet and I are going to Guernsey in the morning, let's

see what we find out by searching the yacht for this blunt instrument and talking to Theo. I think we will do that under caution,' Sandy said. 'What do you think, Richard?'

'Yes, no need to arrest him. I haven't got him clearly as a suspect in my mind, but to use a caution is better safe than sorry. And I will wait until I get Dr Braithwaite's report before I dare go and talk to the assistant and deputy commissioners.'

∞

Downstairs in the living room was Grandad Tom. He was sitting alone and was gloomily flicking through photographs on his phone. He had clearly been crying.

'Where are mum and dad?' Sandy asked him.

Brightening up on seeing his grandson, Tom replied, 'They have gone to see a couple of friends. Get some fresh air, I think your mum said.' Tom put his phone away. 'How did your meeting with the forensic pathologist go?'

'Very good. Well, I think so. We are currently working on the strong theory that Adam Scott must have killed his wife, Vivienne.'

'Wow!' Tom said and whistled. 'What a story that is going to be.' He smiled at his grandson as he sat next to him on the sofa. 'Just because it is highly likely that the husband is the killer, make sure your investigation is not blinkered towards him.'

'It's not, Grandad,' Sandy said. 'We have three other suspects that we are still looking at.'

'Good. I always remember the West Yorkshire Police's Peter Sutcliffe case in the 1980s. The senior investigator was convinced the killer was someone else, a person he called

"Wearside Jack" and wouldn't hear of any other theories,' Tom recounted, now in his element talking about detective work. 'It was always felt that more women were killed after they had Peter Sutcliffe named in the investigation. He killed thirteen women in total.'

Sandy headed in to the kitchen area to make them both a cup of tea.

'Are you able to tell me how Vivienne was killed?' Tom asked.

'Blunt force trauma to her neck. Probably dead before she hit the floor or the deck on the yacht.'

'I had a case…' Tom started.

They both smiled to each other almost laughing. In that instant they both had the same image of Sandy's grandma rolling her eyes, which she did as soon as Tom uttered those words of "I had a case".

Sitting back down again with their drinks, Tom continued, 'In my case, the weapon used was a metal bar that turned out to be a crowbar.'

Sandy jumped up and went and collected his laptop from his bedroom. Richard had forwarded Dr Braithwaite's email with the photographs of the marks on Vivienne's neck.

'Can you see those holes in the middle?' Sandy said. 'They couldn't be caused by a crowbar, could they?'

'Have you tried the National Crime Agency?' Tom asked. 'They have a section called the Forensic Medical Advice Team. They have the most incredible, and probably the best, collection in the world of images of injuries and what may have caused those injuries. It is called the National Injuries Database.'

'This is a case from Barbados, though. Do you think they

would be able to help as it is not a UK police force?'

'It is the death of a British citizen though, and what a famous British citizen Vivienne Jones was. Let's fill their form in and see what they say.'

They spent the next hour or so completing the form, putting as much detail about the case into it that they could and uploaded the photographs of the injury marks to Vivienne's neck. Then the pair of them headed off the short distance to the Cutter Inn to treat themselves to a couple of pre-dinner beers.

Chapter Twenty

As soon as Juliet saw him the next morning at London Gatwick Airport, she rushed over and gave Sandy a big hug, telling him how sorry she was about his grandma passing away. Clare Symonds, the investigation teams lead CSI who was stood beside Juliet then also proceeded to hug him.

After this they whizzed through security. As they only expected to be in Guernsey for a couple of days or so, they only had carry-on luggage. They found somewhere to sit after buying their take-out breakfast,

When his phone started buzzing telling him he had a call, Sandy glanced at it while taking a final mouthful of his bacon bap. He saw it was Celia Longstaff. As much as he desperately didn't want to answer the call, he felt a duty to do so.

'Hello Celia, how are you?' Sandy said as bright, breezy and nonchalantly as he possibly could.

Celia was having none of it. 'Don't you go hello Celia to me DCI McFarlane! Now you tell me what is happening.'

Sandy hesitated fractionally too long.

'So, there *is* something happening. Spill the beans boy.'

'There is nothing too much I can tell you or Adam at the moment,' Sandy said, trying to sound confident. 'I am just at the airport now about to fly to Guernsey to carry out a proper search of the *Magnificence,* and talk to the skipper of the yacht.'

Undeterred, Celia continued, 'When can you tell us what you can't tell us now, then?'

Sandy thought to himself, *it will probably be next week when we will undoubtedly be arresting your precious Adam for murder.*

Instead, he said, 'You missed your vocation, Celia, you would have made a good detective.'

They both laughed.

'How is Adam doing?' Sandy asked.

'He has that deeply annoying ex-wife of his coming around all the time.'

'Well, Adam was married to her, and she is the mother of his two children,' Sandy offered as a possible explanation.

'Don't I know it. I organised their wedding, darling. She has had her hair done and wears lipstick and she has taken to dressing up like she is going out on the town.'

Sandy couldn't help but smile.

'She is such a loser!' Celia said, as she continued her rant.

Sandy laughed. 'I hope you don't call her that.'

'Oh, yes, I do, but Adam has asked me to stop doing it. So, I just do the L shape with my forefinger and thumb on my forehead when I see her.'

'What does Adam think to you doing this?'

'Annoys him unbelievably and that is where I get the win, win of annoying him even further as well as her. Right, ring me next week or I will be annoying you more than you will be able to cope with.'

'I will definitely do that. Before you go, I meant to ask,

how did you cope for all of those hours on the flight back from Barbados without smoking?'

'Alcohol darling! I just got them to keep the champagne coming and told them not to stop until I passed out.'

They both laughed together, and Sandy was laughing so loudly that other passengers were looking at him.

∞

Finishing her phone call at almost the same time as Sandy ended his call, Juliet announced, 'Good news!'

Neither Clare nor Sandy said anything, but just looked enquiringly at her.

'Roger Forbes is back in prison for at least another eighteen months to serve the rest of his sentence.'

'That is good news. Imogen will be so pleased.' Sandy said. 'Who was that you were just talking to?'

'Roger Forbes' probation officer. Imogen told me about it earlier this morning and I was just confirming it.'

Sandy told them about his conversation with Celia, which made them both laugh.

'I wonder why Celia is so anti Adam's ex-wife?' Sandy pondered aloud. 'Celia clearly adores his children and was keen to get home from Barbados not only for Adam, but also for herself to see them.'

'You obviously don't read the gossip columns, do you?' Juliet said. 'As you know Adam left Vivienne for her the first time and Celia is, or certainly was, totally devoted to Vivienne.'

'Apparently they were having a break so that Vivienne

could concentrate on her career and the ex-wife jumped in, which appears to be what she is up to now, but then the ex-wife quickly got pregnant,' Clare added.

'How come it isn't Adam that she is cross with? It was him that strayed,' Sandy said.

'You know the answer to that question don't you. Adam is her blue-eyed boy. As I think you could be building up to be as well Sandy.'

Frightened by that prospect, so looking to change the subject as quick as possible Sandy replied, 'I presume Imogen has signed the consent to retain the tissue samples?'

'Yes, the family liaison officer visited with the form that I had sent them through, listing what we are seeking to retain in Barbados, I then called her to explain.'

'Any issues?' Sandy knew from experience that occasionally there was a preference from a loved one for the body of the victim to be retained by the pathology department until all tests had been done and the body parts returned. Rarely though if it was just for tissue samples that had been made into blocks and slides for examination under a microscope.

'No. Imogen was keen to get her sister home to Wales for a funeral, cremation and memorial service as soon as possible.'

'What about after any criminal investigation has been completed?'

'Ethical disposal she says, by the hospital in Barbados.'

'Well done, Juliet,' a smiling Sandy said. 'I think I will just message Celia about it rather than enter into another conversation with her. Not sure my nerves can cope with it! That woman terrifies me!'

He then sent Celia a message that Roger Forbes was in prison for several more months and that as soon as they could get the relevant paperwork to Barbados, hopefully arrangements could start to repatriate Vivienne's body.

Clare told them that the gate number for their flight was being displayed on the flight information board and they slowly made their way towards the aircraft. As they did this, Celia, as responsive as ever, replied to his message telling Sandy that she and Adam would most likely head to Swansea at the beginning of the next week and not to worry, they would report in as to where they were staying. Sandy thought this would work well as they had developed a good relationship with some of the officers in Swansea police, just in case Richard decided an arrest of Adam was needed.

∞

They walked together to the gate and saw that the Aurigny Airlines plane was one with propellers. Sandy couldn't remember the last time he had flown in one of those. Sitting down he saw that his phone was buzzing again, it was from a number he didn't recognise. In spite of this, he decided to answer the call.

'Hello, is that DCI McFarlane from the Foreign, Commonwealth and Development Office?'

'Yes,' Sandy said. He decided to stand up and walk away from the other passengers and went around the corner from where they were all mingling getting ready to board the aircraft.

'This is an advisor from the Forensic Medical Advice

Team at the NCA. I got your form for the search of the National Injuries Database.'

Just an acknowledgement, thought Sandy. Was this a good demonstration of customer service, or had he submitted it all wrong and was going to be told he needed to make some changes and re-submit? Probably the latter. He should have got Richard Ambrose to do it.

'Have I got something wrong on the form?' he enquired.

'No, nothing wrong with the form. I saw the request come in and was intrigued. Obviously, I, like almost everyone else on the planet know of Vivienne Jones, so I started on the case straight away. I have the result of the search and my report that I can send you now.'

'Wow! That was fast.' Sandy walked back a few steps to see if anyone was boarding the aircraft; they weren't. 'Did you find out anything to help our investigation?'

'Yes, I think so. I did a couple of hours on it yesterday evening and then an hour or so first thing this morning before I did an input into a detective training course.'

Sandy recognised the name, and connected it with the voice. 'You did a similar input a few years ago to my senior investigators course at Hendon, when I was in the Metropolitan Police.' He smiled to himself, it was so nice to deal with someone as experienced, enthusiastic, and efficient as the advisor clearly was. 'What have you found out then?'

'You have to bear in mind that the report and search are for information purposes only for use by the forensic pathologist in Barbados, or I can contact one or two other pathologists that we have on our list here in the UK that are very good and would be able to assist.'

'Is one of them Dr Nicholas Stroud?'

'Yes, he is. Do you know him then?'

'Yes. He was the pathologist who was involved in my last three homicide cases.'

'I will make contact with him this morning and send you a form with terms of reference to engage him if you want me to?'

'I will check if the Detective Inspector in Barbados and the forensic pathologist there agrees first. I am sorry but I have a plane to catch so could you just let me know what it is you have found out?' Sandy didn't even bother to walk around the corner this time, he knew that boarding would be taking place either now or very soon.

'From the images we have it looks like it might be a piece of metal shelving that has caused the injury.'

'Metal shelving!' Sandy repeated, unable to work out how that could be the case.

'It is all in the report and you can see from the images that it is a bracket piece on top of which you attach the shelf.'

It was becoming clearer now to Sandy.

'The holes are where you attach a bungee. You know a bungee strap, to keep anything on the shelf firmly in place. Probably very useful on a yacht that sails across oceans and is being thrown about by the power of the waves.'

Knowing that he really did have to go now and saying thank you and goodbye at the same time, Sandy walked around the corner to find that there was no one there, they had all boarded.

He ran for the plane as the voice on the Tannoy called out, 'Can the last remaining passenger please join the aircraft as your flight is ready to depart.'

Chapter Twenty-One

A few of the passengers, but not that many, glared at Sandy as he shuffled past them to find his seat. Where he found Juliet and Clare laughing at how distressed he looked, this became even worse as he couldn't find any room in the overhead locker to put his carry-on case. A member of the cabin crew came and took it off him and placed it further down the aircraft in a space that he had only just passed by.

'Not like you to be late for anything Sandy,' Juliet laughed as he fastened his seatbelt next to her.

As he did so the plane moved backwards away from the stand. He really had cut it fine.

'Who was it on the phone? Presumably Hannah, and you couldn't bring yourselves to say goodbye to each other?'

'It was actually the NCA, a very helpful advisor from the Forensic Medical Advice Team who told me what they think caused the fatal injury.' Seeing that Clare now was also keenly interested, he added, 'He thinks it may be a piece of metal shelving. They have two cases on the database that are extremely similar. In essence, it is a metal bar. I am hoping that if the report is with me by the time we land in Guernsey, I can show it to you both and send it to Richard and Dave in Barbados.'

The flight took less than forty minutes, and they were soon

taxiing to the terminal. As they only had carry-on baggage and it was a domestic flight, within fifteen minutes of landing they were outside the terminal looking for their lift. Dale Le Toc was there waiting for them; he was the DS who had been helping them throughout the investigation. They looked at his very tiny police car and wondered how they would all fit in it. Then, looking at the boot, which was full of equipment, it was even more unlikely that they had any chance of them all going in the car.

However, Dale was a glass half full type of guy and while putting Sandy's and Juliet's laptop cases in the boot on top of the equipment, he said, 'Get in, and I will pass your cases to you to put on your laps.'

Afterwards, they headed off to their hotel. The Bailiwick of Guernsey is situated in the Channel Islands, just off the coast of Normandy in France. It actually comprised not only the Island of Guernsey, that they were on, but also the Islands of Sark, Alderney and Herm, plus a number of smaller islands, some privately leased from the Crown like the Island of Jethou. Guernsey is a British Crown dependency, but is self-governed, and everything that Sandy and the team were hopefully going to be doing would have to be led by the local police, with which Dale was going to be their link.

It was definitely an extremely pretty island – well, as far as they could see from peering around their cases that were placed on their knees. Only ten kilometres across and very green in places, they saw glimpses of the sea as they headed to the capital, St Peter Port. The older houses looked similar in design to the houses he had seen in the past when visiting Normandy and Brittany in France. Dale told them that there were about sixty-five thousand residents, but as tourism is a major industry, that swells to many more during the spring and summer months. If they got a chance before they left, he told them he would give them a guided tour around the island and show them some of the beautiful beaches as well.

Their hotel, Les Rocquettes, was well situated up a hill from the harbour in St Peter Port. After Dale dropped them off and having checked in, lunch in the restaurant was top of not just Sandy's, but all of their priorities.

During lunch Sandy showed them on his phone the images that had been sent through in the report from the NCA. Clare as a CSI was very interested and now knew what to concentrate on in her search of the yacht, which would hopefully take place either later that day or early the next. Sandy, even though he knew it was still early in Barbados, forwarded the report to Richard and Dave. It would be useful for Dave Ashton to circulate the image of the metal shelving bar to his contacts across the Caribbean, who were hopefully looking out for the catamaran containing Michael and Bradley Lewis.

∞

The other two had already left for the Guernsey Police Headquarters and Sandy hurried off to join them. He had been delayed talking to Hannah. They had decided not to risk making arrangements to meet up on the Saturday, just in case he was still in St Peter Port, so instead had agreed to have Sunday lunch together in Cambridge.

The walk to the headquarters didn't take too long at all

and Sandy looked around at the scenery as he walked, he was intrigued to see a signpost to Cambridge Park as he approached the headquarters in Hospital Lane. The weather was certainly warmer here than at home in Ely and he was enjoying himself. The headquarters was also the main police station for the town. Clare had gone off to meet up with the two local CSIs who were going to help her search the yacht later that evening or the next morning. Waiting outside were Dale and Juliet and they walked to the Candie Investment Bank, which was just situated off the Candie Road itself, and ran opposite the Candie Gardens which were nearby the Victor Hugo statue.

A very pleasant man and woman, who told them that they were the joint managers of the leisure section of the bank, showed them into their spacious office floor. The view was lovely and looked down over the extensive harbour area. They enthusiastically talked about a hotel purchase that they had just made on the island and how this aspect of the business was growing.

They had the files for *Magnificence* with them which included a floor plan of the yacht's decks. Juliet took some pictures on her phone and sent them to Clare to help with her planning. The yacht's skipper was a man by the name of George Dotrice, and Heather, one of the mangers, said that he had been with them since they started with the three yachts three or so years ago.

'Theo,' she said, 'has only been with us for a few months, this trip was his second one for us. Both the clients and ourselves have been impressed with him.'

Looking at the files on the desk in front of him and pointing at them, Sandy asked, 'Is his personal file one of these?'

It turned out it was on the desk and was a very slim folder.

A sheepish Heather informed him, 'We have a confession to make, we never checked any of his references.'

Her colleague said, 'I know that we should have done but George took him out for a half day sail as part of the interview and was very impressed, and as he was only a relief skipper, we didn't feel we needed to do anymore.'

'We have a lot more work for him next year and are looking to employ him,' said Heather. 'Probably permanently, so we will now check his references.'

Picking up the file and looking at the picture of Theo, Dale said, 'I think I know him but can't quite place him. This photo isn't very clear. Have you any others?'

The two managers shook their heads, but Juliet had a thought and produced a couple of photographic stills from the marina clubhouse CCTV in Barbados. These were with Theo and Vivienne and Adam entering, then leaving the restaurant.

Looking intently at the photographs on Juliet's phone didn't seem to help Dale much either. Heather offered to enlarge them and print them off, which when she did, really helped.

'That is not Theo Le Tissier, but Theo Le Feuvre,' Dale exclaimed loudly.

Everyone looked around at him.

'Has he got form?' Seeing the enquiring looks from the two managers, Sandy added, 'A criminal record?'

'Just some low-level drug offences when he was much younger, but I think he got into trouble in England not that long ago and may have served time in prison.'

Heather and her colleague had turned very pale in colour. 'He isn't in trouble here though, is he?'

'We don't think so in terms of the death of Vivienne,' Sandy said, 'but he was one of the last people to be with her, so we just need to talk to him so we can eliminate him.'

The colour seemed to return to their faces, only to go again.

'He might be guilty of an offence best described in lay man terms of getting a job under false pretences.'

Dale added to this. 'Would you have employed him if you knew of his criminal record?'

'Not in the role of a yacht skipper,' Heather answered. 'We have some very rich, powerful, and discerning clients. We wouldn't have risked it. Maybe elsewhere in the organisation, but not in this role, however great a sailor he is.'

∞

They set out for dinner that night in the knowledge that *Magnificence* was arriving in St Peter Port at some time that evening. However, due to the tides, Heather had told them it would be mooring outside Albert Marina until the morning, when it would make its way the few hundred metres to end its voyage in Albert dock, moored on one of the jetties there.

The walk from the hotel to the restaurant was downhill. Due to the light rain, they were walking with their hoods up and a little too fast to take in the surrounding scenery. They did slow down as they passed the sunken gardens and then the war memorial into what was, they presumed, the High Street area.

All three of them looked at each other knowing that they were lost. Sandy came up with the idea that they should head through a side passage, down some stairs and hopefully emerge by the sea and the marinas. He was right, as they arrived outside and overlooking Victoria Marina.

As they had time before their reservation and due to the rain not being conducive to walking around sightseeing – even though Sandy was keen to, the ladies definitely weren't – they visited the Albion House Tavern that was situated directly next to a church and directly on the seafront.

The first-floor bar area looked out over the dock and although the weather meant that the view wasn't that clear, it did seem that there weren't many boats in the marina that they could see. The landlady told them that by April or May that would change, and the marina would be a hive of activity and full of boats.

The restaurant they were eating at was called Pier 17 and looked out over the port.

As they took their seats, Clare pointed at an extremely beautiful large yacht. 'That's it, isn't it? That's *Magnificence*.'

Clare was right, it was the yacht. All three of them looked in wonder at the yacht that they had spent what felt like a lifetime talking about, but was in reality only a couple of weeks, was right there in front of them.

Sandy took a few photographs on his phone, and sent them to Richard and Dave in Barbados. He had already updated them earlier about the change in surname for Theo along with the information that Juliet had gleaned from the Police National Computer, that Theo had a conviction for a robbery that had taken place in London. He had been given a three-year prison sentence, of which he had served half, and on coming out of prison had returned to Guernsey earlier that year.

They asked to move tables so that they could watch and look at the yacht. It had felt out of touch for so long that it had developed a mystical feel to it, so it was good to now have it in sight. So close but still so far. Dale had said that he could arrange for them to get out to it as soon as it arrived if they wanted, but Sandy thought it best to let it dock and then go about their business searching in the relative calm of the marina. They could then talk to Theo at leisure, and take him off to the police station to do this.

The seafood meal at the restaurant was delicious and Sandy enjoyed it. Clare didn't eat seafood but there was plenty on the menu for her to enjoy as well.

As they headed back to the hotel the downside wasn't just the weather, but the walk was now heading uphill. Juliet, as usual, had pushed for a taxi and after being outvoted had moaned all the way back. Sandy felt that he didn't want to abandon the yacht, because for him it was a crime scene, as this was the last place that they knew for sure that Vivienne Jones had been alive. This feeling niggled him all the way up the hill.

As they walked through the doors of the hotel, Juliet had a call from Dave asking if they could be free in a few minutes for a video call with himself, Paulette and Garry.

Chapter Twenty-Two

On each floor of the hotel there was a beautiful atrium area from which corridors led off to the bedrooms. The atrium had floor to ceiling and wall to wall glass windows, which if it hadn't been pitch black outside would have given a beautiful scenic view out to the sea.

With his computer open on the table in front of them, Sandy and Juliet settled onto the sofa. They had resisted the temptation to buy a drink in the bar to ensure they kept to being professional with a clear head. Clare hadn't really got a part to play in the meeting, so told them she would meet them in the morning and had gone to her room.

Before too long they were joined by Dave, Paulette and Garry, who were all sitting together around the computer screen.

'Where is Richard?' asked Sandy, while at the same time wondering if there would be room for him to be seen on screen. The three of them did look bunched up together.

'He is at band practice,' Dave replied, shaking his head as he did so. 'I have had a call from the Royal Cayman Islands Police to say they have sighted the Lewis cousins' catamaran making its way to a dock in a marina at West Bay, Grand Cayman.'

'Wow! that is exciting news,' Sandy said, and as he

glanced at Juliet sitting next to him, he saw she was smiling. 'What did you tell them to do?'

'Arrest them both as per the conditions of the international warrant and then search their boat. I have also asked for them to be interviewed. I sent the detectives there a full briefing package, plus those photos of the injury and those possible shelving images from the National Crime Agency in London.'

'Good news,' Juliet said. 'Were you surprised, Dave, with our news about Theo and that he has a criminal record?'

'I wasn't,' Paulette said. 'Well, not now. Not after we got some more information from the barman Royston from the clubhouse at the marina.'

She now had Sandy and Juliet's full attention.

'What do you mean?' Sandy asked.

'When we originally went there, I saw Benjamin and Garry saw Royston.'

'I wonder why that was,' Garry said, who could be seen smirking on the screen.

Totally ignoring Garry's interjection, Paulette continued, 'I am not sure why Garry didn't find this out in the first place.'

'Why do you question everything I do?' Garry said loudly.

'Because,' Paulette said, looking straight at Garry, 'everything you do is questionable.'

When she said this and how she said this, caused Dave, Juliet and Sandy to laugh out loud.

They were laughing so much that they missed Garry saying, 'Paulette is only at her happiest when she has a list of complaints about me.'

These two, in Sandy's opinion, were as funny together as Morcombe and Wise, Laurel and Hardy or any other comedic duo.

Managing to stop laughing, Juliet glanced at her watch. 'Is it possible please to tell us what you wanted to tell us? I am not sure what the point of this conversation is.'

'The waiter, Royston,' Garry said, 'saw Theo buy at least two, if not three tablets from Bradley Lewis. We presume these tablets were to give him some sort of high. Something like amphetamine or another sort of upper type drug.'

'He, Theo that is, has got criminal convictions for drugs,' Juliet said. 'We all missed it Garry, don't worry – all of us were only interested in Vivienne Jones and her movements.'

'Yes, don't worry Garry, we will have our hands on the Lewis cousins and Theo soon anyway. I presume you have a statement from Royston now though that covers this?' Sandy added.

'Yes, I took it,' Paulette said.

'Any excuse to visit and see Benjamin,' Garry added bringing more smiles all round.

They ended the meeting with Dave promising not to wake them up during their night, but to send through an update on what happens, if anything, in Grand Cayman.

∞

It was late afternoon in Grand Cayman as Bradley Lewis firmly attached the mooring ropes to the catamaran. The weather was glorious, as it had been for the last few days. The constant thunderstorms had stopped, and it looked like the Caribbean was heading into a more settled period. The hurricane season was just about over, which for this year had yielded the odd major storm but no devastating hurricanes.

The stopover in Jamaica had proved fruitful and Bradley and his cousin felt like they hadn't a care in the world. Michael was just coming onto deck when he saw the two men approaching. Bradley feared the worst, well not actually the worst, as these two men had on shirts and ties and were most probably law enforcement and not members of a drugs gang that were likely to rob and harm them.

As they got up to Bradley, the taller of the two men said, 'Are you Michael or Bradley Lewis?'

'Who wants to know?' Bradley replied, loudly.

He moved away from the catamaran and the two men followed him onto the roadway. He continued to walk further away and the smaller man, who it was clear from the muscles showing through his short-sleeved shirt that he worked out, grabbed him by the arm. It was more than just a grab; it was a very strong hold he had on Bradley.

'Get off me,' Bradley shouted, 'Get off me you scum!' Try as he might, he wasn't going to get out of this grip.

The taller man said, 'I am a detective with the Royal Cayman Island Police Service, and I am arresting you on behalf of the Barbados Police Service on the suspicion of the murder of Vivienne Jones.' He then cautioned Bradley.

As this was happening, Michael came off the boat with a large backpack and carrying a holdall, he ran off in the opposite direction. The two detectives didn't know what to do, they looked around helplessly at each other, then at Michael who was running away and at Bradley, who was now smiling at them.

'What, this again? It is nothing to do with us. Didn't her husband kill her? Don't you read the news? I am an American citizen and I demand my constitutional rights.'

In a very short time, a number of police cars started arriving, along with a van which had its blues and two-tone horns going, that brought everyone in the area out to see what was happening. They bundled Bradley into the van which went off conveying him to the police station in Georgetown. The van still had the blue lights whizzing around and the two-tone horns making the most annoying loud noise. Then an unmarked police car turned up which they sent off in the direction Michael had run off in.

Finally, a small van that had two CSIs in it came and the four of them entered the tight living accommodation on the catamaran. One of the CSIs went out as it was just too tight for them all. She set about swabbing the outside rails for any fibres or fluids that might have traces of Vivienne.

The rooms were extremely tidy for two men sharing the living accommodation. A few drawers and cupboards were open as if someone had gone in there hurriedly and had not had time to close them.

The taller detective spoke to his colleague, looking intently at the shelving in the engine room. 'Where are those photos they sent us across from Barbados?'

He got out his phone and looked carefully at the images on there while trying to compare them with the shelving. To be honest it didn't look like it had been apart as it was all firmly fixed in place and on the shelf were a number of hard-cased boxes, with the bungee clips firmly in place. However, they did look identical, and the holes were there in the same places as they were on the photograph.

'This is it. One of these two metal shelving bars are what

was used to kill Vivienne Jones,' the taller detective declared, with a large smile.

They were triumphant and asked the CSI to recover them both forensically.

As they climbed out, firstly onto the deck and then onto the road, along walked Michael Lewis empty handed and with no sign of the backpack and holdall.

'I presume you are after me as well.' He put his hands in front of him to be handcuffed.

∞

The interview room in the police station in Grand Cayman contained the two local detectives, Bradley Lewis and a lawyer, who was an American more suited to the law of international corporate banking than criminal law. The cousins' grandfather had organised the lawyer for his two grandchildren.

The taller of the two detectives was the one asking the questions. 'How do you own a catamaran of the value of the one you are sailing? You don't seem to work, and are bumming around the Caribbean on it.'

'Not sure that is any of your business,' Bradley replied. 'How has this got anything to do with Vivienne Jones, dying?'

The lawyer interjected, 'Keep to topic detective.'

Asserting his authority, the detective raised his voice. 'I am in charge of this interview, not you or your client.'

'Are you really,' the lawyer barked back; he had a deep south American State drawl to his accent. 'My client doesn't need to say anything. Isn't that what you said to him? So, I suggest if you want him to answer any of your questions, stop fishing and stick to what the police in Barbados want to know.'

This was a slick Harvard law school lawyer, and unfortunately the two Royal Cayman Island Police Service detectives were not going to be a match for him.

'OK,' the detective conceded. 'What took you to Barbados?'

'Barely relevant,' the lawyer said.

'It's OK,' Bradley said, putting his hand on the arm of the expensive blue silk suit of his lawyer. 'We went to play a couple of rounds of golf. One at the Royal Westmoreland and the other at Sandy Lane Country club.'

'What handicap do you play off?' the smaller muscled detective asked, now interested in the interview.

'I play off eight and Michael plays off six.'

'Wow! I play off fourteen handicap. We have a couple of half decent courses here if you want me to try and arrange something.'

The lawyer and the taller detective looked at each other in astonishment as to what was now happening.

The taller detective said in exasperation, 'But you never stayed on the island to do that. You left Barbados as soon as you could. Why was that?'

It was the lawyer's turn to put his hand on the arm of his client.

'No comment.'

'Tell us what happened then on the day you got to Barbados?'

'When we arrived, there were no berths left for us to moor at, but the marina said we could anchor up and shelter within the breakwater.' Seeing everyone nodding for him to carry on, Bradley continued, 'We were right next to the yacht of Vivienne Jones and Adam Scott. Michael spotted them first and after we had carried out a few essential chores we headed off to the marina clubhouse, bar and restaurant for a drink and something to eat.'

Bradley shifted on his seat to get more comfortable and paused to rub his hands through his hair and beard.

The taller detective asked, 'You followed the actors there, didn't you?'

'No, we actually arrived just before them,' Bradley answered, feeling a little annoyed with the detective as he had been conjuring up and remembering the image of what had happened in his mind and now that thought process had been broken. 'Do you want me to tell you what happened or not?' With both the detectives nodding this time, he said, 'They had both been drinking and were in an incredibly good mood, so much so it was intoxicating.'

About to say something and interject, the taller detective managed to stop himself.

'Vivienne, and Adam also, to be fair to him, are beautiful, intelligent and witty people, meeting them that night before this tragedy was a highlight of my year.'

'We have examined your phone and there are at least twenty photographs of you and Michael with Vivienne or Adam or the both of them. You were obsessed with Vivienne that night.'

'Of course we were. They are worldwide, global, international superstars and you have the chance to spend the evening with them, wouldn't you be?'

'Had they both been drinking, and did they have an argument?'

'They told us that they never drink at all when they are on a film set or doing promotional work, either for a film or for the brands they represent, so when they do drink they really let their hair down.' He looked around, then remembering there was a second part to the question, Bradley added, 'Adam was trying to control Vivienne telling her that she had had enough and that he was tired, and they should go back to the yacht. Vivienne was having none of it and he raised his voice and grabbed her arm. They did go off after that and I never saw Vivienne again, but I spoke to Adam in the morning.'

'You asked Vivienne back to your catamaran to continue the night, didn't you?'

'Well, it was actually Michael. Yes, he did ask, but she went back to her yacht.'

'One of you went and collected her though, didn't you, or she came across anyway?' the taller detective asked.

Bradley looked genuinely surprised. 'What?' He felt his lawyer's hand again. 'No comment.'

The taller detective took a photo out of a folder he had with him. It showed the CCTV image of Bradley passing over a package to Theo. 'You sold their skipper some drugs, didn't you?'

With no hesitation and not pausing for breath, Bradley said, 'He told me he had a headache, and they were headache pills.'

Both the detectives were flummoxed and didn't know what to say.

The taller detective got out a photograph of the shelving.

'This metal shelving bar was used to hurt and kill Vivienne Jones, was it you or Michael that did it?'

Looking even more confused, Bradley just replied, 'No comment.'

The interview came to a conclusion shortly after that, and a uniformed officer took Bradley off to his cell. He returned after a few minutes without Michael, who he was going to collect.

'He is refusing to come out of his cell.'

The taller detective said to the lawyer, 'You had better go to the cells and have a word with your client to get him to come and talk to us.'

Looking at his gold IWC watch and then standing up and putting on a pair of designer sunglasses, the lawyer said, 'I need to get back to the office, my work here is done. Ring me when my clients are ready to be released.' He passed over a luxurious embossed business card and left the room.

The shorter detective sighed. 'I could do with some of those headache tablets myself now.'

Chapter Twenty-Three

Thankfully the rain had stopped when Dale picked them up the next morning. The drive to Albert dock only took two or three minutes, so they were there very quickly.

It was bitterly cold as they got out of the car in the darkness of the November morning. The cold was made worse by the chill of the wind which was piercing through them. Sandy was regretting not having brought a woolly hat and gloves. He saw that Juliet had come prepared as she was well wrapped up.

They walked through the gate that Dale unlocked and saw that *Magnificence* had already docked. Up close it was a beautiful sight as it towered over them. They correctly presumed that the man in his late forties who was busily tying up the yacht to secure it firmly to its mooring was George Dotrice.

'Hi, George,' Dale said, as he walked up to him. 'It sounds like you have had quite a crossing across the Atlantic?'

They shook hands enthusiastically. It turned out that George had taught Dale to sail a number of years earlier, hence the reason they had greeted each other so fondly.

'Not too bad, as there were two of us to carry the load.' He gave an enquiring look at Juliet and Sandy, and then further up the walkway to where Clare and the two local CSIs were standing. 'What's going on, Dale?'

'I thought Heather or someone else from the Candie Investment Bank would have told you.' Dale looked round and introduced Sandy and Juliet to George.

'We,' Sandy said, indicating to Juliet and himself, 'with the help of Dale, are going to formally interview Theo, and they,' he indicated back behind him, 'are going to search the boat on the off chance that there may be some clues to Vivienne Jones' death on board.'

'I am not sure you will find anything on the deck as we have been well and truly drenched a number of times over the last few days.' George looked up at the yacht. 'We didn't feel like touching the bedroom that Miss Jones and Mr Scott had been in, or their bathroom, so that will be as it was left.' He suddenly looked troubled. 'It has unnerved me a bit that she was killed onboard, and I presume by Adam Scott in that bedroom, hence I couldn't go in there.'

'Obviously we will go in and have a look for ourselves,' Sandy said, 'but what else is in there?'

'A galley kitchen and another spare bedroom, much smaller than the main one, a lounge area where you can pull out a double bed, my cabin, which Theo had been using, but I normally use this one, so I took it back when we left Antigua, so he then used the spare crew cabin. Other than the engine room and lots of storage cupboards, that is about it.'

'Surely, Theo isn't still asleep, is he?' Sandy asked, wondering why he hadn't appeared on deck or come to see what was going on down the gangway.

'Theo?' George looked confused. 'He is not on board anymore.'

'Not on board?' Sandy said, realising his voice had suddenly gone up an octave and sounded quite shrill.

'It didn't need both of us to moor the yacht this morning, we often work single-crewed anyway, as this suits the clients.'

'Where is he then?' Sandy said, controlling his voice this time.

'He knew one of the people out sailing in the marina yesterday evening and when he asked, I told him to grab his things and jump off the yacht and go home. He had been away a few weeks.'

Looking at each other, the three detectives' shoulders slumped; they had missed out again on a key action for their investigation.

Seeing their forlorn faces, George said, 'He doesn't live far away,' and he pointed in a non-descript way back over the seafront area. 'He is not the most talkative of people, which was fine by me as we were sailing on a shift type system, but he did tell me that he has a flat and a sort of a girlfriend who lives either in a flat next door or nearby. Then his mum lives about a mile or so away from Petit Bot Bay. You will easily find him, I'm sure.'

As he was keen to get home himself, George sorted them out the spare set of keys, which was, as it turned out, a large bunch of keys that he wanted Dale to return to Heather at the bank when the CSIs had finished.

∞

Their next move should, of course, have been to go and wake Theo up in his flat. It was, Dale had told them, only a few

189

hundred yards away. However, Juliet and Sandy couldn't resist the temptation to walk up the steps and onto the luxurious yacht.

As they got onto deck, Dale informed them that this yacht was now, and had been for a few years, considered as pocket size in the super yacht world. This yacht though, even in the second-hand market, would have a value well in excess of a million or so pounds.

On the upper deck, most of the area was taken up with the yacht's equipment which looked extremely high tech, and there was an enormous steering wheel in the middle of all of the dials. Behind this was a seating area with the seats covered in a luxurious white leather. There was also almost identical seating behind this, but out in the open. At the front was another area where you could clearly sunbathe. When Dale pointed this out, all three of them could only laugh as the weather in Guernsey that November morning was the complete opposite to sunbathing weather.

They only glanced downstairs which was on two levels. Firstly, where the galley kitchen and lounge area was, then down into the bedrooms, and as Clare and the CSIs hadn't opened the locked door to the bedroom that Vivienne and Adam had shared they didn't see inside this. The second one, although small, was luxurious and had twin beds in. They were surprised how small both the crew cabins were, but they looked very cosy and comfortable enough. These sorts of yachts normally have a crew of three or so, especially if one was going to host and cook in the well-equipped galley kitchen, so it would have been a tight fit. Heather had told them that Imogen Jones, when she had booked it for her sister, had asked for only one crew member for privacy and sailing around the Caribbean made this feasible, especially as Vivienne and Adam were going to host and cook for themselves.

As they got off the yacht, they were surprised how flimsy and low the railings were on the deck, and at the back, where the little motorboat was stowed, there were no railings. Bearing in mind that on the night Vivienne went into the water, the little motorboat wasn't even in that position – it was moored alongside, as they had used it to get to the marina clubhouse and it was a free drop into the sea.

They left Clare and the other two CSIs to their work, and after less than a two-minute drive arrived and parked outside flats that were arranged in an L-shape. They were of a modern build and were in three stories. Juliet said they were called maisonettes; the upstairs flats, one of which was Theo's, was only one bedroom and on one floor.

They climbed the stairs to the corridor that Theo's flat was on, and Dale banged on the door. Although the door had glass in it, it was frosted and the only window onto the corridor had a net curtain. They could only make out that the window was into a kitchen and as far as they could see nothing had been disturbed.

Dale knocked again, harder now, still no reply from this flat but the noise brought the neighbour directly next door out. She was an elderly lady, most probably in her seventies, and was fully dressed.

She shouted, 'What are you doing making such a racket at this time of the morning?' The lady looked extremely irritated but, as she was dressed, they clearly hadn't woken her up.

As soon as Dale showed her his police warrant card it was like a switch had been turned on, and the old lady became extremely pleasant; she was of an age that still totally respected the police.

'The young fella came back yesterday evening. I hadn't seen him for weeks; he banged and made a lot of noise for about twenty minutes or so and then went off. He has not been back today at all.'

'Do you know where he has gone to?' Dale asked.

'I thought he would go over there,' she indicated to the other flats on their level in the L-shape. 'The young girl he hangs about with wasn't there at the time he got back, I don't think, and he went off.'

'Any idea where?' Dale asked again.

'The only person who might know is his mother and she doesn't live in St Peter Port.'

'What sort of neighbour is he?' Sandy asked trying to find out something more about Theo.

'A very pleasant young man. He has only been here less than a year and he never has any people round or any parties, which I was dreading when I saw him move in. Plays his music a bit too loud at times.'

∞

'What are we going to do next?' Dale asked, looking at Juliet and Sandy while they walked back to the car. 'I presume we are going to head to Petit Bot Bay?'

'I would say yes. We need to get our hands on Theo Le Tissier or Le Feuvre. Whatever his real name is,' Sandy said.

They drove out of St Peter Port and along the coast to the pretty seaside village of Petit Bot Bay. Sandy had seen a signpost for it when they first arrived, not long after they left the airport.

Dale told them that in Guernsey they have at least twenty-seven beaches, all of them beautiful, from the flat, mostly sandy beaches in the north and west to places like Petit Bot Bay in the south with its dramatic cliffs.

Even though a late autumn walk or even a winter walk on a beach did often appeal to Sandy, it was the last thing on his mind that cold, miserable November morning.

They parked in a small car park by a firmly closed tearoom that had a notice on the door saying "back in April". A cup of tea or coffee would have been a nice tonic to the disheartened feelings of the detectives. They looked down at the bay, and it did look lovely and would especially do so on a spring or summer's day. The cliffs down to it were also spectacular.

The cottage that Theo's mum lived in was not far away. Dale knocked hard on the door which was opened by an attractive woman no older than fifty years old. After Dale had introduced themselves, they were shown into a small and cosy front room. It was evident that Theo was not there. Sandy was sure he heard the woman say her name was June Le Tissier. There was just about room for them all to fit in and take a seat.

'What has he done now?' a worried looking June asked, glancing at all of them. 'He did seem troubled when he arrived last night. I put it down to the long and hard sailing he had been doing over the last few days, in fact it's probably been weeks that he has been away.'

So, Theo had been there. They had again missed him.

'We need to speak to him about the death of Vivienne Jones,' Sandy said.

'I couldn't believe it when I saw the news of her going missing,' June replied. 'My boy was sailing her and Adam Scott around the Caribbean. I told everyone.'

'Did you speak to Theo about what happened?' Sandy asked.

'He rang me from Barbados and told me she had fallen off the back of the boat while drunk one night and was missing.'

'How did he seem to you at that time?'

'It was only a short call, but he seemed distracted.' She looked around the room. 'He is my only child and we went through a lot with his dad, I know him better than anyone.' June then jumped up out of her seat. 'Who would like a hot drink. It is so cold outside, and that wind is bitter.'

Although they were keen to go and find Theo, the background information they were getting from his mum was invaluable to their investigation.

June returned with a tray that had four steaming hot cups of coffee and large chunks of what she told the UK detectives was a Gâche Melée, a spiced apple cake. She had baked it fresh that morning as she knew Theo loved the traditional Guernsey cake, but he had gone off before it had been fully baked.

There were a hundred and one questions that Sandy wanted to ask about Theo, but he thought he would stick to his time with Vivienne and Adam.

'Can you tell us about all of the conversations that you had with him while he was with Vivienne and Adam?'

'Theo didn't know who it was that he was going to be skippering when he flew to Antigua, just that it was a VIP couple. Gosh! He hit the jackpot with those two didn't he!' June looked round the room at them, smiling. 'He rang me straight away and told me.'

'When else did he talk to you about on that part of the trip?'

'A couple of days later. He was more than a little bit infatuated with Vivienne and he said Adam was charming and great fun, but he had a bit of an edge to him.'

'What did he mean by that?' Juliet asked.

June just shrugged her shoulders. 'What does "got an edge" even mean? Young people talk a different language at times.'

'When else did you hear from him, and what did he say?' Sandy enquired.

'That was it until Vivienne went missing, and I have told you about that. He was then in Antigua, and told me he would be home a bit later than planned as he was going to help bring the yacht back to Guernsey. He seemed very down, and I just wanted him home.'

'Can you tell us what you meant by "went through a lot with Theo's dad"?' Juliet asked.

A look of pain crossed June's face; even though it must have been years ago, the scar of what she was about to tell them still ran deep it seemed. 'He was an alcoholic and used to beat me horribly, whatever he could get his hand on he would strike me with it, or just his fists.' She paused. 'When Theo was about eleven his father beat me so badly I spent four weeks in hospital. Theo went to my parents and then we came to live here, which was my grandparents' house.'

'What happened to him?' Juliet asked. 'Theo's dad I mean.'

'He went to prison for four years and then died about four years later. Luckily, I never heard from him again and neither did Theo as far as I am aware.'

Knowing that they could come back and that they needed to get their hands on Theo, Sandy asked, 'Did Theo tell you where he was going this morning?'

'To his girlfriend's, he said. They have been together only since he moved back to Guernsey. She lives on one of the flats nearby him. She is barely out of her teens, so not sure where this relationship will go.'

∞

They then headed back to the block of flats that they had been at that morning, passing a sign to the German Occupation Museum. Guernsey, during the second world war had been occupied by the Germans for a period of four years and the legacy of the oppression of the occupation lingered afterwards for decades .

The flat that Theo's girlfriend lived in, who was a girl by the name of Susan Walters, was opposite where they had been earlier. They went by the elderly lady's flat without being seen and Dale banged loudly on the door. There was no reply and after a short time Dale banged again. The door was eventually opened by a very slight, slim girl who was, as June had described, hardly out of her teens. So, about ten years or more younger than Theo.

'What do you want?' she shouted. 'Banging on my door so loudly. I was asleep.'

'We have come to talk to Theo Le Tissier,' Dale said, barging past her and into the small flat.

The other two followed his lead and also went straight in.

'Get out of my flat now. I will call the police on you!' an even more agitated Susan shouted.

'We are the police,' Dale said, showing her his warrant card.

This seemed to agitate Susan even more, and as they went from room to room looking for Theo, she shouted, 'Shouldn't you have a warrant to search like this? This is my property; you can't do this.'

The flat contained one large room that had a lounge and a kitchen within it. There were two mugs on the kitchen top and also the ash trays had more than one reefer in them. Sandy detected a faint trace of cannabis but no more, and he thought that Susan might have a good point about needing a warrant. They could though argue that they were in pursuit of a criminal and this was the address that they believed he had gone into.

There was a bedroom that had a divan bed and a wardrobe. No trace of Theo in the wardrobe and to be fair he couldn't have got in there as it was full of clothes just dumped in there. A number had the labels on, and Sandy wondered if Susan had been shoplifting.

That only left a bathroom which had a toilet, sink and a bath with a handheld shower. The flat was quite filthy; it was the sort of place you wiped your feet on the way out rather than on the way in.

The three detectives left rather dejectedly to Susan's shouts that she hadn't seen Theo and would warn him off if she did and they could expect a complaint from her solicitor.

As they walked past the elderly lady's flat, the door opened dramatically, but the elderly lady took a step back into the hall to make sure she wasn't seen.

'Is he back in his flat?' Dale asked.

'No. He is in there. He hasn't left,' she whispered.

'There is no sign of him in there though,' Dale said. 'We have searched it.'

'I can assure you he has not left unless he jumped out of the window at the back, and I would have heard him scream in pain from the fall,' the elderly lady insisted.

'My grandad told me about the case of Shannon Matthews, a young girl who had been abducted, and was hidden in the bottom of a divan bed. Maybe he is hiding in there. He is meant to be only small isn't he.'

'I will call for uniform back up,' Dale said, as he got onto his phone to the station. 'Let's wait downstairs for them to arrive.'

In literally five minutes two uniform officers turned up and went with them to the flat. They banged on the door but with no immediate response. A few moments passed and they banged again. Again, no immediate response, then eventually the door was opened by Susan shouting and screaming about it being a police state and this was oppression. Almost all the flats now had people out of them, those downstairs looking up and the others on the same floor looking along at the scene that had developed.

'We have come to arrest Theo Le Tissier for fraud and the

involvement in the death of Vivienne Jones.'

There was an audible gasp that went round the watching crowd on the mention of Vivienne's name.

In they went, and Juliet and Dale checked the divan drawers. They were both empty, but Theo could have fitted in them. Was he now elsewhere in the flat? Sandy had another idea, again from a story of Grandad Tom's police career. He once told him of the time as a uniform officer, when he was driving the night crime patrol detective around, that they had been trying to arrest a burglar and he had hidden around the bath behind the panel.

They went into the small bathroom, only Sandy really fitted in the room, he pulled the unsecured panel away and there he was, there was Theo wrapped around the bottom of the bath. He sprang out at speed, knocking Sandy off balance, but Sandy was still able to make a tap tackle learnt from his rugby playing, over went Theo into the lounge area and Sandy fell on him. Susan then jumped on Sandy's back and bit his shoulder hard making him yelp loudly and roll out of the way.

The two uniformed officers then took over and one of them, with the help of Sandy as best as he could, managed to handcuff Theo. Susan, on the other hand was much harder to detain as she kicked, spat and tried to bite anyone who came close. Eventually she ran out of steam and the other uniformed officer, Dale, and Juliet carried her out, still screaming with her hands handcuffed behind her back, to the now arrived police van and re-enforcements.

Chapter Twenty-Four

In the medical examination room adjacent to the cell block in St Peter Port police station, the force medical examiner looked at the bite mark on the top of Sandy's right shoulder.

'The bite has broken the skin only in a couple of places where her incisors are,' the medical examiner said, prodding with blue gloved hands, not as gently as Sandy would have liked. 'You will feel a bit sore for a few days, and if you are not up to date with tetanus and hepatitis I suggest you come along to my surgery tomorrow morning and we will sort you out.'

'Good job you were wearing all of those layers, your coat, suit jacket and shirt,' Clare said, smiling as though she found Sandy's discomfort amusing.

She was busy sticking a ruler scale next to the wound and taking photographs for any court case against Susan, which the Guernsey police would now initiate.

'I am glad she hasn't damaged my clothes,' Sandy said, examining each piece as he put them back on. 'I am just going to write my statement and then I will come through to the meeting room to see what your search revealed.'

Forty-five minutes later, and with his statement about the assault completed and a second mug of tea in his hand, Sandy and the others settled around the table in the meeting room to be briefed by Clare. Unfortunately, neither Richard nor Dave Ashton could join them via a Zoom meeting link as they were otherwise engaged at that time.

'I will start with the bedroom,' Clare began. 'I am not sure why I was surprised, but I was, that the room was fairly untidy, and the bed had not been made. There was in the room either hanging up, or on the floor, a lot of Miss Jones clothes, and let me tell you she has some beautiful clothes.'

The local female CSI interjected, 'Her shoes are gorgeous! We have recovered all of the clothing; in fact, all her belongings, and we are in the process of packaging them up to return to whoever is her next of kin as they are of no forensic or evidential value. There are also a lot of Mr Scott's belongings which we are trying to itemise separately.'

'Is there anything in her belongings which could be of interest to our investigation?' Sandy asked.

'Was she wearing any jewellery when she was found or was any jewellery taken off her at the autopsy?' Clare asked.

Juliet added, 'What about that incredibly beautiful gold and diamond Cartier watch she always wears? Did you see that on her body?'

Being suddenly bombarded with questions none of which he was sure he could answer, Sandy remarked, 'What Cartier watch? I have never noticed her wearing one before, and I am sure I would remember if I saw this being removed from her wrist at the autopsy.'

'She was wearing it when we saw her before, you know, those times in Eaton Square. You missed it as you were no doubt too busy being entranced by Vivienne's beauty,' laughed Juliet, as she showed Sandy the watch on Vivienne's right wrist on a number of social media pictures.

'Anyway, two more areas to discuss,' Clare continued. 'In the lounge area underneath the seat was a medium-sized black leather Prada clutch bag that was open and contained bright red lipstick, but nothing else.'

They looked at the photographs Clare had taken; Sandy shrugged his shoulders, not sure if this took them anywhere.

For her last point, Clare said, 'In the front cabin where Theo used to reside, until he was moved out, is this shelving.'

Clare again showed them photographs, this time of the identical type of metal shelving bar they were looking for, and exactly what they had seen that had been taken out of the catamaran in Grand Cayman. It would appear that these were a standard fit in a luxury yacht or other similar vessels.

'I wasn't sure it was worth us taking them as it all looked firmly in place, that was until George Dotrice popped back to get some more of his belongings. He told me the shelving had been unstable for a long period of time and that Theo must have taken it apart and fixed it. Did a good job, he said. So, I have taken both shelving bars and exhibited them separately. Not photographed to scale for the National Injuries Database as yet, though.'

∞

Before they discussed an interview strategy with Dale and Juliet who was going to accompany him in the interview, Sandy sent off two messages. The first one to Adam asking about the Cartier watch and the handbag being empty. He then let Richard know about the search. He had already sent him a message about the arrest of Theo, within which he had omitted to say that they had been given the run around all over the island, and how he had been assaulted by Theo's girlfriend.

He had only just finished writing and sending the message to Richard when his phone buzzed, and Sandy had a call from the man himself, Richard.

'Great work,' Richard said. 'Sorry I didn't respond earlier; I was at my daughter's final assembly at primary school.'

Richard didn't seem to know anything about the Cartier watch being taken by them in Barbados. He also didn't know what was happening on Grand Cayman with the Lewis cousins as Dave was dealing with it, but he did know that Dave had given up on trying to fly to Grand Cayman himself as there were no direct flights. He was now trying to get them brought to Barbados.

'I thought you were in charge of this investigation,' Sandy said, laughing with Richard.

'I wish you were,' Richard said sincerely.

Before they had a chance to discuss the next steps to take, they had to end the call as Sandy had an incoming call from Adam Scott. He put his phone on to the speaker function as he was keen for Juliet to be a witness to their conversation, bearing in mind that Adam was their prime suspect.

'Hello Sandy,' Adam said. 'I thought we had Vivienne's watch here, but I have gone through all of the bags I brought home, and it is not in them. I have just chucked everything in a spare room.' He paused for a few moments. 'Sorry, just remembering that Vivienne always said I was useless at looking for anything and she was right, things I thought were lost were under my nose all of the time!'

'We have only just noticed that the watch was missing and that Miss Jones always seemed to wear it.'

'You are very observant, Sandy,' Adam said.

Sandy moved out of the way of Juliet's elbow, narrowly avoiding her jab. He should have given her credit for spotting the watch.

'The watch was her pride and joy,' Adam continued. 'I didn't buy it for her, it was her gift to herself for winning her first Oscar. She always took it off at night, that's why I thought I picked it up when I packed up things from our bedroom.'

Not wanting to say to Adam that he didn't do a very good job of clearing all of the belongings out of the yacht, Sandy said to him instead, 'You did leave the odd thing behind that we have now collected, we will send back your belongings to you and Miss Jones to her sister.'

'It was all a bit of a rush as I didn't want to stay on there any longer. I was feeling traumatised so I might have left the odd thing or two.'

'You probably don't know the answer to this, but would Vivienne have had anything else in her black clutch bag?' Sandy asked.

'Let me think now,' Adam paused for a short while, the detectives pictured him scratching his head. 'She normally carried a small packet of pocket tissues, no cash but two credit cards in there. There is I believe a small pouch somewhere in the bag that she kept them in. I think she paid for the meal the previous night with one of them.'

Clare, who was still in the room, whispered, 'I checked

that pocket and nothing in there.'

'Thanks Adam, I have got to go now but I told Celia I would call early next week.'

'Appreciate it. I have sent Celia back to London for a few days, I couldn't cope with her anymore at the moment!'

Cramping your style with the ex-wife maybe, thought Sandy, probably a bit unkindly.

Adam added, 'We do plan on visiting Imogen next week though to discuss the funeral arrangements and a memorial service. Sorry, got to go myself.'

∞

'What do you want me to prioritise next, Sandy?' Clare asked as Dale and Juliet went off to plan and then interview Susan.

It had been felt that as Sandy was the victim of the assault, he should have nothing more to do with Susan's time in custody.

'I know it has been a long day for you already, but can you firstly get the photographs of the shelving metal bar completed and sent to the National Injuries Database. Probably need to remind DS Dave Ashton to make sure that is done in Grand Cayman as well. Then, in terms of scenes left to examine here, we have Theo's flat, Susan's flat and then Theo's mum, June Le Tissier's, cottage. That will be a quick one so maybe do that first.'

'OK, boss,' Clare said, smiling. 'I will get one of the local CSIs to go and do the cottage and I will take the photographs and upload them.'

'I will go and check with the custody officer on the

chances of keeping Susan in custody overnight to allow her flat to be examined tomorrow morning,' Sandy said.

He also wanted to find someone with a couple of painkillers for his shoulder as the ones he had taken earlier were wearing off.

He didn't need to go far as he was met by the custody officer coming to find him.

'DCI McFarlane, can I have a word with you? The solicitor for Mr Le Tissier has asked if his client can have a rest period now and be interviewed in the morning.'

Sandy was torn between striking while the prisoner seemed to be vulnerable and to hold an interview now or acceding to the wishes of the solicitor. He thought that they should probably have a quick interview that evening.

However, the next comment by the custody officer made that not possible. 'The solicitor thinks that Mr Le Tissier is emotionally drained and having a psychological collapse of some description. He has asked me to get the police medical examiner to see his client.'

This decided things so there was no choice other than to leave an interview until the morning.

As the custody officer was about to leave, Sandy asked, 'I presume you will be looking to keep Susan in custody overnight as well?'

'Oh yes, no problem. We have signed off an authority for a search at the addresses. I know they take time to organise.' He winked at Sandy. 'And we will keep them both in custody for twenty-four hours as a minimum.'

The custody officer went off to call the force medical examiner and to find Sandy a couple of painkillers that he knew they had in the custody block area.

He was not sure why he had not noticed it before, but he saw that he had a couple of missed calls from Hannah. When he called her, she answered straight away.

'Hi Sandy, how are you getting on in Guernsey?'

Although she seemed to be sounding bright and breezy, Sandy instinctively knew that there was something wrong.

'What's wrong, Hannah?'

'Nothing really and everything really. I am just feeling very emotionally fragile at the moment, which as you know isn't me, or is it me? I don't know anymore.'

'What has brought this on?' Sandy asked, while sitting down.

No sooner had he done this than the custody officer walked in with his two tablets, so he stood up again and pulled his water bottle out of his backpack, a drink would help him swallow the tablets.

'What was that about? Why do you need to take painkillers?' Hannah asked in a concerned voice.

'It's really nothing to worry about, I got bitten when arresting someone here in Guernsey, but the bite hardly broke the surface. I am OK. Let's not talk about me, tell me about you.'

'I had a rubbish day in court and the judge told me off for leading my victim. She was a victim of rape for goodness' sake. I normally shrug things off, but the defence barrister was so nasty to her I wanted to punch him.'

This brought lots and lots of laughter from them both. They enjoyed each other's company so much; they just didn't get to spend enough time together though.

Chapter Twenty-Five

Although none of the team had particularly wanted to go out the previous evening, they had forced themselves to walk down to the waterfront and had then enjoyed a curry at the Taj there. Dale had joined them, and they had all gone across and looked at *Magnificence* moored in the harbour. It was a very beautiful yacht.

During the evening meal, Clare had told them that they had found nothing at the examination of June Le Tissier's home. She made them all laugh when she told them the photographs of the shelving metal bars that had been sent by the police in Grand Cayman had been sent to the National Injuries Database with no scale attached, so she had got them to re-submit them.

The next morning, Sandy had booked himself onto the day's last flight out of Guernsey heading to London. Juliet had agreed to stay if needed and Clare, was volunteering to also stay and keep her company. As Sandy walked towards the police station, he felt very guilty, but he needed to get home and spend some time with Hannah and his family as his boss, D/Supt Watson needed him to be in the office all of the following week, so that meant a week in London.

By the time he settled into a room from which he could monitor the interview, he saw that Dale, Juliet, Theo and his solicitor were already in place and the caution and introductions had been completed.

'Before you begin questioning Mr Le Tissier,' the solicitor said, 'I need to raise a point. Although this morning he has been deemed fit to be interviewed, due to his fragile emotional state I would ask that you take your questioning slowly and gently.'

Sandy looked at Theo. This was the first time that he had had a real chance to see him in person, lying on top of him in the flat and then seeing him being dragged off in handcuffs was not conducive to actually seeing what he looked like. Sandy saw a young man, slightly younger than himself and of small build. He did look gaunt with hollow cheeks and his hair was dark, quite long and unkempt. He clearly had not seen a hairdresser before he had set off on his Caribbean journey. Sandy also saw that his right leg was bouncing up and down wildly and, try as Theo might, he was unable to keep it still.

'The name you are using, Le Tissier,' said Dale, 'is not your real name, is it?'

The question made Theo look up from the mysterious spot on the desk he was focussing on to stare at Dale. 'It is my name,' he said.

'It is not your surname, that is Le Feuvre,' Dale said.

'I don't use that scumbag's name. I haven't used it since I was seventeen. He ruined my mum's life and almost ruined mine.'

Theo spoke with such venom that everyone was surprised, including his solicitor, and everyone stared at him.

Dale recovered first. 'Le Tissier is your grandad's name

then and your mum's maiden name.'

'That's right, my grandad was incredible to me, and he taught me to sail before I could hardly walk and to manoeuvre big yachts like *Magnificence* through oceans and to sail even bigger yachts, but I prefer the ones where I can be in charge by myself,' Theo said, animated now and not the sullen character he had been just before. There was such a contrast of emotions he was displaying.

'Your grandad was Peter Le Tissier then?' said Dale.

Juliet and Sandy, who were watching, hadn't a clue who Dale was talking about. Seeing Juliet's confusion, Dale answered his own question.

'He was an Olympic sailor and won medals when he competed, and in world championships. He even sailed in the America's Cup. It is a sailing competition that two nations compete in, and the boats and the whole event costs multi-millions of pounds.'

A smile at last crossed Theo's face. 'Yes, that is my papa. He sadly died when I was seventeen. He was the one who paid for and insisted that I took all of my yacht master and ocean-going courses. I even got to be part of the Olympic fringe team, hence I moved to Portsmouth and Weymouth in England to start with.'

Good, they have got him talking and have built a good rapport with him, thought Sandy.

Dale asked, 'You got the job with the Candice Investment Bank by false pretences, didn't you?'

Looking angry again, Theo said, 'No I didn't!'

'Do you think that they would have employed you with your previous convictions to look after VIP customers like

Vivienne Jones and Adam Scott? Of course they wouldn't.'

'If they had enquired into my references they would have found out,' Theo said, looking back down at the spot on the table he had focused on before. 'One of the references I gave them was my probation officer, for goodness' sake.'

'Before we talk to you about your time with Miss Jones and Mr Scott, can I just ask you about the evening before she went into the sea from the boat.'

Sandy liked the way Dale phrased "went into the sea".

'You bought something off an American in the marina clubhouse bar that we believe is an illegal substance. What was it?'

'I didn't buy anything; you are making it up,' Theo said, again displaying his temper.

Selecting a photograph from a folder that Juliet had with her on the desk, she passed it across to Dale, who after glancing at it passed it over to Theo and his solicitor. Theo visibly shuddered on seeing himself in the photograph, which had been downloaded from the CCTV. It showed him taking possession of a small packet from one of the Lewis cousins.

Without even being asked a question, Theo said, 'No comment.'

His solicitor added, 'My client needs a break.'

∞

As soon as the detectives left the room after having switched off the recording equipment, the solicitor and Theo went into a deep conversation. When he left the monitoring room and walked to meet Juliet and Dale, Sandy looked through the glass window and saw this animated conversation going on. *Not sure that is what I would describe as needing a break... the solicitor said that Theo was allegedly tottering on a nervous breakdown*, Sandy thought to himself. Theo looked like he was raging in there, he most certainly had a lot of pent-up emotion inside him.

No sooner had they settled down in the canteen with a cup of tea for Sandy and coffee for the other two, when in walked a grinning Clare Symonds and the other two local CSIs.

'What are you all grinning about?' Sandy asked, now smiling himself even though he had no idea what for, the smiling was just infectious.

'You will need to wait, boss,' Clare replied. 'Do you want the good news or the bad news first?'

'Good news,' Juliet said, before Sandy had a chance.

'No. You will have to have the bad news first,' Clare laughed. 'We have finished examining both Theo and Susan's flats.'

'What time did you start this morning?' Sandy said, surprised that they could have finished already.

'Seven a.m., while you were no doubt still lying in your bed!' Clare replied. 'There was nothing of note in Theo's flat. Not long after we arrived the old lady next door made us bacon sandwiches. She had gone to the shop yesterday in preparation, somehow knowing we would be there today. When I told her I was a vegan, she went and made me scrambled egg, which of course I don't eat either. Then she made me toast, with the finest Guernsey butter, she told me. The toast would have been fine, but it was covered with butter. I didn't have the heart to tell her it was no good for me either.'

'When you have finished dragging out your story of the saga of breakfast can you tell us what the good news is, Clare, if the bad news is that you couldn't have breakfast,' Sandy said, smiling.

'No, the bad news is there was nothing at Theo's address.' Clare smiled, milking it again. 'The good news is this...'

She produced an exhibit bag with a small amount of what looked like cannabis inside.

A clearly disappointed Sandy said, 'Is that it! A bit of cannabis that amounts to only enough for a caution.' He looked around at Juliet and Dale shrugging their shoulders in disappointment.

When he looked around, he saw that Clare had reached again into her exhibit bag and there, sat on the table was a gold, diamond encrusted Cartier ladies' watch.

'Where did you find that?' Sandy said in delight.

'Behind the bath panel where you found him hiding,' a smiling Clare said. 'I am worried about harming it by dusting it for fingerprints or using any chemicals for trying to find DNA.'

'We had a call yesterday morning from a high-end jeweller called Ray and Scott in Saint Sampson, just north of us here in St Peter Port,' Dale said, and then as it dawned on him, 'they said someone had been in to get a watch valued, which they were dubious about. I hadn't got anyone to attend but was going to get someone to go and see them today.'

'It must have been Theo who went there after he left his mother's. She said he had the use of a scooter to get around with,' Sandy said. 'Or is that just wishful thinking?'

Dale went off to organise someone to go with Clare to check if it was the same watch, recover the CCTV and get advice on how best to swab the watch. This was handy as the solicitor had just come out of the room and told them that they were ready to continue. One of the local CSIs returned with printed-off pictures of the photographs they had taken of the Cartier watch to assist them in the interview.

∞

As they left the meeting room, Clare had taken a call telling her the fingerprints they had found on one of the metal shelving bars was that of someone called Theo Le Feuvre. Returning to the interview room, Dale and Juliet looked and felt jubilant; that someone was also known as Le Tissier and was the man sitting in front of them.

This was an investigator's dream, having evidence to put to a prisoner. They now had so much that they were rubbing their hands with glee. They only hoped he didn't return to saying "no comment".

Dale asked the first question. 'I hope that you had a good break and are now ready to answer some more of our questions.' Seeing Theo nod, he said, 'You told the police, when you were spoken to in Barbados, that you went to bed after returning from the marina clubhouse.' Seeing Theo nodding again, he went on, slightly raising his voice and thrusting his words forward. 'That is not true, is it? You accosted Miss Jones, stole her credit cards and her Cartier watch and threw her into the Caribbean Sea.'

The fire was back in Theo's eyes as he shouted, 'I didn't!

Don't you dare accuse me of murdering her.' Regaining his composure as instantly as he had lost it, he said, 'You know I didn't murder her; it was Adam Scott who did that.'

'Did you see Adam do anything to her that supports what you are saying?' Dale asked.

Sandy, now back in the monitoring room, shouted out to himself, as there was no one else there, 'Don't let him off the hook by letting him distract you, talking about Adam Scott!'

'Yes, I saw him grab Vivienne quite roughly and tell her that they were going back to the yacht and to stop flirting with the Americans.' Theo paused and took a deep breath. 'The row must have continued after I had gone to my cabin.'

'Get back to the watch and the metal shelving bar,' Sandy said, again out loud to himself. It was often so frustrating monitoring an interview when you so much wanted to be the one asking the questions.

As is if hearing him, Juliet asked, 'Did you ever notice Miss Jones wearing a beautiful Cartier watch?'

A visibly stunned Theo, now knowing they must have found the watch, said, 'Yes, I did.' Then, quick as a flash and surprising the interviewers and Sandy who was watching, he said, 'I found the watch in the lounge area of the yacht not long before I got back to Antigua. It was on the table, and I knew it would be valuable and of personal significance to the family, I decided to look after it and bring it back to England to give back to Mr Scott.'

He had possibly dislodged their argument, as part of the offence of theft-stealing was that you need to have the intention of permanently depriving the owner of their property.

Dale was going to try and dismantle this defence straight away, and as Juliet produced photographs of where the watch had been found and photographs of the watch itself, he said, 'I don't think this is giving it back to the owner's family, is it?' He gave Theo a few moments to take in the significance of the photographs and the hiding of the watch. 'Hiding the watch underneath a bath isn't giving it back to the owner, is it?'

The solicitor looked bewildered as Theo had clearly not told him about any of this. He just shook his head.

Theo said, 'No comment.'

'What about going into Ray and Scott's to sell it, almost as soon as you had got back on the island?'

Before his solicitor could stop him, Theo said, 'I was just inquisitive, that was all. Doesn't mean I intended to sell it.'

'Let's talk about this metal shelving bar,' Dale said, showing other pictures of the shelf in place and the metal bars taken down.

Sandy could swear that he saw a moment of fear cross the face of Theo, who paused for such a long time that everyone, probably including his solicitor, felt that he would make no comment. In these situations, interviewers normally let the person they are interviewing fill the gap, rather than ask a question themselves.

'How do you explain that we have found your fingerprints on one of the metal shelving bars?' Dave enquired.

Not needing any more time to think, Theo said, 'It had come loose so I had taken the shelf apart and on the way back to Antigua I had fixed it. That's why my fingerprints are on there.'

The solicitor, totally bewildered about any significance of metal shelving bars and clearly cross that he had not had any disclosure of what they had wanted to talk to his client about, added, 'I feel this has all been a bit of an ambush. I want us to stop the interview and for me to take instructions from Mr Le Tissier.'

Chapter Twenty-Six

One of the other detectives in the CID office took Sandy to the airport, and they had to race as he was cutting it a bit fine to make the last check-in time. In places tight, the narrow lanes of Guernsey made it slightly scary, but Sandy just made it in time.

On the flight home he felt guilty that he was leaving Juliet in Guernsey; she had been away as much as he had, and she was a mother with two children and had her husband at home as well. Juliet had been insistent that she should stay, especially as she was taking part in the interviews. Although he was due in the office in London on the Monday and all of next week, he had arranged with the boss, D/Supt Watson for Juliet to have the week at home.

After having had dinner with just his mum and dad, Sandy had gone straight to bed. It would appear that Grandad Tom had gone out with a number of ex-work colleagues, a great group of retired detectives like him, for a drink and to play a card game called Clag, whatever that was, but apparently they all enjoyed playing the game. Tom had decided that now was the time to go back to his own house and start to face living there alone.

The weather that late November Saturday morning was cold, very cold, but Sandy's early morning run turned out to be for him a pleasure as he ran his usual circular route around the cathedral, through Ely and then along the River Great Ouse back to his home. He had, as he ran, mentally processed what information he needed to update Richard Ambrose on when they met later for their Zoom chat. He had also thought about how he could get back into the Ely Tigers rugby team that he used to play for; as he was now in his early thirties, his time for playing was slipping by fast and he wanted to make sure he kept in the team as long as he could.

The one person he hadn't thought about was Hannah; she was there waiting for him when he got back home. His mum and dad had already gone out leaving Sandy and Hannah alone. Whether his parents genuinely had things to do or it was a deliberate ploy, Sandy didn't care. It was great to have the house and Hannah all to himself for a change.

As Sandy had settled into his bedroom to join the zoom call with Richard, he had received a call from Juliet telling him that Theo had made no comment interviews that morning. Dale had spoken to one of the Crown Law officers who had agreed to charge Theo with a fraud offence for obtaining employment by deception (not declaring his previous convictions) and handling stolen property (the Cartier watch.) This, they thought, would act as holding charges while the authorities in Barbados decided what they wanted them to do with him.

After an interview with Susan that afternoon, Juliet and Clare were on the flight home, Juliet joked that she could stay no longer as she had run out of clean knickers.

It was a pleasure to see Dave Ashton on the Zoom call along with Richard.

'Always in a bedroom somewhere Sandy,' Dave commented, which made them all laugh. 'Before we talk about what is happening in Guernsey, is it possible please to talk about Bradley and Michael Lewis. I have their lawyer and the police in the Cayman Islands breathing down my neck. There are some other big shot lawyers flying in from New York City early Monday morning and they are threatening to create a diplomatic incident unless we release them.'

Although Dave was leading on this side of the investigation, it was Richard who had made the decision to arrest them, and it was pleasing to see he was clear in his decision making.

'I am happy we have the grounds to keep them in custody until at least Monday when we have the results of the forensics on the metal shelving bar. My only regret is that we haven't got Adam Scott in custody as then it would be even more appropriate to have all of the suspects in custody at the same time.'

'What do we know about the Lewis cousins, where did they get their money from?' Sandy asked.

'Their paternal grandfather is a billionaire,' Dave said. 'He owns the catamaran and another yacht, which is probably even bigger than *Magnificence*. The boys have a large trust fund.'

'And what do they do with it? They wander about the Caribbean peddling drugs,' Sandy said, shaking his head.

'Let me tell you about Theo Le Tissier, whose real name as you now know is Le Feuvre. The Cartier watch that I asked you about, we found him in possession of it – he had hidden it.'

'Brilliant!' Richard exclaimed. 'It is him, tell me it is him?'

'He has come up with an explanation, that he found it after Adam had left the yacht and he was going to return it to him.'

'Oh dear,' said Richard; the elation had lasted only moments.

'I have seen Vivienne wearing that watch on the CCTV from the marina on the night she was murdered,' Dave said, 'How much do you think the watch is worth?'

'It has been valued,' Sandy replied, smiling.

'That was fast work,' a clearly impressed Richard offered.

Still smiling, Sandy replied, 'No, not me actually. Theo had it valued, saying he was curious. It is worth somewhere in the region of one hundred thousand US dollars.'

Richard whistled.

'Might be as much as ten times that if a Vivienne Jones memorabilia hunter is after it in the future,' said Dave.

'A law officer to the Crown there has agreed for him to be charged with handling it, but they need some sort of decision from yourselves in Barbados soon, as to what you want doing.'

They concluded the call with an agreement to meet again at nine a.m. (Barbados time) on Monday, when it would appear that the Assistant Commissioner Seymour Garner was going to join them.

∞

On the Sunday, Hannah and Sandy had made a decision that they would spend the whole day together, just the two of them. This meant no service in the cathedral for Sandy once again, and his suggestion of having the day out going for a drive in his Morgan car had also met a big *no* from Hannah.

They eventually decided on a day in Cambridge, which would include a visit to the Fitzwilliam Museum. As the museum on a Sunday didn't open until midday, they had a lazy breakfast and were then taken into Cambridge by Gregor, Sandy's dad. He was going to have Sunday lunch with his father. John McFarlane had originally wanted to tag along with Hannah and Sandy to visit the museum, he had also received a firm, but polite, no from Hannah.

When Gregor dropped them outside Hannah's house to deposit their cases, as Sandy was going to travel from there the next morning to his work in London, he switched his phone off. He had already heard from Juliet that she had got home safely the previous evening and they had dealt with what was happening. Susan had been an interesting interview, she denied all knowledge of ever seeing the Cartier watch but had told them that Theo had told her that he had done something stupid on the yacht and had lost it (meaning, she thought, his temper). Sandy had made the decision to de-arrest her for handling stolen goods (the Cartier watch) and take a statement from her as a significant witness.

Having had a leisurely walk to the museum, they admired the front of the large building – well, Sandy did; it was in his view an incredible example of a neo-classic building with a Palladian architecture type structure to it. This architectural style originated from the Venetian architect Andrea Palladio. The 19th century architect to the Fitzwilliam Museum had successfully followed Palladio's design concepts.

The museum has an outstanding collection of pieces

stretching from antiquity to the modern. Definitely a world-renowned collection of over half a million beautiful works of art, masterpiece paintings and historical artefacts. Hannah knew how much Sandy was fascinated by the art, and whereas she normally went ahead and then waited for him to catch up, today she stayed with him. The masterpieces he lingered with were those by Titan, Canaletto, Rembrandt, Rubens, Turner, Monet. There were even drawings in there by Leonardo Da Vinci, who was Sandy's favourite artist.

As they were walking up one of the magnificent stone staircases, Sandy said, 'My grandad told me the story of the man who allegedly tripped here.' Sandy demonstrated a trip and did in fact almost fall over, which brought laughter from them both. 'This man, though,' Sandy continued after steadying himself, 'knocked over three 17th Century ceramic vases. Can you imagine that happening?'

'How awful for him. I bet he was devastated.'

'My grandad says that they all wondered if it was deliberate and thought about investigating it as criminal damage. They were worth well over a hundred thousand pounds.'

After a bit of exploring, they found the vases that had been incredibly and beautifully repaired and now housed in a glass display case.

'I think he knocked them over deliberately,' said Sandy.

'I don't think you can rule out that he did trip?' Hannah replied.

'Always the defence lawyer!'

'I will have you know I prosecute twice as much as I defend! It is just that there were these Chinese vases worth an absolute fortune just sitting on a window ledge.'

'They had been sitting there sixty years without this happening before, and survived three hundred years without being broken.'

They wandered further through the museum, having a lovely time together.

'They did have an actual theft here almost ten years ago now. It was of Jade.'

'They convicted them, didn't they?' Hannah said. 'I think I saw it in the news.'

'They did a fantastic job, yes. There was a local DCI, who my grandad tells me is wonderful, and the excellent person leading it was from Durham as he had a previous similar theft at Durham University.'

'How much was the Jade worth?'

'I think I read, in total with other thefts, over fifty million pounds. I am sure the thieves had no idea what they were dealing with.'

When they walked into a side display room, Sandy stopped in his tracks.

'What has happened?' Hannah asked, concerned.

'These are not normally on display,' Sandy said as he pointed to two statues. 'They are believed to be, and I personally believe them to be, by Michelangelo.'

The statues were in bronze and of two males, one older than the other, they were both riding on magnificent panthers. Hannah did look at them with wonderment but was now worried how she would get Sandy out of the museum, remembering how many times, when they were in Florence, that he went back and visited Michelangelo's statue of David.

'I know it is disputed, but the detective work to try and

prove these are by Michelangelo is fascinating and although different, it's as good as any detective work I do,' Sandy said, looking around for a chair to sit on and spend longer to gaze at them.

Hannah was desperately looking around hoping there wasn't one.

After spending a lovely afternoon in the museum they grabbed an early Sunday evening meal on the way back to Hannah's house.

'I am sorry how I have been over the last few weeks before your grandma died, but however much I try to not be and to live in the moment, I can't do that.'

Looking at Hannah, Sandy could see how anxious and nervous she was. They had had a wonderful day together and he wanted to just enjoy that and not get into a heavy relationship discussion. Although that was what he wanted to say, he didn't.

'Tell me what you are thinking?' He took her hand, and they sat on a nearby bench even though the weather was damp and cold.

'I always look for outcomes,' Hannah said, not looking at him but continuing to hold Sandy's hand. 'I love our relationship together here and now, but is this still how we will be in five, ten, or twenty years' time? Still busy with our careers, meeting up when we get time? Is that as strong as our commitment will be to each other?'

Sandy didn't reply immediately. He thought he was totally committed to her and what was wrong with carrying on as they were. He also knew what Hannah was alluding to but was unsure what he thought, as he, as no doubt most other men hadn't thought that far ahead.

'Is it OK if I process this a bit in my own mind and give you my true feelings on it?' Seeing Hannah nod, he added, 'I love you so much that I can't imagine a future that you are not in, so just give me a bit of time please.'

On hearing Sandy say he loved her, Hannah put her arms around him and hugged him, not hearing his final comments.

Chapter Twenty-Seven

After a restless night, Sandy left Hannah sleeping as he caught a train to take him to the Foreign, Commonwealth and Development office in London. The train was full of early morning commuters heading into the big city. He looked around to see if his dad was on the train, having boarded it earlier on in the journey at Ely, but couldn't see him. A quick response to his message told him that his dad was working from home this week so he could be there to help make the final plans for Sandy's grandma's funeral. Sandy would have the flat to himself, which wasn't really what he wanted.

The first person Sandy needed to see on arrival at the office was his boss, Jane Watson. As he dropped his bags on top of an empty desk, he was met with "hello stranger" from the Detective Constables that were already in the office before him.

Jane waved him in when he stood in her doorway shortly afterwards. 'How are you, Sandy?' she asked, putting down her phone that she had been looking at.

Not wanting to say the usual answer of "I am fine", or "I am good, thank you", Sandy knew he could be honest with his boss.

'I am generally feeling a bit out of sorts at the moment, Jane.' He sat down and brushed his hand through his strawberry blond hair. 'It is not just that my grandma died who I was very close to, I am unsure what the future should hold for me.'

Looking at Sandy and giving him full eye contact, Jane said, 'I will be honest and tell you that I really need you to be here, but your health is the most important thing that matters to me. Please go home and talk to someone, if not professionally, then anyone you trust. Ring me when you need to as well.'

Sandy stood immediately. 'No, but thank you.' He was shocked that he was almost being sent home. 'Being here will not be a problem. I will go and chair the team meeting, but I see there are only a couple of DCs in the office today.'

'If you are quite sure, Sandy. Why don't we cancel the team meeting and instead can you go through the two officer's workloads that are here. DC Billy Tudor has lots of cases that haven't had any work done on them. The families whose loved ones have died abroad from suspicious circumstances need to know what is happening, if anything. We all know we do what we can for them, but this is only a fraction of what they rightly feel we should be doing.'

Drawing a seat up alongside Billy Tudor, Sandy said, 'Billy, let's go through the files in your in-tray and see if we can make any progress with them. I can sign them off if need be.'

Billy, an experienced officer with twenty-nine years police experience, looked disapprovingly at Sandy. 'You don't need to worry about me, governor, all my work is in hand. I have been a detective since you were in short pants.'

Not one to lose his temper, Sandy was very close to it

now, only just keeping control. 'Why have you got sixty cases still open to you?'

Not getting the hint and making it worse by winking at Sandy, Billy said, 'They are no trouble sitting in there and it stops me being allocated anymore work as the sergeants, you, and the other Chief Inspector can see how much work I have on the go.'

Still biting his tongue, Sandy asked, 'What are you doing on any of them?'

'The odd phone call here and there. You know,' Billy replied, starting to get the hint that he was in a bit of trouble. 'I thought you were one of the good guys Sandy, you are too nice to be talking to me like this. I am going to get a cup coffee.' With that, Billy got up and walked off.

Was that what people thought of him. Just a nice guy, too good to be true? Granted, Sandy knew he had had a sheltered, privileged life so far, and that might be the reason why he couldn't work out what to do next with Hannah, he just had been cushioned from life's harsh realities.

As Sandy worked through Billy's files by himself rather than with Billy, he shook his head. Being nice then was his flaw as a detective, not a hard drinker or a womaniser or a maverick or someone with a vile temper, no, his flaw was being nice!

He could do something about the obviously correct accusation of detective experience, but that was growing. The trouble was they only really dealt with one or two cases at a time here, they didn't have the capacity for the volume he might get if he went back to one of the Met Police's homicide teams, or, he could leave policing all together and make use of his law degree from Cambridge and go to bar school as his grandpa John McFarlane would want.

∞

As the morning dragged on and with his gloom worsening, Sandy was pleased to see he had a call from the Forensic Medical Advice Team at the National Crime Agency.

'DCI McFarlane, do you want the good news or the bad news?'

Why does everyone do this, Sandy thought, playing along with it. 'Bad news first, please.'

'We are better to do this via a Zoom call so I can show you what I am talking about. I will send you an invite now.'

The advisor rang off and Sandy logged out of Billy Tudor's case files and switched to his emails to await the invite. The FMAT advisor did seem very excited, so the good news might be very good news.

'I will share my screen with you,' said the advisor when they connected. Up on the screen came an image of a metal shelving bar. 'This is the one recovered and photographed from the catamaran on Grand Cayman.'

'I am sorry that the first images you got weren't to scale,' Sandy said.

'Not unusual to be honest, but not as bad as the time we got asked to look at a head wound injury and the image they sent us still had the wound all bandaged up.' They both started laughing. 'I replied and said we are good but not that good.'

Things sobered up a bit when the next image shown was the injury mark at the back of Vivienne Jones' neck.

230

'We used a technique called digital superimposition and image overlay and as you can see,' the advisor said, showing another image of the two together. 'The holes do not line up. This can't be the murder weapon.'

Sandy realised now what the good news was likely to be. 'Please tell me that the shelving bar from *Magnificence* does match?'

'You spoil sport, that was my good news. Let me show you.' Sharing his screen again it was clear that the image overlay showed a perfect match between the injury and the image of the shelf bar. 'The holes are slightly bigger and wider spaced than the one from the catamaran.'

A very excited, Sandy felt his gloom lifting. 'How do we produce this in evidence then?'

'As much as I would love a trip to Barbados to give evidence, I can only put these findings into a report, which I will do now. You, or the detectives in Barbados, need to share it with a forensic pathologist to interpret.'

'The resident pathologist for Barbados did the autopsy so it could be sent to him. Not sure if he has done this sort of thing before though.'

'If not, you could try Dr Nicholas Stroud, he's done this sort of work on a number of occasions in the past.'

Sandy knew Dr Stroud well and would make contact with him if the pathologist in Barbados gave him the go ahead. Looking at his watch there were at least two hours to go before the meeting with Richard and his Assistant Commissioner, time to get back to the cases of Barry Tudor. He suddenly realised why Barry thought he was a mate. Sandy had laughed at one of his jokes.

Once, when Barry had come into work really quite late and when he was about to leave early that same day, Juliet had said to Barry, 'Why are you going so early? You only came in late.'

Barry made a lightning-quick reply, 'I always think it best not to be late at both ends of the day!'

He was onto Barry now.

∞

Long before two p.m. Sandy was logged on and waiting. He somehow managed to stop himself phoning Juliet to update her, so he could at least let her have one complete day off. He knew she wouldn't be impressed and would have wanted to know, so he might weaken and call her later.

'DCI McFarlane, welcome,' the booming voice of Seymour Garner said. 'Can we focus on the two Americans in Grand Cayman first – have we anything that we can keep them in custody for? There is a huge political storm coming, and if we don't act quickly and correctly will engulf us all.'

Even though he could sense the urgency in the Assistant Commissioner's voice, Sandy did want to put some order to their conversation. He could see Richard and Dave in the room with Seymour.

'Richard, I sent you a report across earlier in your morning. I see you haven't opened it yet, but that might help us.' Watching Richard open up his laptop and switch it on, Sandy continued, 'I think it is important that we maybe look at our four suspects under the headings, Motive, Means and Opportunity. Is that, OK?'

He saw nods all round, but before he could say anything, Richard, clearly now reading the report, smiled widely. 'Wow!'

'Shall we start with the heading "Means"? The "means" used to kill Vivienne Jones was a metal shelving bar.' Sandy then shared the image overlay of the Lewis family catamaran. It was clear that the holes didn't line up. Looking at the three earnest faces sat in the room in Barbados, he added, 'I think we probably could loosely say they have a motive if we said they got angry because Vivienne spurned their advances. The opportunity is only if she somehow made it to their boat, but that is not very likely.'

Looking firstly at Richard and then at Dave, Seymour's voice wasn't booming now, it was more like urgently shouting.

'Get them released DS Ashton, immediately, and let's hope they don't sue us.'

'I think it will be fine,' Sandy said, seeing how forlorn Richard looked – he actually had no idea whether it would work out fine or not. 'They were, to be fair, most probably dealing drugs all across the Caribbean, but I am sure they will be brought back to work in the family business now. Let me go back to means...'

He saw Dave begin to make a fast retreat out of the room, no doubt to get the Lewis cousins released.

'Dave,' Sandy shouted. 'Can you stay to just hear this bit, it will only take a couple of minutes.'

Dave sat down again as Sandy showed the image overlay for the injury and the shelving from *Magnificence*.

Even though Richard knew what they were seeing as he

233

had just seen it, he said, 'Wow!' again.

'This is the means of killing Vivienne Jones.'

Sandy looked at his phone that hadn't stopped buzzing with calls, the four missed calls were from Clare Symonds, then a message asking him to call her immediately as the fast-track DNA on the shelving bar from the *Magnificence* had come back as matching Vivienne Jones.

'I have just got a message from our CSI that on this shelving is Vivienne's DNA. As you know, the fingerprints on it are Theo Le Tissier's.'

'I didn't know about the fingerprints,' Seymour said, again staring intently at Richard.

'He has an explanation that he mended the shelving, which he did, and that is why his fingerprints are on there.'

'Motive for Adam Scott is that of controlling his wife. Motive for Theo is of robbery – he has possession of Vivienne's extremely valuable watch. Her credit cards have also gone but have not been used.'

'Surely Adam Scott wouldn't have used a weapon, and his fingerprints weren't found on the weapon, were they?' Richard asked.

'No, only Theo's,' Sandy answered.

'They would both have had the opportunity as both Scott and Le Tissier were on the yacht that night,' Seymour said. 'And surely Adam Scott would not have thrown this woman he idolised into the Caribbean Sea, would he?'

'No,' Sandy said, 'all of the evidence we have points to Theo.'

'DS Ashton why are you still here?' Seymour said. 'Get those American's released immediately. You,' he pointed at

Richard, 'come with me now to see the Deputy Commissioner and then the Director of Public Prosecutions and the Attorney General to agree a charge of murder for Mr Le Tissier, and for the extradition process to be started straight away. You,' he pointed at the screen at Sandy, 'need to make sure he is still in custody in Guernsey.'

Chapter Twenty-Eight

When the conversation had finished Sandy sat feeling stunned. He leaned back in his seat, put his hands through his hair and let out a big sigh. Across the room from him he could see Billy Tudor, who was pretending to be working hard on his computer while watching Sandy out of the corner of his eye.

Sandy somehow held back from shouting out, 'Yes!' to the news he had just heard from Barbados and answered instead the incoming call from Juliet.

'I thought I told you to take the day off and work from home this week?'

'Not a chance,' Juliet replied. 'I am booked on the flight this evening to Guernsey.'

'What do you mean?' Sandy said a bit surprised, then it dawned on him. Clare had been talking to her. 'Juliet, I can't let you do this. It's not fair.'

'I am making the choice. I am part of the interview team with Dale, and we will be interviewing Theo Le Tissier first thing in the morning.'

'What has Clare told you then?'

'Clare, who is she?' They both laughed. 'Clare has told me about Vivienne's DNA on the shelving metal bar and the image overlay.'

Having moved away from Billy Tudor and into a side corridor, Sandy said, loudly and excitedly, 'This is excellent news, isn't it Juliet? How did Clare know about the image overlay – they rang me?'

'Clare was the person who uploaded the image, and she got a match notification. I so agree, Sandy, great news. Have you told Richard and my cousin yet?'

'Yes, had a Zoom call just a few moments ago. They are off to see the Deputy Commissioner and then I think the Director of Public Prosecutions and the Attorney General.'

'I have to go, Sandy, and pick the kids up from school and then pack ready for Guernsey. Send me a message as soon as you know anything from Barbados.'

Later that evening after he had finished his dinner and spent more time working on Billy Tudor's case load, Sandy received a message from Richard asking if he was available for a Zoom call.

Appearing on the screen was Dave Ashton and Richard.

'We managed to get Bradley and Michael Lewis released,' Dave said, speaking even before any of them could say hello to each other, 'before the big shot lawyers arrived.'

'How did they take it? Have you got a big complaint heading your way?' Sandy asked, then added, 'Good evening to you both too, or should I say good afternoon for you.'

'Sorry, Sandy. I will be honest with you, I have been so worried about an unlawful detention complaint, in fact, worried sick,' Dave said, indeed looking extremely stressed.

'No need for you to worry,' Sandy said. 'Richard made the decision!' They all laughed, although Richard's laugh may not have been as fulsome as that of the other two.

'The Royal Cayman Island Police have released the catamaran to one of the grandfathers' lawyers. Not before the police on the instructions of the FBI did some telematics searching on the boat,' Dave said looking at Richard rather than at the camera on the laptop. He had clearly not given Richard this information.

'What are they?' a confused Richard asked. 'Telematics? Never heard of it.'

'I thought that was something to do with cars, not boats,' Sandy said.

'Same principle,' Dave explained, now talking to the screen and Sandy. 'The catamaran had a sophisticated GPS navigation system. They have downloaded the chip and replaced it. The FBI are sure that their route around the Caribbean will match other narcotics intelligence they have.'

'Where are they now?' Sandy asked. 'Still on the Cayman Islands?'

'No, they have long gone, went on the first flight to Miami.'

'OK guys,' Sandy said, standing up, 'I have a bit of clearing up to do and I need to get ready for the morning, then bed for me. I will talk to you tomorrow after Juliet lets me know how she gets on with interviewing our friend Theo Le Tissier.'

'Whoa! Hold on!' Richard exclaimed, which made Sandy jump and then sit back down. 'I haven't told you what we wanted to speak to you about.' He then started smiling, and before Sandy could say anything, added, 'We have got permission from the DPP to prosecute Mr Le Tissier for the murder of Miss Vivienne Jones.'

'What!' Sandy shouted. 'Really?'

'No, I am making it up.' Seeing that Sandy now looked confused and then deflated, Richard said, 'Of course I am not making it up! After the interviews are completed tomorrow, we then have to sort out extradition.'

'Brilliant news! Well done to you both. From what I found out when I was in Guernsey, the extradition route will be to London first and then on to Barbados.'

'Equally well done to you Sandy, and Juliet as well,' Richard said. 'The Deputy Commissioner is unsure though; he is still convinced it is Adam Scott. It is always the husband, he unhelpfully kept saying in the meeting And I need to warn you he also kept saying if DCI McFarlane has got this wrong, I am going to swing for him.'

Sandy could hardly sleep that night with a mixture of unbridled pleasure, getting someone charged with murder was an incredible feat and feeling for any homicide detective, but he also had a feeling of extreme worry because of Carlos Bishop's words. What if they had got it wrong and it was Adam all along, like the whole world of social media seemed to believe.

∞

On his way into the FCDO office the next day, Sandy had called Juliet, who was more than excited with the developments in the case. Before the interview with Theo, she told Sandy that she had a meeting with Dale and his bosses and the law officer to the Crown, and she would let them know what the Barbados government and police there were hoping to achieve.

Before the Zoom call had finished the previous night, Richard had asked Sandy to make sure he let Imogen Jones and Adam Scott know. Assistant Commissioner Seymour Garner was keen to hold a press conference, to let the world's media know the briefest details of the developments in the case, then say no more, so the criminal justice process could take precedent.

Doing this was an extreme problem for Sandy, as his boss had insisted she needed him to be in the office in London all week. It was amazing how little they, and the consulates around the world, were able to do for British citizens who died abroad, but Jane Watson was determined that they would still try and find out where they could what that little was, and to do it.

Jane was sitting in her office when he arrived; Sandy saw that she was on her phone, but her nod to him was enough of an invite to allow him to take one of the chairs in her office.

'Sandy,' Jane said as soon as she finished her call, 'I hope you are making progress on the officers' workloads. I also need you to go to a couple of meetings tomorrow for me and a conference on Thursday that I was supposed to be speaking at. I will give you my presentation.'

This news was a blow to Sandy and his plan to ask Jane for time to travel to Swansea to see Imogen and then visit Sussex to see Adam.

'I have a problem with some of what you want me to do,' Sandy started hesitantly, but still trying to get eye contact with Jane. 'The government and police in Barbados have made a decision to prosecute Theo Le Tissier.' Seeing a slightly confused look on Jane's face, Sandy said, 'He was the skipper of the yacht *Magnificence*.' Putting his hands through his hair, which Sandy seemed to be doing a lot of recently, he continued, 'I really need to go and see the next of kin, her sister, in Wales and her ex-husband in Sussex before they hold a media briefing in Barbados.'

Jane didn't say anything for quite a few seconds, and it was clear to Sandy that she was thinking about what a solution could be. 'I did think that DS Ashton could help with this, but she is not here. I think this is for the best and the right thing for all involved and especially for the family if you go and do this now. Take the day to do it and then be back to sort things out tomorrow.'

As soon as he got to a desk in the large open plan office Sandy searched for train times from London to Swansea and then rang Imogen. His plan was to see her first and then as soon as he got back to London, head out to see Adam, hopefully in the early evening. He would book one of the department's cars and a driver to help with the trip to Sussex.

'Hello, Sandy,' Imogen said on answering. 'I was going to ring you this morning but I have a hundred and one things to sort out at the moment.'

There was an incredible business-like tone to Imogen's voice and her whole manner on the phone. 'What are you sorting out?' Sandy asked, knowing that what he was hoping to be able to tell her later in the day would shatter Imogen's appearance of normality.

'Vivienne's body is being re-patriated today and lands in London Heathrow this afternoon. The coroner for West London is going to open an inquest and immediately transfer the authority to my coroner in Swansea.'

Wow! Sandy thought, *does Richard know about this?* If so, why hadn't he told him?

Before Sandy could say anything, Imogen kept on talking, 'We have decided, well that is Celia and myself, to hold a service to celebrate Vivienne's life at the end of next week at Westminster Abbey. The dean and his staff were wonderful when we met them yesterday.'

'Yesterday… are you in London, Imogen?'

'Yes, I am at Eaton Square now. Adam arrived yesterday afternoon, but too late for the meeting with the dean. It is the guest list we are having problems with, even though there is seating capacity for over two thousand, we can only use part of the abbey, so we are limited to seven hundred and fifty people and two hundred of those are going to the media. We would like you and DS Ashton to attend, and Adam mentioned DI Ambrose and DS Dave Ashton from the Barbados Police to attend as well if they can.'

'Don't move from Eaton Square and tell Adam not to either,' Sandy said, as he leapt to his feet grabbing his coat and backpack in his other hand and sped out of the office. 'I will be with you all as soon as I can.'

Deciding that Horse Guards Road rather than Whitehall was best for getting a taxi to Eaton Square, Sandy ran through Great Charles Street and managed to get a black London taxi almost immediately, as one was dropping off a couple at the Churchill war rooms.

As the taxi sped along to Victoria and then towards Belgravia, Sandy realised that the service would probably clash with his grandma's funeral as that was going to be held on the Friday of the following week. He did want to, and felt it was right to attend Vivienne Jones' service, but his grandma and family must come first.

Chapter Twenty-Nine

As he walked up the steps to enter the house in Eaton Square, he looked at the house next door; he had visited there on a number of occasions in the past to see Viscount Peveril and his sister Arabella Montague, who lived there. Sandy wondered if any of them were at home, he felt he was missing their company.

Imogen showed Sandy into the downstairs lounge area; there was no open fire in this house as there was next door, but an extremely modern, pseudo open flame fire which Sandy was pleased to see was switched on. The weather outside was freezing.

Sitting in the corner of the room behind a desk was Celia, she was on the phone and had her laptop open in front of her, and strewn across the desk were a number of papers and leaflets.

In walked Adam and with him was his ex-wife, Rosamund Scott. This relationship was looking pretty strong, and Sandy wondered if he was going to get any feedback from Celia about it during their time together this morning. They went and sat next to each other, on one of the sofas opposite the chair that Sandy had been positioned in by Imogen, who sat on another chair next to him.

While Celia was finishing off her phone call, Sandy

addressed Imogen and Adam, who both seemed to him to be energised, having something like the service to focus on had clearly lifted them both.

'Which day next week is the thanksgiving service?'

'Thursday,' Imogen replied before Adam could. 'We do need to know numbers as soon as you are able to let us know. We have allocated four seats for yourselves.'

Sandy breathed out a sigh of relief. His grandma's funeral was on the Friday, meaning Sandy would be able to make both services.

'I have got a lot of information to update you all on,' Sandy said as he saw Celia position herself on the other side of Adam.

Before he could say anything, Celia interjected, 'I spent all day yesterday waiting for your call. I kept checking my phone for messages, there were none. Where was that call as promised from DCI McFarlane, I thought, has he abandoned us?'

They all laughed, mostly because of the tone that Celia used.

'There is a lot going on, Miss Longstaff. I have some quite shocking news to tell you all.' These words brought about a change of mood in the room. 'As you know, we believe that Vivienne was murdered by being struck on the back of her neck.'

'Are you sure about that now?' Adam said. 'Because last time I was told anything was in that interview room in Bridgetown, and it was all a bit vague.'

'Yes, we are sure, and we believe that a piece of metal shelving was used. We have been able to match up the marks on Vivienne's neck with a piece of metal shelving that we have seized from *Magnificence*.'

'It all comes back to the yacht again,' Imogen said, shaking her head. 'I wish I had never chartered the damn thing; it is a towering bad omen.'

'The metal shelving we have recovered has Vivienne's DNA on it in one or two of the holes.'

The first to cry was Adam, followed by Imogen. Both Celia and Rosamund grabbed his hand. Imogen sat in her chair all alone sobbing quietly to herself.

'We have in custody Theo Le Tissier, the yachts skipper, his fingerprints were on this shelving.'

'You are saying that Theo has killed Vivienne?' Adam asked in utter surprise. 'I can't believe it, he showed no signs of anything to suggest he was violent, in fact quite the opposite. Why would he do such a thing?'

'The motive we think is robbery. We found Vivienne's Cartier watch in his possession.'

This brought about tears from all of them now, including Rosamund.

Knowing that he had to go on with his final piece of information, Sandy added, 'The Barbados Police have been given the authority to prosecute Mr Le Tissier for murder, which isn't his real surname, but the one I think we are all going to use.'

'I presume he has admitted what he has done?' Celia asked. She had taken her glasses off and was mopping up her tears with a tissue.

'Not so far, but we are interviewing him again this morning. It looks like there will be a trial in Barbados sometime later next year. He has to be extradited to there first.'

Realising it was time to go and leave this family to grieve in private, as he stood up to be shown out by Celia, he looked at Imogen and wanted to give her hug as she looked all alone and very isolated.

Sandy could hear Adam saying again to her, 'I am so sorry Imogen. I am so sorry.'

∞

Despite the weather being bitterly cold, Sandy decided to walk back to the FCDO offices. He had a hat and gloves in his backpack which helped fend off the cold.

He desperately felt he himself needed a hug. Sandy knew it was not his grief, his despair, his loved one that had died but this didn't mean to say the emotion of it all hadn't affected him. So, another character flaw of his to add to being too nice, he was too emotionally invested, too emotionally engaged, too emotionally involved with his cases. Was that a good or a bad thing? Sandy was unsure. After he arrived in Victoria, he increased his pace and walked along Buckingham Palace Road, past the palace, and deciding on St James's Park rather than Birdcage Walk, he made his way to the office.

Just as he arrived, he received a call from Juliet.

'How did it go?' he asked after firstly pulling off his gloves and then his woollen hat.

'Not so good,' Juliet said despondently. 'He did speak but it was mostly a no comment interview I am afraid.'

'What about the image overlay and his DNA on the metal shelving bar?'

'He said that it had been lying in the lounge area and on the way to Antigua he had picked it up from the floor where it had somehow moved to, wiped it and fixed the shelving in the cabin.'

'What about Vivienne's DNA, though?'

'He had no idea about that,' Juliet said. 'He was shocked when we told him he was going to be prosecuted for murder and seemed to go into that subdued shell that he was in last week.'

'Did you explain that the extradition process will be starting, and that the world's media will soon know all about him? Thinking about it, Juliet, I think we should warn Theo's mother that she is going to be inundated with media requests.'

'I will go round there with Dale before I fly home. I have nothing more to do here so might as well get the flight back to England this evening. The media will have to be careful though, won't they, so as not to jeopardise a fair trial.'

Agreeing with Juliet, but with the hand that was holding the phone now freezing Sandy said goodbye and sped indoors through the nearest FCDO office door that he could find. He also realised, kicking himself as he went and sat down at a desk, that he had failed to tell Imogen or Adam not to tell the media, including social media, anything. He quickly sent a message to them both, then, as an afterthought, added in Celia, saying that they must not tell anyone about the update in relation to Theo Le Tissier as it could harm any future trial. You fool Sandy, he said to himself, forgetting to do this due to the emotion of it all.

The sandwich and tea he had got for his lunch were quickly eaten by Sandy as he read through Jane's presentation for the conference later in the week. The conference involved a number of bereaved families' key stakeholder groups. These were always difficult meetings for civil servants, like Sandy in reality was, as he knew that he fully agreed with them that the FCDO, if they could find the funding and the resources, should do more for these families.

On looking at his watch he was pleased to see that the time was now not too early to ring Richard in Barbados.

'Richard,' Sandy said, 'thought I would let you know as soon as possible that I have updated both Imogen Jones and Adam Scott.'

'Good morning, Sandy,' Richard replied. 'It's a lovely morning here, the sun is shining brightly already. What's the weather like there?'

Looking out of the small rectangular windows Sandy could see it had now started raining. 'Wet, freezing cold and miserable,' he said, while still gazing out of the window. 'You can come and sample it yourself if you want and are able to, as you and Dave are invited to Vivienne's service of thanksgiving which is here in London a week on Thursday.'

'Really, a trip to London!' Richard sounded excited. 'I will definitely see what we can do. Thanks for letting me know the update. I am leaving home now for Bridgetown as I am in meetings all morning, firstly about the media conference and then extradition.'

∞

Standing outside the Barbados High Commission Offices in Great Russell Street, London, Juliet and Sandy realised that they had arrived too early, but they were not early enough to have time to go to one of the nearby coffee shops.

The rest of the previous week and weekend had gone by without any dramas, other than when Richard, who had made it to London with Dave, had rung Sandy to tell him there were a few bumps in the road on the British side, to do with extradition, and could Sandy accompany them to a meeting at their High Commission in London.

Here they were for that meeting. Very quickly people started turning up; Richard and Dave, who were staying with siblings in London, they also had with them someone from their DPP's office, then a person from the law offices to the Crown in Guernsey, and finally, a high ranking and severe looking civil servant from the British Ministry of Justice. He was the only one not to shake anyone's hand on arrival in the meeting room.

The bad news was he was chairing the meeting. 'We have received the papers for extradition from Barbados, they are in two parts,' he said, while holding them up for all to see. 'The first part is from Guernsey to the UK.'

'Isn't Guernsey part of the UK?' Richard asked.

'No, it is a crown dependency and has a separate judicial system.'

'Quite right, young man,' the civil servant said, looking at Sandy over his half-rimmed glasses. 'This is not an issue and we have agreed this.' He looked at the law officer to the Crown from Guernsey and they both nodded to each other as if in agreement. 'The problem lies with the UK's extradition to Barbados.'

'What's the problem?' Juliet asked.

'The problem is...' The man checked his notes. 'Mr Theo Le Tissier, formally known as Le Feuvre, is going to be tried for an offence of murder.'

'Why is that a problem?' Juliet asked again, confused as to what was the issue.

Suddenly it all clicked into place for Sandy.

'They still have the death penalty in Barbados. We cannot send a man or woman to be tried in a country where they could be sentenced to death.'

'We have not used the death penalty,' said the woman from the Barbados DPP's office, 'since 1984, and the last time there was a mandatory sentence of death was in 2010. I am sorry, this is crazy.' She looked and talked as if she was cross, which she clearly was. 'I sent you the criteria for this and the circumstances of the death do not fit. The Caribbean Court of Justice struck out mandatory sentencing of the death penalty for us in 2018. So, come on, agree to the extradition.'

The man seemed unmoved.

'I have two options to resolve this issue,' Sandy offered. 'We have recent precedents that I have been involved in, plus numerous others I am sure, where, for example, Barbados in this case can send a letter that would assure the British Government that a death penalty sentence would not be used.'

'And the other option?'

'We could try Theo Le Tissier here. There is a law from the 1800s that allows that to happen in cases like murder that has happened abroad, and the defendant is a British Citizen.'

'That, I am afraid,' the man said smugly, 'wouldn't work because Theo is not a British Citizen but from Guernsey.'

'Actually, he was born in England and has a British

251

passport through his late father,' Sandy said in reply.

Richard, Dave and Juliet smiled at each other enjoying the ping pong match between Sandy and the man from the Ministry of Justice.

'OK, so both of those options could work,' the man said, while putting his papers back in his briefcase.

The meeting had ended and the woman from the DPP office in Barbados told them all that, as soon as it was business hours in Barbados, she would make the calls to see what could be arranged.

When they left the High Commission offices, Richard and Sandy arranged to meet up later that evening for a drink and dinner.

As they parted, Richard whispered to Sandy, 'There is no way that Deputy Commissioner Bishop will ever let the British hold a murder trial for this. If I ever mention to him that it was your idea,' Richard smiled mischievously, 'you would never be able to set foot in Barbados again!'

Chapter Thirty

The media were out in large numbers all around the entrance to Westminster Abbey. The dean had refused to allow them to film Vivienne Jones' thanksgiving service, but this didn't stop them filming and trying to talk to the people to get quotes as they arrived. It was an event even larger than any movie premiere that there had been before. The attendee list was full of A list actors. Sandy and Juliet while they were stood around the corner waiting for Richard and Dave to arrive, saw Harrison Ford, Brad Pitt, Dame Emma Thompson, Emily Blunt, George Clooney, to just name a few.

Looking across at the abbey they saw a building in its present form that had been there since the 1200s. There had been a church on the site going back a further two hundred years before that. It was a place of worship that had stood the test of time and had hosted the coronations of forty British Kings and Queens over all those centuries. It had also seen the weddings and funerals for monarchy, statesmen, poets and authors.

On the arrival of the two Bajan detectives, they quickly walked past the camera crews and the reporters. It looked as though they hadn't been recognised but against the cast list attending why should they have been? They were not celebrities.

There had been no holdups with the repatriation of

Vivienne's body, and everything was on schedule. The actual family funeral was taking place the next day in Swansea, the same day as Sandy's grandma – hers in Ely. Imogen and Adam had agreed to cremation as they didn't want to create a shrine, memorial or tourist attraction in any graveyard.

The family came into the abbey just before the coffin. Adam walked in with who they later found out to be his brother and sister, and also Celia. Rosamund arrived separately with their children. They had clearly been choreographed to be apart. Vivienne had apparently been an excellent stepmother to the two girls. The last to arrive was Imogen and a friend of hers. As soon as she took her seat everyone stood on the dean's instructions and the organ started playing "The Arrival of the Queen of Sheba" by Handel. Violinists and a solo trumpet accompanied the organ as the pallbearers slowly and rhythmically walked up the long aisle of the abbey. The music may have been more often used for a wedding entrance, but it worked beautifully on this occasion.

The dean welcomed everyone and talked about Vivienne, then he read a piece of scripture and gave a short talk from the Bible. The Welsh singer, Sir Tom Jones, then sang his famous song "Green, Green Grass of Home". A psalm came next, followed by Katherine Jenkins leading the whole congregation in singing "Praise my Soul the King of Heaven", which had been Vivienne's favourite hymn.

When Adam stood to speak, the four detectives looked at each other, unsure whether he would be able to hold himself together without crying. Dave and Sandy had been two of the only people in the whole world, other than his family, who had seen him cry almost every time they had met him.

Adam did extremely well, he was after all an actor and able to hold himself together, no doubt treating it as though he was playing a role. He talked of the beauty, kindness and charisma of Vivienne, how it had enchanted him and millions of people worldwide. The person the world saw on the screen was a far more incredible person in real life, he told them. He recited the words from the prologue in Shakespeare's play, *Romeo and Juliet*, citing that their relationship had been similar to that of those two star-crossed lovers; they were two people in love who had been forced to be apart by circumstances on more than one occasion, which was out of their influence and control. Adam then sang very softly with no accompaniment the words from a song from the musical *West Side Story*, "Somewhere". There was not now a dry eye in the abbey, including Adam, who was helped back to his seat by his sister.

The dean of the abbey then read a eulogy written by Imogen, which spoke of them growing up together and included Vivienne's movie career and how proud their mother and father were of her before they themselves had died.

The service concluded with Sir Bryn Terfel singing, "Trees"; Vivienne had loved it when she had first heard him singing this song and had played it over and over again.

As soon as the service had finished, Sandy only had time to wave an acknowledgement to Imogen and say goodbye to Dave and Richard, so that he could make his train back home to Ely ready for his own grandma's service.

∞

The house in Ely was full of people when Sandy walked through the front door. There was a debate going on about whether younger children should go to funerals or not. This was clearly about Aileen's two sons who she thought should be going to their great grandma's funeral the next day. Her husband and the two grandfathers were not so sure.

'Sandy, what do you think?' his youngest sister Isla asked him.

Stroking her dog who had enthusiastically run up to him for attention as soon as had entered the lounge area, Sandy said, 'Don't get me involved in this discussion, please.'

'Seriously, what do you think?' Aileen now asked.

All of his life for some crazy reason these two sisters of his had always, wrongly in his view, totally valued his opinion, wanted his attention, wanted his endorsement.

'I know how much their great grandma adored them,' Sandy said, seeing them both looking intently at him, 'and I also know that she would be delighted that they are there for her. Maybe not at the cremation but definitely at the cathedral.'

That was the end of the discussion; Aileen's big brother had supported her. On going to his bedroom to get changed and leave his bags, he saw that Hannah's bag was already in the room, Sandy hadn't seen her in the lounge so wondered where she was. Getting changed as quickly as possible he went back downstairs to see that Hannah was in the garden, almost in the dark as there was only a small outside light. She was on her phone. Work calls, someone told him.

A delivery arrived of an incredible number of pizzas. Sandy had initially thought his dad Gregor had considerably overestimated the pizza order, but they seemed to get through them all. As the family started to leave, Isla's husband Andrew suggested a drink in the Cutter Inn.

It turned out that only four of them went in the end, the two couples, Andrew and Isla along with Sandy and Hannah. There was lots of teasing of Sandy that he must have been a "C" list celebrity as none of the TV channels had shown him arriving or leaving Westminster Abbey earlier that day.

Leaving Isla and Hannah in deep conversation, Andrew and Sandy went outside for a breath of cold in fact very cold fresh air. They sat down at one of the outside tables and gazed across at the Great River Ouse shimmering in the light of the full moon.

'I am glad that Isla seems to be happier than the last time I saw her just before I was heading off to Barbados,' Sandy said. He had promised himself he wouldn't say anything unless invited to, but he couldn't help himself.

An extremely strained, troubled but at the same time resigned look crossed Sandy's brother-in-law's face.

'I think she is, but I'm not always sure.'

'What do you mean?'

Looking inside the large bay window, Andrew could see Isla. 'I know she didn't want to worry you but Isla has had three miscarriages, the last one was at over ten weeks gestation.' Andrew looked very glum; he was not looking at Sandy but through the window at his wife. 'The doctors don't think she will be able to carry full term.'

Now looking through the window at his youngest sister, Sandy put his hand on Andrew's arm. 'I am so sorry for you both.'

'Isla told me that she knows that I will make a wonderful

257

father and she told me that we should divorce.' Tears were rolling down Andrew's face. 'So I would then be free to meet someone else and have children with them.'

Moving across now to put his arm around Andrew and give him a hug, Sandy said, 'This must be so hard for you both.'

'I told her although my life will have a hole which children would have filled but that is miniscule to the hole that my life would be without her. We are not going to divorce Sandy; we will work through this. I can assure you of that.'

∞

There was a very sombre mood in the McFarlane household the next morning. One of the funeral directors' limousine cars arrived and picked them up. They drove to Tom's house where Katherine and Gregor got out and went into another smaller limousine to accompany Tom. John McFarlane, who had been staying with Tom, joined Sandy, his youngest sister and their partners. Then the hearse arrived carrying the coffin of Margaret Fisher. She came one last time to say goodbye to the house that she had lived in for almost fifty years.

The Fenland Crematorium was a twenty-minute drive away and the journey took place in almost an eerie silence in the car that Sandy was in, as it made its way following the hearse and the car in front. Sandy saw that his sister Aileen and her husband were following behind them.

The service at the crematorium was taken by one of the canons of the cathedral who was also going to lead the service of celebration and remembrance for the life of

Margaret Fisher which was to follow. There were lots of tears, especially when the canon pressed the button for the curtain to close and the coffin to move backwards. How sad and final it all felt, there was no one who was not crying.

When they arrived back in Ely at the cathedral, a number of people had already arrived, and also waiting for them were Aileen's two sons, Margaret's great grandchildren. Although playing no part in the service, The bishop and dean of Ely were also present. *We can also have "A" list celebrities*, thought Sandy.

The number of guests at the most amounted to one hundred and fifty people, only twenty percent of the number Westminster Abbey had had in it yesterday and with no TV cameras or journalists waiting outside, but to the family and friends Margaret was equally, if not more, important to every one of them than Vivienne Jones.

The canon led the service, and the organist played the music to the hymns but other than this the family of Margaret contributed everything else. Tom himself did the eulogy and told the congregation how he and Margaret had met, when he was a young constable in uniform walking the streets of Ely. They were almost inseparable from that very first meeting. They married very young as a fairly modern police house became available in a nice part of the city. Margaret's mum and dad were not keen, but their love had stood the test of time regardless of their young age. Tom told them all he would have been nothing without her and was not sure how he could continue to be anything now that she was gone.

Katherine read a poem and Isla read Psalm 23, "The Lord is my shepherd". Aileen read from the Bible, Colossians chapter three verses twelve to fifteen.

Then Sandy stood and walked very slowly to the front of the cathedral. He looked around at the people gathered there for the first time as the family were sat in the front rows. He saw the rows and rows of smiling people who his grandma had touched in some small, or for some of them large way.

'My Bible verse is about love,' Sandy said, looking around at everyone, he didn't need any notes or the Bible to prompt him. 'My grandma was the most loving person I have ever met or will ever meet. Her faith and love were unwavering and were not only an inspiration to me and her family but to many others. She showered us, her family, with love and generosity continuously, it was never failing. Everyone who met my grandma felt her love, for example the shopkeeper, the postman, the nurse, anybody and everyone. Immediately after meeting her they would feel her love and good wishes because that is just how she was.' Sandy couldn't now stop the tears rolling down his face and the lump in his throat getting bigger and bigger, he saw almost everyone else similarly crying. Softly, pausing and composing himself he said, 'Grandma chose love always. She always chose love.'

Sandy then opened the Bible he was holding and read Corinthians chapter one, verses one to eight.

Chapter Thirty-One

The letter from the Attorney General in Barbados, providing all of the necessary assurances, arrived in December and the extradition processes kicked into gear. Theo had already been brought to London and was housed in a prison there.

Over Christmas dinner Sandy had told his grandfathers about the stance that the Ministry of Justice had taken in relation to needing assurances that the death penalty wouldn't been used.

'Hypocrites!' exclaimed John.

'What do you mean, Grandpa?' Sandy asked as soon as he had finished his mouthful.

John, who still practised as a barrister and lectured at Cambridge University on medio-legal studies, looked around the packed table of his family members and saw he had an audience and said, 'Well, the death penalty for murder was abolished here well over fifty years ago, in 1969. Suspended from use for five years before that. However... High Court judges at the Royal Courts of Justice, sitting in the privacy of the Family Division today hand out death penalties.'

'What do you mean?' Tom asked, now totally intrigued.

'They make decisions not on a rare, but an occasional basis,' said John, enjoying himself greatly, 'to withdraw life support or decide that expensive, untried, and experimental treatment abroad is not good use of NHS budgets. Those babies, children and adults sadly have a death sentence and die.'

None of them had thought about this before and had to agree with John. He looked at Tom hoping that they could have a verbal sparring match or a difference of opinion about what he had just said, but this didn't happen as Tom remained quiet for a change.

When Sandy arrived in Harrogate on Boxing Day to spend a few days with Hannah and her father, she loved this story as John had been her mentor.

Howard had let slip that Hannah had been offered a place that she could take up at any time in a prestigious barristers' chambers in Leeds. Sandy didn't let on that he knew, and this spurred him into thinking through their future together through the blind panic of the worry of losing her.

As the New Year progressed, he suggested buying a house together which was met with a good level of enthusiasm. They looked in Cambridge but the ones they liked were too expensive and the suggestion of Ely to live in was being thought about by Hannah. Property in the north was cheaper, she mentioned on more than one occasion.

Easter came and went and the two of them floated along much the same as they had been for the last two years or so.

It was amazing how quickly the trial for Theo Le Tissier arrived. The team hoped they were ready. Sitting on the plane heading to Barbados for the trial, Sandy made a decision that something needed to be done for their relationship, whether to let Hannah go and move to Leeds, if that is what Hannah really wanted, or to make their future more solid. He was travelling alone as Juliet had flown there the previous week.

The trial had begun but had not really started because as soon as the jury was sworn in legal arguments were in full flow. The legality of the international arrest warrant, the legality of the search of Susan's property, the legality of the extradition. The arguments went on and on.

The defence attorney was Reece Prescod, and he was apparently exceptionally good, and the DPP, Elliot Sobers, himself was prosecuting. He was described by Richard as a safe pair of hands who ran an efficient prosecution service for Barbados, he did this by being good at moving paper around, mostly to his incredibly able deputy who got on with it. The deputy was Faith Maynard and luckily for them was the number two for the prosecution at the trial. Presiding over the trial was Honour Madam Justice Gabrielle Weekes. Sandy had asked if Paulette was related to her at all, but apparently not.

Having been originally placed in a hotel not far from the courthouse, Sandy had changed it to the one he had stayed in before. Hannah was coming the following weekend for the last week (hopefully) of the trial, not to go to court, she said, as that was a busman's holiday, but to acquaintance herself with the beach and the Caribbean Sea. Richard, Dave and Juliet had all offered to drive him into court each day. For Sandy, the trial needed to conclude within two weeks as that was all Jane Watson could spare him for and that was why he had missed the previous week's legal arguments.

∞

It was Richard who collected Sandy on Monday morning and they went straight into a meeting room near the courtroom the trial was to be heard in. Sandy was surprised there were so few cameras outside, then he heard that a whole courtroom had been set aside for the media to use with a live video link from their court, Number 3 Supreme Court.

The DPP was a large man in his early sixties with tight, grey curly hair. He seemed troubled.

'I don't know what to do about calling Mr Scott as our first witness,' he said with a worried brow.

'We must call him first, Elliot,' said Faith Maynard, a petite lady in her late forties. Her black shoulder length hair had been straightened and was held back with a gold clip. 'He has to start our case.'

'I just feel it has the opportunity to start us on the wrong track with the jury before we get our best evidence to them,' Elliot the DPP said, walking about while talking. 'The negative media against him must have been read by the jury, and when Reece Prescod finishes with him, the jury will think the wrong man is in the dock.'

Elliot was even wringing his hands now.

For Sandy he had long ago come to this realisation with the case, after Theo had been identified as the most likely offender. The murderer was either Theo, as they, the prosecution team were sure that the evidence suggested, or it was Adam Scott who had killed his wife.

There was no time to debate this further as they had been called into court. Faith was going to win anyway; she knew how to manage her boss. As Sandy entered the courtroom, he saw Imogen and said hello. Standing next to her was Celia, who kept putting a vape to her mouth.

'I don't think you will be allowed to vape in the court room or in fact in the whole Supreme Court complex,' Sandy whispered to her.

'Who is going to stop me?' Celia said, looking Sandy threateningly in the eye. 'Not you, sonny boy,' then, looking at the security guard on the door, 'and certainly not him.'

'She has given up smoking, Sandy, and unless she is continuously vaping she is beyond tetchy. Best to just let her be. Her nerves with this trial are bouncing about like a highly coiled spring,' Imogen said, while shaking her head.

The jury, shuffling into their places in the courtroom, was made up of seven women and five men. Does this play into being on Adam's side? Sandy didn't know, all he wanted them to do was listen to the evidence.

When they stood for the entrance of Madam Justice Gabrielle Weekes, Sandy was surprised by how young she looked; of all the lawyers in the court she was the youngest. Only early forties, her black hair was plaited closely to her head. She wore striking red lipstick and her make-up was beautifully applied. Her half-moon glasses were gold plated and, the thing that surprised Sandy the most, Justice Weekes was smiling.

Following a nod from the judge, Elliot Sobers, the DPP, stood and faced the jury. 'Members of the jury. Let me say at the earliest opportunity, thank you for your service that you will carry out in this trial. I apologise that last week you were not needed due to various points of law that the defence Mr Prescod and I have been discussing with the judge.' Elliot, as he said this, nodded towards firstly the defence attorney and then the judge. 'I am presuming that all of you will know the public image and person that was Vivienne Jones. I presume all of you would have read the media over the last six months in relation to her death.' Elliot looked down at his notes, then reading from them said, 'Although not used by me, Twitter, Snapchat, TikTok, Facebook, Instagram, plus other blogs and conventional media have posted...'

On using the word posted, Elliot checked he had said it right, the judge smiled and nodded the affirmative.

Elliot continued, 'Have posted opinions on what happened to Miss Jones in the press of a button that reaches millions upon millions. Almost all of the people reading these posts (he was enjoying saying the word post), will believe what they are reading although there maybe not a shred of truth to them. I urge you all to put that out of your minds please and only make your decision on what you hear, either from the witness stand or read, as agreed by my learned colleague Mrs Maynard.'

Sandy thought Elliot had been very clever not to mention almost all of those media and social media stories which believed that Adam Scott was the murderer.

∞

The first witness to be called was Mr Scott. He entered the courtroom walking very confidently, wearing a light blue linen suit with a gleaming white shirt and dark blue tie. He looked every bit the movie star. There was a hush throughout the court as he stepped into the witness box and said the oath.

Dave Ashton had spent time with him going through his

statement and had told him to stick to this statement. Dave had told the other detectives that he wasn't sure how much Adam was listening to him, and he didn't want to push it so as not to be accused of coaching.

Faith Maynard was standing and took Adam through how he and Vivienne had met, married, and divorced, then met again and re-married. Adam was a wonderful orator, and the court were enthralled. Sandy glanced at the jury, they couldn't take their eyes off Adam; that included the men and not just the women.

'Talk us through the night that Miss Jones died, Mr Scott.' Faith asked. 'Before you went to the Speightstown Marina clubhouse, did you and Miss Jones have anything to drink?'

'Yes, we had been swimming near a beach on the south coast of Barbados, we had some cocktails after that and then after we had moored, we had a few more cocktails,' Adam told her but spoke directly to the jury. 'I don't want you to think that Vivienne was a big drinker, she never touched a drop when she was on a film set. This was just a few days of us both letting our hair down.'

'What happened at the marina clubhouse?'

'Theo,' Adam gesticulated to Theo in the dock, 'took us there and we had a few drinks and a meal. I was tired and wanted to go back to the yacht, and then I went to bed and that was the last time I ever saw Vivienne...' Adam started to cry.

Faith waited patiently for him to compose himself. 'I know Mr Prescod will ask you this. You were cross with Miss Jones and grabbed her, why did you do that?'

'I regret that greatly. I really do. I shouldn't have done

it,' said Adam softly, just loud enough for everyone to hear. 'I just wanted to get her attention, to convince her that it was time to go back to *Magnificence*.'

'When you got back to the yacht, you say you went to bed. Where was Vivienne and where was…' Faith turned and pointed to Theo Le Tissier, 'the defendant?'

'Vivienne was pouring herself a whisky and then said she was going to sit in an outside area of the yacht, and…' Adam paused as if he was trying to picture the scene again, this wasn't something Sandy or Dave Ashton had specifically asked him. 'Theo was still sitting in the lounge area, but I didn't notice what he was doing.'

Faith decided there was no need for any more questions and she sat down.

Reece Prescod stood and said, 'You killed Miss Jones, didn't you!'

In an instant Elliot Sobers was on his feet. 'Your Honour, objection.'

The judge, not smiling at all now, said to Reece, 'Mr Prescod, the witness Mr Jones is not on trial here, it is Mr Le Tissier.'

'Your Honour, if I had been allowed to finish my sentence before being interrupted, I would have said, that is what the media is saying, how are you coping with that?' Reece said, smiling as he was getting maximum impact of his words. 'I would also ask Your Honour, that you tell the prosecution to not act like a wrestling tag team.' This comment brought laughter from around the court. 'This witness was one that Mrs Maynard was leading on, not Mr Sobers.'

Before the judge could reply, Adam said, 'I was not coping

with it very well, but trying to cope with the loss of Vivienne is far, far worse.'

'During your cruise, how did you find Mr Le Tissier?' Reece asked.

Looking straight at Theo, surprisingly not with any venom, hate or disgust, Adam said, 'I found him to be extremely good at sailing the yacht. He was polite, courteous, and a very nice young man.'

'The police have put together reports that Miss Jones may have been at times the subject of domestic abuse by you. Is that right?'

Elliot Sobers fought the urge not to object.

'I never, ever, physically struck her. I wouldn't, I loved her.'

'Domestic abuse is a lot more than just physical violence, Mr Scott. No more questions.'

Her Honour Justice Gabrielle Weekes decided it was time for lunch and as Mr Sobers had a point of law he wanted to discuss, the jury was given an extra half hour. Sandy's job now was to make sure that Celia Longstaff didn't assault the defence attorney and yes, he, sonny boy, would make sure that didn't happen.

Chapter Thirty-Two

Celia told Sandy over lunch that she was not stupid, but she was now vaping so much she was probably inhaling nicotine at the rate of sixty cigarettes a day.

When they returned to court, Sandy had a good look at Theo. He was now clean shaven, and he had had his hair cut short, gone was the long scraggly look he had when Sandy had last seen him almost six months ago in Guernsey. He had put on weight, prison food obviously agreed with him or the opportunity of being fed regularly did. He looked smart in his suit, he had the look of a young professional about him, definitely not that of a murderer, whatever one of those looked like.

As soon as the judge entered the courtroom, Elliot Sobers was on his feet. 'The questioning of Mr Scott in relation to domestic abuse,' he said looking squarely at Justice Weekes, 'has I think opened the door for us to include Mr Le Tissier's previous conviction for a strikingly similar offence.'

'No,' the judge said, before Elliot could say anything else.

Reece Prescod smiled and looked around at the defendant, as if it was his work that had got the motion denied.

'Are you not open to have a discussion about it?' Elliot asked.

'No. Too deeply prejudicial,' the judge said, unsmiling.

'Next point or shall I call the jury back in.?'

'We have had trouble getting two of our next witnesses to court. Bradley and Michael Lewis have been served with witness orders in the United States but we have had no contact, and it would therefore be safe to assume that they are not coming.'

'I am not going to authorise international arrest warrants for them.' Justice Weekes then smiled and said, 'Something the Barbados Police seem to have used against them already.'

'Our trouble is Mr Prescod is not agreeing to their evidence being read,' said Elliot Sobers, scowling at Reece Prescod.

Rising to his feet Reece said, 'It is the bit in their evidence that insinuates, wrongly, I must add, that the defendant bought drugs off them.'

'Nothing more I can do for you, Mr Sobers, call your next witness and let's have the jury back in court.'

The next witness was Royston, the barman from the Speightstown Marina clubhouse. He was dressed very smartly in a suit but without a tie. Elliot took him through his evidence, and they covered Vivienne and Adam drinking and eating, the argument that he observed, and the buying of drugs by Theo from Bradley Lewis.

Looking straight at Royston after standing, Reece said, 'Were you alarmed by the actions of Mr Scott towards Miss Jones?'

Not knowing what to say Royston looked around for Elliot Sobers to help him, or someone, or anyone to help. Did he say no, if so, that would that mean that he condoned a man being more than assertive with a woman? If he said yes, why then didn't he act to protect the woman?

'I don't know what I thought and I can't answer that question.'

'OK,' Reece Prescod said, smiling, he had scored another point against Adam Scott. 'These drugs, that is the term that you used, isn't it? If they are drugs and not headache tablets as Mr Le Tissier states they were, why didn't you as barman intervene and stop it, and report what happened to your manager and the police?'

If there was a hole, Royston would have dived into it. He contemplated whether he could get away with fainting; in fact he did feel extremely light-headed. 'They must have been headache tablets then.'

After a brief discussion between Elliot and Faith Maynard it was agreed there would be no further questions for Royston, and the prosecution had decided not to call the waiter, Benjamin.

Following this, Benjamin, now being allowed to sit in court, walked in holding Paulette's hand. She was not in uniform and smiled at Sandy as she walked past, clearly pleased to see him again.

'Those two got together then?' Sandy asked Richard.

'It was inevitable, wasn't it?' Richard said, smiling.

'What does Garry think to it, I always thought he was in love with her?' Sandy murmured, with an equally big smile.

'Maybe, but he gets on great now with Benjamin, they go to the gym together, and that annoys Paulette greatly,' Richard said laughing.

The final witnesses' statements for the day were read out by Faith Maynard. They were from the man who had found Vivienne's body and then the evidence from the two CSIs.

The next witness to be called the following morning was to be Dr Barry Braithwaite, the resident forensic pathologist of Barbados.

On the drive back to his hotel, Sandy, who was normally a half full type of personality, was always half empty when it came to a court case. He didn't know why he was like this, but it was just the way it was, maybe because he had no control. He felt the prosecution had had a bad day. Richard agreed with him, who was a half empty type of guy.

∞

The next morning before court began Sandy spoke to Imogen, Adam and Celia.

He asked nosily, 'How is Rosamund?'

Answering for all of them, Celia said, 'We...' Adam frowned at her. 'OK, I decided that it would be a better look if she wasn't here at court with Adam and stayed in England.' Moving closer to Sandy she whispered, 'He is going to marry her.' Pausing, she then said with her sly smile, 'Again!'

Sandy started to move to take his seat as court was about to begin for the day.

Celia shook her head. 'Fifth wedding.'

In response, Adam said, 'Only three women though, Celia, only three women.'

'As if that makes a difference.'

Standing in the witness box with a huge file of papers in front of him was a very smart looking Dr Barry Braithwaite, dressed in a dark check suit with a bright yellow bow tie. After he had taken the oath, Elliot Sobers took him through the examination of the body at the deposition site and then at the autopsy. Barry covered his examinations of the body and its organs, and the jury seemed to get a bit squeamish when he spoke about decomposition and fish damage to the fingers, hands and feet.

'Tell us about the marks you found on the rear of Miss Jones' neck?' Elliot asked at the same time as Faith Maynard, who was managing the technology, managed to put the image up on the screens for the jury to see.

The judge and Reece also had a screen and there was a larger screen that the others in court could see. Sandy looked around and could see Imogen flinching as she looked at the neck of her sister. Dave had warned them what to expect that morning when the pathology evidence was being presented in court.

'As you can see there on the screen,' Barry said pointing to his screen, 'the two tramline marks and even more faintly the holes in the middle that are evenly spaced. That, we believe, was caused by a piece of a metal shelving bar taken from the yacht *Magnificence*.'

Faith put up the image of the shelving, first when in position in a cabin of the yacht, and then the second image when it had been taken down so you could just see the shelving bar.

Moving onto the next screen in her presentation, Faith showed the digital superimposition and image overlay that the UK Forensic Medical Advice Team had supplied.

'On looking at these images,' the pathologist said, 'you can see a perfect match, weapon to injury.'

'That is how you believe Miss Jones died, by being struck

274

by this shelving on her neck?' Elliot Sobers asked.

'Absolutely; the metal shelving bar would have been used with force, power and accuracy on the neck and it is quite probable that Miss Jones would have been dead before she hit the deck,' Barry Braithwaite said firmly, leaving no one in any doubt of his opinion.

Rising to his feet, Reece Prescod said, 'As you know, the defence in this case have not had a chance to examine Miss Jones' body ourselves as she was hastily cremated.'

Elliot went to stand and make an objection, but anticipating this Justice Weekes waved him down.

'Mr Prescod, are you disputing the actions of the coroner or are you going to dispute the pathology that Dr Braithwaite has carried out? If it is the latter, produce your defence pathologist that I can't see mention of in any of the papers.'

'Sorry, Your Honour, neither of those are going to be points I make.' Looking back to the pathologist from the judge, Reece said, 'As I have just said to the judge, I am not going to argue with any of your findings or dispute on behalf of Mr Le Tissier how Miss Jones died. However, this, what did you call it,' he consulted his notes, 'digital superimposition, is all a bit of computer-generated imagery isn't it? You can do anything with CGI, look at the movies, some of which Miss Jones starred in had CGI animations.'

'I don't profess to know how the technology works but I can assure you this is not CGI; it is a simple look at those holes and whether they match up. In this case, yes, they do,' Dr Barry Braithwaite replied very firmly.

'OK, if I was to accept what you say about this piece of shelving being the weapon that killed Miss Jones, are you able to say who wielded it? There were two people on that yacht that night with Miss Jones.'

'No, I cannot.'

There were no further questions for Dr Braithwaite.

∞

After the lunch break, the first witnesses' evidence was read. This was Clare Symonds' evidence, she was distraught that she had not been called to Barbados to give live evidence, but her evidence wasn't in dispute. Juliet and Clare had prematurely planned all that they were going to do around the court case and how Juliet was going to show off her island. The main two pieces of her evidence were taking possession of the metal shelving bar and the Cartier watch.

The fingerprint and lab technician from London did make the trip to Barbados and he was the next witness. He had an impressive list of qualifications, maybe not quite as impressive as Dr Braithwaite, but certainly impressive.

Elliot Sobers asked him about his examination of the metal shelving bar. The bar had been brought to Barbados amongst other exhibits by Juliet from England the previous week. On the tabletop in front of the fingerprint expert was the piece of shelving. It was the first time that Sandy, Richard and the others had seen the murder weapon in real life and not as a photograph.

'I first checked it for DNA,' the expert said, and picked it up to demonstrate, indicating where he found the DNA of Vivienne Jones, 'inside three of the small holes.'

'You also found fingerprints on the shelving bar, didn't

you?' Faith Maynard was back at her computer presentation and showed the picture of where the fingerprints had been found.

'Yes,' the expert said. 'As you can see there, I was able to find them as shown on the screen.'

'Whose fingerprints are they?' Elliot Sobers asked.

'Mr Theo Le Feuvre. Now known as Le Tissier.'

There was murmuring around court when he said this and even the jury looked confused.

Justice Gabrielle Weekes spoke. 'Mr Le Tissier has used his mother and grandfather's name since his late teens and that is what he is known as and is his name for this trial. There is nothing sinister in this and nothing for you to read anything more into.'

'Were you surprised there was no DNA anywhere else on the metal shelving bar?' Reece Prescod asked in cross examination for the defence.

'Not really. I was just pleased I had found it.'

'Please pick up the bar and hold it for me where you found the fingerprints,' Reece instructed.

The fingerprint expert did this and grabbed the bar at its end, placing his fingers roughly where the fingerprints had been found. He had thick, broad fingers so it didn't match up perfectly with Theo's small hands.

'Where did you find the DNA, which holes?' Reece Prescod asked, smiling.

There were murmurs again all around the court and Elliot Sobers was talking in earnest with Faith. Sandy and Richard looked at each other. They hadn't even thought to check it. The holes were directly underneath where the fingers were placed.

'How could the defendant have swung the metal shelving bar and struck Miss Jones? His fingers would have been in the way and it wouldn't have been the clear, powerful and accurate strike that the prosecution are alleging, would it?' Reece said, now looking deadly serious.

'You are right,' the expert said, 'I never thought about that. Brilliant!'

There was no doubt that was exactly what Reece wanted him to say.

Having no further questions, Reece sat down.

Elliot Sobers, not one to re-examine a witness, had to this time. 'Could an explanation be that after the attack the bar was wiped clean, but obviously not inside each of the holes. Then, when Mr Le Tissier was fixing it back in place in the cabin, he would have left the fingerprints you found?'

'Yes, that makes sense.'

Reece Prescod added, 'I don't need to re-cross-examine the witness, but I do need to stress that it doesn't have to be Mr Le Tissier who was the one that wiped the shelving bar clean, if that is what happened.'

That was a good place for the court to adjourn for the day. Sandy had time for a quick swim in the sea and walk on the beach before he had his dinner alone in the hotel. He would be relieved once Juliet had given evidence, so that they could spend time together.

Chapter Thirty-Three

As it turned out, the next day in court was taken up with statements being read and legal arguments in relation to the interviews that had taken place with Theo in Guernsey. Reece argued, probably rightly so, that the interviews in Bailiwick of Guernsey were carried out following different statutory processes. Justice Weekes after having reflected on it and read through the interviews, felt there was nothing controversial in them and certainly no admissions, so would allow them to be included in evidence.

Having found a meeting room to sit in, Sandy spent all day on his laptop working on his, and others in the team's, cases. Billy Tudor had retired a few weeks earlier and Sandy had allocated to the team his outstanding cases but kept one or two for himself, increasing his workload considerably. From the room he was sitting in, he could see outside and the brilliant sunshine of the Barbados day made what he was doing even more unexciting.

Another thing that Sandy did was to have a good look online at all of the media reporting in the Vivienne Jones case. Unfortunately, a number of the reports still had opinion pieces that Adam was the one who should have been on trial, not Theo. One newspaper ran a poll: "Adam Scott or Theo Le Tissier, who do you think killed Vivienne Jones?".

The next morning DS Juliet Ashton was called into court. Dale had been desperate to be a witness as well, but Juliet had got the nod ahead of him as she was coming to Barbados regardless of whether she was a witness or not.

There were four interviews that took place on three separate days and Faith Maynard asked the questions and Juliet gave the replies that Theo had given. Sandy looked at Juliet; he was very proud of her. He saw how smart she looked in a brand-new, light grey pinstripe trouser suit and how confidently she talked.

The reciting of the interviews took all morning, and it wasn't until after the lunchtime recess that Faith enquired, 'DS Ashton, what the jury haven't been able to get a feeling for is how any of these questions were answered by Mr Le Tissier.' Faith paused and thought for a moment as she wasn't sure that she was expressing herself well. 'I mean, did he just flatly answer the questions in a monotone voice or was there any passion involved?'

'Do you mean did he get cross, lose his temper? Yes, he did at times. Once when he was talking about his late father, he was extremely agitated.'

'What was his psyche throughout the interviews? Why did he act like this?'

Reece Prescod almost fell over jumping to his feet. 'I must object to this, Your Honour. The sergeant isn't a clinical psychologist.'

Before the judge could answer, Juliet said, 'I was present in the interviews, and I can give an opinion which the jury can accept or reject. I have been in literally hundreds of interviews, so I have an incredible amount of relevant experience.'

Her Honour Justice Weekes, while looking at Juliet and not Reece, said, 'DS Ashton go ahead and answer Mrs Maynard's questions.'

'We had to delay the start of the interviews as it was felt by Mr Le Tissier's solicitor that he was not emotionally fit to be interviewed. That is recorded on the custody record,' Juliet said, looking straight at Reece, daring him to say anything.

'Why do you think that was?' Faith asked.

'Oh, come off it,' Reece muttered, but everyone heard, and Justice Gabrielle Weekes looked down at him and her stare was enough to make him freeze and make no more comments.

'I don't know,' Juliet said, not wanting to step out of her expertise. 'It could be that he was overcome because he had done something, or that he was overcome about what could be about to happen to him.'

Looking at Theo, Sandy saw that he was sitting in the dock as expressionless as he had been throughout. This was the first time the jury were getting to know anything about him as, up until now, he had been invisible to everyone and was just sat there quietly. The court case was all about the lawyers, like gladiators sparring with each other, and the judge was the ringmaster. Sandy wondered what Theo was thinking, especially as he had no control over proceedings. He was viewing the trial as a spectator, just like all the others who were watching were. It was, however, all about him and his fate. Sandy pondered how he would feel if it was him in the dock. Would he have been so passive, quiet and invisible?

'What motive could Mr Le Tissier possibly have to murder Miss Jones?'

'There are a number, in my experience, of motives to commit murder. One motive that I have only come across myself personally once, was where the murderer enjoyed the act of killing. Another could be a loss of face; you get this with the teenage gang members in London and Birmingham, killing each other through knife crime.' Juliet took a sip of the water that was in a glass beside her. 'What could be the case here, is the desire to control someone. You get this in domestic murders more often than not, when the murderer feels control is slipping away from them.' Juliet paused again, looked around the courtroom and then faced the jury. 'What we believe, though, is that Mr Le Tissier's motive could possibly be that of greed. He killed Miss Jones to steal her diamond-encrusted gold Cartier watch that we found in his possession.'

Thinking this was an ideal place to stop, Faith sat down asking Juliet to stay as Mr Prescod may have some questions for her.

'You mentioned a motive of controlling someone,' Reece said before he had even stood up properly. 'That would be a motive that would fit Mr Scott in this case, wouldn't it? He tried to control Miss Jones in the marina clubhouse, didn't he? We have heard evidence in this court about this already, haven't we?'

Faith and Elliot were locked in conversation, presumably about whether they should object or not. They didn't, and Justice Weekes, acutely conscious she had allowed latitude to the prosecution earlier didn't intervene either.

'As I have already said that motive definitely happens in cases of domestic homicide,' Juliet replied.

'You say theft is Mr Le Tissier's motive, but he said he found the watch left on *Magnificence* and always intended to return the watch to Mr Scott. Can you prove that is not the case?'

'No, but he hadn't returned it had he? And it was found hidden by him,' Juliet said.

There were no more questions and Juliet was released as a witness and the court was adjourned for the day. Dinner that evening for Sandy and Juliet was eagerly awaited by them both.

∞

The next morning the first witness to be called was Susan Walters. Standing outside the court, this was the first time that Sandy had seen her since she had bitten his shoulder. Susan was a small slim young woman, she had pleaded guilty to assaulting him and had received a conditional discharge; Sandy had been awarded two hundred pounds compensation, not a penny of which he had seen as yet.

There was a point of law that Reece Prescod wanted to raise with the judge before the next witness was called.

'I would like to object to the evidence of Miss Walters. She only made her statement to get herself out of custody for any offence associated with the death of Miss Jones. Her evidence is compromised.'

As quickly as he could, Sandy went into his backpack and took out his key decision log. He walked up to and sat next to Faith Maynard showing her the specific entries that he'd made in Guernsey.

Without discussing it with Elliot, Faith said to the judge, 'Your Honour, DCI McFarlane, the British detective involved in the investigation is able to help with this. Can I have your permission to ask him about this in the witness box?'

'Yes, of course.'

This was a real surprise to Sandy and not what he had arrived in court that morning prepared for. He took the oath anyway.

'Your Honour, in my bound book that I have here, I can show you and Mr Prescod where I made a decision that Miss Walters was a suspect, then when she wasn't a suspect for any offences involved in this case, and then a further decision when Miss Walters was classed as a significant witness. After this, her statement was taken. It shows quite clearly the timings for her status.'

Sandy handed over the book with the relevant pages, edges folded over, to the judge who after scanning the pages handed it over to Reece Prescod.

But before he was even able to properly look at it, Justice Weekes pronounced, 'All pretty straightforward to me. Call the jury to come in and the next witness, Miss Walters.'

They passed each other as Sandy went back to take his seat. Susan didn't recognise him, but even so, Sandy gave her a wide berth, her teeth were vicious.

Richard gave Sandy's arm a pat as he sat down saying, 'Well done.'

'How long were you in a relationship with Mr Le Tissier?' Faith asked.

'We are still in a relationship,' Susan said, affronted.

Sandy and Richard looked at each other and shrugged –

this seemed improbable.

'Over one year now,' Susan added, smiling at Theo in the dock.

'What did he tell you about what had happened when he was in Barbados, with Miss Jones and Mr Scott?'

'He loved being able to skipper them about and felt honoured. He sent me some photos of him with them.'

'What did he tell you had happened when he came home though?'

'Theo was very upset when I saw him the first morning he came home and came to my flat. He told me that he had done something stupid on the yacht, and had lost it.'

'What do you think he meant by that comment?' Faith asked softly.

'I don't know, he didn't say, but he was very shook up. I think he meant he lost his temper.'

Not wanting to push it any further Faith sat down and said to Reece, 'Your witness.'

Reece shook his head; he was not going to engage with Susan Walters. Did that mean she knew more than she had told the police and the court?

As Susan went to leave the court, she walked up to the dock and said to Theo, 'I still love you Theo.'

Madam Justice Gabrielle Weekes felt that they had heard enough for the week so wished everyone a good weekend. She firmly reminded the jury not to discuss the case with anyone.

Chapter Thirty-Four

Pleased that court had finished early for the day and the week, Sandy arrived in good time to pick up the car he had hired for the weekend.

He was also in place waiting in arrivals at Grantley Adams International airport for Hannah when she would come through the automatic doors.

The flight from London had arrived and it didn't take long for Hannah to walk through the doors with her baggage. The embrace the two of them shared was as though they hadn't seen each other for months rather than less than a week.

When they had driven to the hotel near Holetown and Hannah saw the beach and the sea, she was quite clear with Sandy that this was the spot where she was going to stay for the week, she wasn't going to move until they travelled back the following Friday evening.

This was the opposite of what Sandy had planned, for the weekend at least, hence why he had hired a car. Other than a long weekend away staying at The Lodge Hotel in Old Hunstanton he could hardly remember the last time they had been away on holiday together.

The next morning when Sandy woke up there was no sign of Hannah. He found her reading on the balcony, jetlag had meant that she was wide awake at least two hours earlier.

As it was just getting light, Sandy convinced Hannah that they should go for a drive around the island and stop for breakfast whilst they travelled, and they would still be back late morning to have the rest of the day on the beach.

They headed north and Sandy took a detour early on to show her his favourite police station, the one in Holetown. Hannah was unimpressed. He then took her to show her the Speightstown Marina. Hannah was much more impressed with this. The marina was already a hive of activity with boats and yachts moving about and the Caribbean Sea was beautifully calm and a bright azure blue in colour.

They made no more stops but went around the north coast and down the east side of the island where the coast became a lot rockier and the sea a lot wilder, a real contrast to the calm sea they had near their hotel.

A late breakfast at a beach café in St. Lawrence Gap was a welcome time to stop. The beach and sea here was very beautiful and was already filling up with tourists and some local people taking their spots on the beach for the day. Sandy recalled to Hannah the chase and arrest of Marlon which brought much laughter from them both.

Having had a lovely morning driving round the beautiful island of Barbados, they settled onto the sun loungers on the beach.

Sandy realised what a lucky man he was as he was supposed to be here in Barbados working. Not bad for a boy from Ely in Cambridgeshire. His mind wandered to thinking about what Imogen, Adam and Celia were doing now and if they were OK.

Giving Hannah the excuse that he needed to go back to

the room for something, Sandy rang Imogen.

'Just checking in to make sure you are alright. I am sorry I rushed off yesterday without checking in with you all.'

'We are fine, I think,' Imogen said in a whisper, 'hang on.' Sandy could clearly hear a door opening. 'That's better. It is all very claustrophobic in our villa here. Adam makes a big pretence in court of him being OK and coping reasonably well, but then comes back here and just sits drinking in the chair on the terrace by the pool. Celia is a bundle of nerves and lashes out with that tongue of hers, mostly at Adam but me too and my friend, who has now moved out to the Sandy Lane Hotel.'

Feeling Imogen's distress, Sandy was glad he had rung. 'Trials are particularly stressful for the families involved, I will see if either Dave Ashton or I can visit tomorrow.' Sandy was not sure how he would be able to fit this in as he hadn't yet told Hannah his busy plans for the Sunday.

'Get Dave to give Adam a call and I will see you on Monday. The biggest problem I have is this...' Imogen hesitated. 'It is now abundantly clear to me that if it wasn't the defendant Theo Le Tissier that killed Vivienne, it had to be my brother-in-law, Adam Scott!'

∞

An early walk on the beach on the Sunday and a leisurely breakfast had taken place before Sandy outlined the plans for the day.

A trip to see an incredible garden and then a late Sunday lunch with Juliet and her family was what was planned.

Expecting a cry of "no, I want to stay on the beach", Sandy was surprised when Hannah said, 'That will be lovely.'

Only a twenty-minute drive from Holetown in the centre of the island in a beautiful setting of lush hills was an incredible place called Hunte's Gardens.

They took a self-guided tour wandering around in the sunshine admiring the rare and exotic plants. As they went deeper and deeper into the gulley, they saw that the garden had transformed all of the terraces, which were filled with cascading vines in vivid reds and yellows along with the many vibrant colours of the plants, bushes and trees throughout the garden. Small birds including hummingbirds were everywhere seeking nectar and food from the flowers. It was a most relaxing and tranquil setting. The smells were also intoxicating.

Sandy was so pleased that he had brought Hannah to see without doubt one of the most beautiful gardens in the world. They were even more pleased when they went to get refreshments that Anthony Hunte himself was there and he told them all about the garden and the history of how he had developed it from the sinkhole that had made the gulley. They were equally amazed when he told them that just him and one fulltime gardener kept the place going. The recorded classical music playing on the terrace as they sipped their refreshments and listened to Anthony was a perfect end to a most lovely Sunday morning.

The peace and relaxed feeling that Hannah and Sandy were experiencing was soon shattered when they turned up at Juliet's mum and dad's house. The music blaring out into the garden when they walked into it, was a combination of reggae and other hits from the seventies and eighties.

Juliet's dad was busy on the BBQ with ribs and chicken thighs and wings sizzling away on it, to which he kept adding lashings of jerk sauce. Juliet and her mother were busy inside cooking a big pot of Bajan pepper pot beef and there was also rice and beans cooking away.

The embrace between Hannah and Juliet was so sincere and lovely. They hadn't seen each other for almost six months.

'Did Sandy tell you about my sparkling performance in the witness box?'

'He did mention it,' Hannah replied. 'We went past the Supreme Court complex yesterday, very impressive buildings to have a court case in.'

'How are the five of us going to eat all of this food?' Sandy asked, but just as he did so, he saw Dave and his family arrive and Dave's father, who was Juliet's uncle with another young family, presumably a second family.

'What we don't eat, I will finish later,' Juliet said laughing. She tapped her watch. 'I have already done my ten thousand steps today so I will be alright.'

Having a sudden thought and leaving Hannah and Juliet in deep conversation, Sandy slid around the corner of the house and frantically searched his phone for an email, but he couldn't find what he was looking for.

He glanced back around the corner and saw that Juliet's mother had joined her and Hannah, who was admiring the all-in-one leopard print jump suit Juliet's mum was wearing.

He caught Dave's eye and gesticulated for him to come and see him. Looking through his own work phone, Dave found the images that Sandy was looking for; it was as Sandy thought. He told Dave what he was going to try and find out which Dave was very impressed with.

'How did you get on when you spoke to Imogen and Adam this morning?' Sandy asked, as they headed back to the group in the garden.

'I went and visited, rather than called. Adam was in his usual position, but not drinking, which I thought was good. He had a video call planned with Rosamund and his two girls early this afternoon which he was looking forward to. He felt that he should just go back to England and let the court case go on without him, but Celia won't let him.'

Dave then stopped walking to make sure no one overheard him, 'Imogen,' he said, 'was just moving out to stay at the Sandy Lane Hotel, to join her friend.'

'Is she having second thoughts about Adam...' Sandy glanced around to make sure no one was listening, '... maybe being responsible?'

'I am not sure about that,' Dave said, looking unsure as to what Imogen was actually thinking. 'It was Theo's fingerprints being on the wrong end of the metal shelving bar that has thrown her. The bar must have been wiped, so whose fingerprints were on the end that would have been held when it struck Vivienne?'

∞

The last thing Sandy wanted to do the next morning was leave Hannah and go to court. A day with her on the beach was far too enticing. They hadn't woken early enough to have a pre-breakfast walk on the beach. The afternoon had headed into the evening at Juliet's family home and the after-effects had meant they were feeling sluggish that morning.

Leaving the keys for the hire car to be collected in the hotel reception, Sandy went outside to wait for Richard to collect him. It had been too late yesterday evening to call Dale as it would have been the middle of the night in Guernsey, but the email Sandy had sent had spurred Dale into action. Dale had found what Sandy was looking for and was getting it examined. Hopefully he might have a result that day, he had also contacted the company involved; they were in the United States and would, if needed, send confirmation.

As Richard arrived, Sandy had a wide grin on his face and when he told Richard what he was trying to discover, the half empty man said it might amount to nothing and it was all too late now anyway!

Already in court when they arrived were Adam, Celia and Imogen. They were sitting together but had arrived separately for the first time, which the watching media had thought significant and so were seeking comments.

The prosecution had decided to rest their case. Elliot Sobers had handed over to the defence. Reece Prescod told the jury that he wouldn't keep them too long as he intended to call only two witnesses that would satisfy them that they would not be able to be sure, beyond all reasonable doubt, of Mr Le Tissier's guilt.

The first of the two witnesses was the manager of Ray and Scott's jewellers in Guernsey. Dave had collected the Cartier watch from a safe at the Barbados Police HQ and it was the first time that it had been seen in court.

Dave brought it in just as Juliet arrived, who was clearly

nursing a sore head that morning, but when she clasped eyes on the beautiful gold, diamond encrusted watch, they lit up. No wonder she had noticed it the first time she had seen it on Vivienne's wrist in Eaton Square, London, and remembered it from all that time ago.

'Do you remember seeing this watch before?' Reece asked, as Dave handed it to the witness.

'Oh yes, it is an incredibly beautiful, rare and in fact unique watch.'

'Who brought it for you to see? Can you see them in the court this morning?'

The witness, dressed in a three-piece pinstripe suit looked very smart, prim and proper, he didn't gaze around the court but looked straight at the defendant in the dock.

He didn't point but just said, 'Yes, he is sitting in the dock over there.'

'What did he ask you?'

'Could I provide a value for the watch for him,' the witness replied.

'Value,' Reece repeated very loudly, 'no mention of selling it?'

'No, just for me to value it.'

Having asked that question, Reece sat down, leaving Elliot for the prosecution to stand and ask, 'How much did you value the watch for?'

'It was really difficult as it is a one off and much more difficult now as the watch was designed and made for and worn almost continuously by Vivienne Jones. I did a search of what I could purchase a similar watch for, and it was roughly 80,000 Guernsey pounds.'

'I am not sure of exchange rates for the Guernsey pounds, how much in say sterling or US dollars?'

'One hundred thousand US dollars,' the witness said.

That brought about gasps from around the court, including from one or two members of the jury.

'A value well worth stealing for,' Elliot said, glancing down at Reece, who surprisingly didn't object.

The manager of Ray and Scott's left the witness box. *Not bad*, Sandy thought, *a paid trip to Barbados care of the criminal justice system for just a few questions.*

He checked his phone and saw that he had a number of missed calls from Dale and an email from him which, when he read it, brought a big smile to Sandy's face. He should really go out of court and call Dale, but when the next witness being called was Theo Le Tissier, he couldn't leave his seat.

Chapter Thirty-Five

As Theo Le Tissier made the short walk from the defendant's dock to the witness box, he was accompanied by a prison officer. In comparison he looked small and unable to cause anyone any harm, let alone what was being alleged against him in this court over the last few weeks.

As he gave the oath, Reece Prescod, his attorney, had to tell him to speak louder to make sure the jury, judge and the prosecution attorneys heard his replies.

The hush around the court was palpable as they all awaited the defendant's view on what was being alleged against him. Sandy didn't exactly feel sorry for him, but his strong emotional intelligence did pick up how alone Theo must be feeling. His mother, June, had not made the trip across, only Susan had expressed any love for him. The only person on his side in the courtroom was Reece Prescod. The victim though was not Theo, it was Vivienne Jones, her life had been snuffed out long before it should have been.

'Tell us about you as a sailor, Mr Le Tissier.'

'I have been sailing since I was a very young lad.' This must have been rehearsed as a first question as it was the subject Theo loved the most. 'My maternal grandfather taught me. He was a brilliant sailor.'

'You are not too bad yourself, are you?'

A beaming smile crossed Theo's face. 'Thank you. I was on the fringes of the British Olympic team and over time have become more efficient with large, motorised yachts as well as smaller sailboats.'

'Have the Candice Investment Bank that own *Magnificence* and two other similar yachts been happy with your work?'

'Yes, very happy. They told me that they wanted to offer me full-time employment. Previous clients, and Miss Jones and Mr Scott, had told me and them what a good job I had done or was doing.'

'We will talk about your time with Miss Jones and Mr Scott shortly,' Reece said, looking back at Adam as he did so. 'DS Juliet Ashton told this court about you being a bit emotional in your interviews in Guernsey.' He had avoided using the words "lose your temper". 'Tell the court about your upbringing; I know you understand the words adverse childhood trauma – describe how this has affected you.'

Theo started to cry, and if Reece wanted the jury to feel sorry for Theo, he was well and truly succeeding. Reece was very good, very good indeed.

'I grew up in a home filled with domestic abuse. This horrible man, I can't go as far as to call him my father, used to beat my mum up so badly sometimes that he put her in hospital, and he was incarcerated. I was pleased when we left.' Theo had to stop as he started crying even louder.

'Take time to compose yourself. We can all understand why you might get emotional at times. Moving forward to your time with Mr Scott and Miss Jones; you saw Mr Scott get very cross and grab Miss Jones on more than the one occasion that we discussed with Mr Scott last week in this court. Is that right?'

'Yes, twice at least when I was present; there was another occasion earlier in the trip before we got to Barbados.'

Elliot looked at Faith, and then they both looked round at Richard and Sandy who could only shrug and shake their head as this was the first they had heard of it. When Sandy looked at Adam, he shook his head back at him and he saw that Imogen had her head in her hands.

Sitting near them were two people Sandy hadn't seen or heard enter the court. They were both extremely smartly dressed in full uniform. Seymour Garner smiled at Sandy and sitting next to him was the towering mountain of a man, Carlos Bishop, who just glared at him. What he had just heard helped to confirm his thoughts that it was Adam all along.

'We agree with the prosecution evidence that the metal shelving bar caused the injuries that Miss Jones died of. Where was that shelving bar?' Reece asked.

'It was in the lounge area in a small recess, it was in the way in my cabin, so I moved it there.'

'So, obvious for anyone onboard to see?'

'Yes,' Theo nodded as he said this.

'The prosecution allege that you stole the Cartier watch. That is not right, is it?'

'It was lying on the table, and I picked it up for safe keeping to return to Mr Scott,' Theo said. 'I never had the chance though as I was arrested shortly after getting back to Guernsey.'

'Did you kill Miss Jones to steal the watch?' Reece asked. While he asked this question, he was shaking his head at the jury, he had been using body language and head movements to help convince the jury of what Theo was saying.

'No. I most certainly did not,' Theo said most emphatically.

∞

The court adjourned for lunch. Sandy carefully avoided Carlos Bishop and made his way to the room he had been using the previous week to phone Dale. Richard had gone off to call Paulette and Garry to see if they remembered seeing the metal shelving bar and the Cartier watch in the lounge when they had searched it on the first day Vivienne had gone missing.

What Dale told him excited Sandy greatly, and he knew he needed talk to Elliot Sobers, Faith Maynard and Richard as soon as possible.

Opening up an image on his laptop and seeing their confused, intrigued and worried faces, Sandy pointed out to them the heart rate reading from Theo's fitness watch. They still had this in the exhibits store in Guernsey, but he had got it examined. The internationally well-known fitness watch company from the United States had also made a statement based on their reading of the information on the fitness App, which had confirmed it as well.

'Theo had a normal resting heartrate of sixty beats per minute,' Sandy said. 'When we look at the night in question, shortly before they got back to the yacht that heart rate had suddenly spiked up to eighty-five.' Sandy made sure they were all following what he was saying. Crammed in the room he could see that they were all transfixed. 'Possibly this was the time when he took the drugs he had bought from Bradley

298

Lewis.'

Sandy then moved to the next image that took into account the heartrate during the time after they had got back on board the yacht. The spike in heart rate was alarmingly sky high, it almost went off the scale, two hundred or more beats per minute and then slightly reduced for five to ten minutes, it then spiked again, not as high as before, but still very high.

Looking at the faces of the others, Sandy didn't have to say anything as they knew the significance of what he was showing them. He couldn't resist it though, pointing at the two spikes.

'This is the time of the murder, and this is the time of disposing of Vivienne's body into the sea.'

'We can't use it, unfortunately,' Elliot said, 'it is too late in the trial.'

'Of course it isn't,' Faith said to him, loudly and emphatically. 'Let's get the judge to decide.'

As usual Faith Maynard won the argument and Sandy rushed off to find someone who could print off the images and information, multiple times for the defence, judge and jury. Elliot went to find Reece and then to speak to Justice Gabrielle Weekes.

Following an extended lunch break they all assembled in court, with no jury. Faith led on the legal argument rather than Elliot as her heart was passionately in it. She outlined what the information showed and suggested that they could introduce it by putting it to the defendant in cross examination.

Theo had his head in his hands in the dock.

Reece said in rebuttal, 'Your Honour, this is preposterous for this to be included now. It is not new information that has just come to light. The police have had it almost six months. The fact they had failed to do the necessary enquiries is down to their incompetence.'

Justice Weekes, who had had time to think about this over lunch and had now listened to the argument, paused, looking at the images and reading the statement from the fitness company again. Sandy and Richard felt like nervous wrecks, their stomachs were full of butterflies and Sandy thought he felt a little bit sick as they waited for her decision. The few moments felt like a lifetime.

When Reece went to speak again, Justice Weekes put her hand up, she had heard enough. 'I am going to allow it.'

Sandy and Richard wanted to cheer.

'The evidence is so clear; it would be wrong not to allow the jury to hear about it. You can of course, depending on how things turn out in court, Mr Prescod, take my decision to the Appeal Court in due course.'

Reece did manage to get an adjournment to the following morning so he could take instruction from Theo during the afternoon.

∞

The next morning in court there was no sign of the Deputy and Assistant Commissioners, but sitting in their seats were Paulette and Garry. They were both pleased to see Sandy and greeted him warmly.

Theo returned to the witness box as the jury filed in and took their places. Richard and Sandy were disappointed that it was Elliot Sobers and not Faith Maynard who was doing the cross examination. They hoped that they had no need to worry.

'The story that you have been telling in court, I am afraid, doesn't add up. You killed Miss Vivienne Jones, didn't you?'

Theo didn't reply. He was not sure it was an actual question or a statement.

'Let's start then with what you said about Mr Scott grabbing Miss Jones on other occasions. You never mentioned it when first spoken to, or in any of your four interviews, did you?'

'No.'

'Is that all you can say, no?'

'Yes.'

Sandy wondered if Theo was taking too far the clear Reece Prescod advice, of making as little comment as possible.

'We have spoken to Mr Scott again and looked at the photos of the two them on both of their phones and we can find nothing to back up previous instances of him grabbing Miss Jones.'

Theo didn't reply. Elliot seemed to be wading through treacle.

Faith passed around a series of photographs for the judge and jury to see of the lounge area of *Magnificence* taken by Clare Symonds in Guernsey.

'Where is the recess that you mentioned that the metal shelving bar would be clearly visible from?' Elliot asked.

Looking at his provided copy of the photographs, Theo said, 'These were taken in Guernsey, and I had already repaired it in the cabin long before this.'

'I know that,' Elliot said, starting to get irritated by the answers. 'Where would it have been? Where is the recess?'

'You can't see it in the photos. It is just out of view of this one.' Theo showed one of the photos to the jury but not to Elliot.

Even Richard and Sandy were starting to get irritated, and Juliet looked fit to burst.

'The two officers that searched the yacht in the Speightstown Marina are in court today and they say they never saw the metal shelving bar in the lounge.'

'They wouldn't have done, would they? Sorry, but they were looking for Miss Jones, she was a bit big to fit in this small recess.' Theo thought he had made a joke, but no one laughed.

'The watch then,' Elliot said, 'you say was on the table in the lounge and when you returned to the yacht on your way to Antigua you took possession of it.'

'Yes.'

'Constable Paulette Weekes says she would have definitely remembered seeing a gold, diamond encrusted Cartier watch on that table, but she didn't.'

Theo didn't reply. Elliot seemed to be making statements and not asking questions.

'Trying to sell it in Guernsey it would have been too hot to handle where you are well known, you needed a value so you could sell it in England or across in continental Europe.'

'No. I was always going to return it.'

Faith handed out the images of the fitness watch readings to Theo, Reece, the judge and the jury who seemed fascinated when looking at them.

'These are readings of your heart rate taken from your fitness watch. Is that correct?'

'Yes.'

'You have an average heart rate of sixty beats per minute. Is that correct?' Elliot asked, showing the first of the images.

'Yes.'

'Look at the next two images from the evening that Miss Jones was murdered. The reading shows your heart rate raised on three different occasions. The first, possibly when you took the drugs, the second, when you killed Miss Jones.' Elliot paused there to let his words and the significance of the image sink into the jury's psyche. 'Then the third is when you threw Miss Jones into the Caribbean Sea.'

Theo didn't reply.

'That is what really happened on that night, isn't it, Mr Le Tissier? Your fitness watch tells the story of what happened, clear for us all to see.'

'No. I am not sure about the first spike, maybe I was agitated by the behaviour of Mr Scott.' Theo paused to think for a moment. 'The second two are when I went to my cabin, I couldn't sleep so I did a short intense fitness workout, and the last one must have been my cool down.'

Looking at each other, Richard and Sandy thought good work by Reece Prescod, he had come up with a wonderful rebuttal to the evidence for Theo.

Elliot, exasperated, not even expecting an answer, said, 'Come off it, Mr Le Tissier, your cabin was tiny, it was too small for any workout. You killed Vivienne Jones and blaming Mr Scott is not going to work.'

He was right, he got no answer. Elliot sat down. Reece didn't need to re-examine; his defendant had done well. Richard and Sandy did regret Faith not cross examining.

Chapter Thirty-Six

There was no more evidence for the defence to be called, and the judge decided that the next morning would be appropriate for short, she emphasised short, closing statements. She would then sum up in the afternoon and have just a few words on Thursday morning before letting the jury take time to consider their verdict.

With the afternoon free, Sandy and Hannah went and visited Sandy Lane beach. However, they did nothing but talk about the case. Sandy was extremely nervous and anxious. He thought about ringing Grandad Tom to relax him with his wise words, but didn't. Hannah was worried; was the evidence enough for the jury to be sure, beyond all reasonable doubt, that it was Theo and not Adam who had killed Vivienne? Seeing Sandy's conflicted face, she told him that yes, she did think so. The key for her was if Adam had done it, yes, he might have struck her in a fit of anger – he clearly had a temper – but would he have carefully put the metal shelving bar back in the recess as Theo said? Most importantly for her, would he have then thrown the woman that he no doubt, loved, adored and idolised into the sea? She thought not.

The next day Elliot Sobers for the prosecution stuck to

a short statement, but did cover all of the main points of evidence. It was quite compelling. Sandy had mentioned to him Hannah's thoughts on the bar and the throwing into the sea by Adam, but he didn't want to talk about Adam. However, Reece Prescod for the defence did, and that was all he talked about in his closing statement, that Adam could have equally done it instead of Theo.

The judge laboriously went through every piece of evidence and then talked about the law and how to apply it when she advised the jury.

The team and Hannah went out for a meal that evening as the Thursday evening was going to be Sandy's and Hannah's last one on Barbados and he wanted it to be special. Everyone was subdued in the restaurant in Holetown. Even Paulette and Garry's slapstick fun with each other wasn't happening. Juliet was staying if the case ran on into the following week. She was missing her husband and children greatly but knew it would only be a few more days.

On the Thursday morning, Sandy's anxiety had increased and he went for an early morning run on the beach. The only way he knew how to relax himself was to exercise and running did it for him. When he got back to the room Hannah was smartly dressed as she told him she would accompany him to court that day. Sandy was so deeply touched as it was her last full day on the beach and in the sea.

At court, when Elliot and Faith found out Hannah was a fellow attorney they invited her to sit with them, but she declined to be sure of sitting next to Sandy. When she saw Richard, he was more of a wreck than Sandy.

The judge gave the jury her last-minute instructions and

told them there was no rush, the court had allocated all of the following week to the case if they needed it.

Standing outside the court to enjoy the Bajan sunshine, Hannah told Sandy about her busy week ahead in court in Nottingham and Sandy told her about his boring first part of the week ahead in the office in London. He felt a wave of missing his grandma that hit him from nowhere whilst he was talking.

Lunchtime came and went, the afternoon started to drag on when Dave Ashton rushed out to tell them the jury was on their way back. They had a verdict. Hannah grabbed both of Sandy's hands and kissed him. Seymour Garner was running along the road trying to be in court in time. The media who had been filming pieces to camera outside were packing up their equipment and in their droves speeding into their allocated court room.

Imogen, Adam and Celia looked shell-shocked and asked what this meant, but no one knew other than it wasn't a question the jury wanted answering, it was definitely a verdict.

Whether she should have done it or not Hannah grabbed Sandy's hand firmly and kept a tight hold. Sandy wanted to do the same for Richard but decided against it, the man was a bundle of nerves.

The jury filed in expressionless, did any of them look at the defendant? Yes, one or two did, what did that mean? Her Honour Justice Gabrielle Weekes walked in. Everyone stood.

The foreman of the jury stood, he was a man in his early sixties who had been dressed smartly throughout the trial in a suit and tie.

The clerk said to him, 'Have you reached a verdict that you all agree on?'

'Yes, we all agree,' he responded, very loudly and firmly.

'On the count of the murder of Vivienne Jones how did you find the defendant, Theo Le Tissier. Guilty or not guilty?'

The foreman now looking directly at Theo, without any hesitation, without building up any suspense or anticipation he said loudly, emphatically and confidently, 'Guilty. Yes, guilty.'

∞

The courtroom exploded in a cacophony of noise. Hannah and Sandy embraced and before Sandy could do the same with Richard, the judge shouted for everyone to calm down.

Justice Weekes, looked directly at Theo, who looked expressionless; had he expected this verdict all along?

She said to him, 'You will be sentenced in four weeks' time. I will make an order now for reports to be available for me well before this date. You must talk to the allocated court officer.' The judge then looked around at the jury. 'On behalf of the court, I would like to thank you all for your service. You are very welcome to return for sentencing if you wish.' Justice Gabrielle Weekes then looked around at Elliot Sobers. 'Please can you read out to the jury, in case they are unable to attend, Mr Le Tissier's relevant previous conviction.'

Elliot read out the robbery conviction and its circumstances. The jury members audibly sighed as if in relief on hearing this.

The court was adjourned and before Sandy hugged

Richard, he went up to Adam and Celia who were in tears. Was Adam's nightmare now over? Sandy thought not. Imogen was even hugging Adam, she had now clearly in her head and heart reconciled with him.

The Assistant Commissioner shook Richard and Sandy's hands. 'Brilliant work by both of you.'

He had forgotten his speech that he was going to make to the media outside the court, and poor Dave had been dispatched to collect it from his desk.

They assembled outside the Supreme Court building, where dozens of reporters were taking photographs or filming. Seymour, Richard and Adam stood with their backs to the court doors. Sandy, Hannah and the rest of the team moved around so that they could see and hear what was happening.

'I personally, on behalf of the Barbados Police, want to highlight my thanks for the bravery of Miss Vivienne Jones' family, her sister and her husband,' he pointed to both Imogen and Adam, 'for their dignity throughout our investigation process and the trial of Theo Le Tissier. My only mention of him is that he has now been convicted and will spend an extremely long time behind bars, here, and then after it is felt due time has elapsed, we will extradite him out of Barbados to serve his remaining term in England or his home in Guernsey.' Finally, looking at Richard and the rest of the team, he said, 'Thank you DI Ambrose and your team for your painstaking work to bring this case to its rightful conclusion.'

He took no questions although there were lots being shouted out.

Adam then went to the front and said, 'Thank you Sandy,

Dave and Richard for your incredible investigation.'

Sandy looked around, hoping that Carlos Bishop was there to have heard this, but he wasn't to be seen.

Adam continued, 'Theo Le Tissier has taken away from us and I mean by us, not just her sister, or me or her stepchildren, but the whole world, who has lost this beautiful, immensely talented and lovely person. He has snuffed out her life but not her legacy, and through the body of her film work she will live on to be the legend that she always was going to be, and now will be.'

Adam had nothing left to say and walked over to join Celia and Imogen. The reporters were not going to let him get off as lightly as they had Seymour Garner, but he was not going to answer their questions.

Richard, unplanned, started talking to the media, 'Can I please ask that the media, and particularly those on social media, stop, please stop this vile trolling of that man,' he pointed at Adam, 'and his family. Accept the evidence that the court has made a decision on.' He then walked off surrounded by complete silence to usher Adam and the family back into the court complex.

∞

Elliot and Faith came and spoke to the family and then headed off back to their offices. The grin on both their faces would take a long time to fade. The family all embraced Sandy more than anyone else as he really had been their main contact throughout.

Celia on her embrace said, 'Well done sonny boy, you

were as good as Arabella Montague said you would be.'

Sandy had to smile when he looked and saw how Juliet, Hannah and Paulette were towards Adam, smiling, laughing and flicking their hair!

The team met up for a late afternoon drink in a nearby bar before Richard took Sandy and Hannah back to their hotel. The team were in extremely high spirits and Paulette and Garry were at each other again about who had made the most important contribution to the case. Juliet was slightly distracted as she was urgently trying to get business admin at the FCDO to book her on the BA flight the next morning with Hannah and Sandy. The person who was late turn cover couldn't seem to find the original booking to confirm the return, but convinced her it would be OK.

Outside the hotel reception, Richard told Sandy he would come in the morning and take them to the airport. He asked if they could still be colleagues, friends, and always keep in touch.

Although Sandy wanted to call his two grandfathers and tell them about the court result, he had switched his phone off. He knew he didn't need to update them as the world's media would already have been running the result on their newscasts.

Getting changed quickly and making their way out to the beach with a large cocktail to see the sun dip down over the horizon and out of sight into the Caribbean Sea, Hannah looked at Sandy and wondered why he seemed so very nervous. She thought he should be on a high with the adrenaline pumping through his veins, maybe it was just relief it was all over.

Getting himself in position and fiddling with something in his pocket, Sandy was looking to time the sun going down perfectly.

Hannah got her phone out of her bag to take some photographs of the sunset, when her phone started to ring, on looking at who was calling she saw it was John McFarlane, Sandy's grandpa. She answered the phone, much to the loud noise of exasperation from Sandy.

'He wants to know why you have got your phone off and not answering his calls,' Hannah said.

'Why is he ringing at this late a time in England?' Sandy wondered aloud, watching the sun go down and almost out of sight. 'Grandpa, what can I do for you?'

'Brilliant! Well done with your court case. The reason for the call is that I have been approached by a third-year student at Cambridge University asking if I can help him. I told him my grandson would be the best one to talk to him.'

'What about, Grandpa?' a very dejected sounding Sandy said.

'His best friend, who is also his sister's fiancée, has been found dead in a hotel room in Vienna. He thinks he has been murdered.'

Author's Note

Many people will think that the inspiration for this story came from the case of Natalie Wood and her husband Robert Wagner, and they of course would be one hundred percent correct. Natalie went missing off her yacht *Splendour* (I named my yacht *Magnificence*) and was found drowned in 1981. Her roles in the films *Rebel Without a Cause*, and *West Side Story* captivated me while growing up. What must Robert Wagner have felt with the media painting the picture of him as a suspect throughout. Inspiration was also taken from the lives of Elizabeth Taylor and her two-times husband, Richard Burton. I also took some inspiration from the case of Sam Heslop who went missing from a catamaran near the US Virgin Islands, and finally, from the tragic case of drowning in Lancashire in 2023 of Nicola Bulley. The horrendous media and social media intrusion and vile comments directed at her husband, family and the excellent senior investigating officer, Rebecca Smith, was truly awful.

However, my first thought to include this as an investigation in the series came from my close friend, Dave Marshall, when he told me about his fascinating and successful investigation in Antigua, where he recovered the bodies of four people who had been murdered on a yacht in 1994 near Low Bay, Barbuda. The yacht was registered in Guernsey, hence I used this as my place of registration as well. The daughter of two of the deceased, Bonnie Floyd, has written a brilliant book called, *Bound to a Promise*.

I spent over thirty years as a police officer and the majority of these years were as a detective. I served as a detective in every rank, finally as the detective chief superintendent (head of the detective branch) of the Cambridgeshire Constabulary. As a detective, I led over a hundred major crime cases, a number of which were homicides or suspicious deaths. I absolutely loved this opportunity. The rank I enjoyed most, though, was the rank that Alexander McFarlane holds, that of a DCI. I am best known for my work as a detective around the UK for my role, over many years, as the national policing lead for the investigation of child death, as well as for my role as the senior investigator at the deposition site for the recovery and forensic investigation into the deaths of Holly Wells and Jessica Chapman, two ten-year-old girls from Soham, who were murdered by Ian Huntley.

In October 2019, my wife Debbie and I had a chance encounter in a remote hilltop village in the Atlas Mountains (Morocco) with a couple from Melbourne – Professor Anne Buist and her partner Graeme Simsion. They are both authors and were working on a romantic comedy novel together. Graeme authored the bestselling novel, *The Rosie Project*. When I told him I had a detective crime novel in mind, he proceeded to give me a fifteen-minute masterclass on how to author a novel. Coincidently, both Professor Buist and I were to be keynote speakers at a conference two weeks later in Melbourne, relating to children who had been murdered by a parent. This chance meeting cemented my thoughts to author the novel I had been talking about for years.

This didn't occur, however, until the first lockdown arrived due to the COVID-19 pandemic. Even though I was still busy with my safeguarding work and writing a number of reviews, I decided to write a first draft of a novel during this period. That novel, *Greed is a Powerful Motive*, and the second and third ones, *Missing but not Lost*, and *Death at Chateau Peveril*, have been published by my brilliant publisher Cranthorpe Millner, to whom I am immensely grateful for all they do for me.

Acknowledgements

To my wife Debbie, who is and has always been my greatest supporter in all that I do. Debbie was the first to read this novel and then painstakingly helped me to carry out a first edit for every page of it. For this and everything, I am truly grateful.

To all my family: my children Daniel, Rebecca and Matthew; and my father-in-law Sydney Barton and sister-in-law Ruth Chaplain-Barton for reading and commenting on the story.

Also, to my close friends who have taken the time to read the novel and to give me feedback. Thank you to Judi Richardson, Lorri and John Kendall (my Canadian family), Joanne Procter, Andrew Harrison (my writing and sourdough buddy), David Marshall (my work buddy and who gave me the initial spark for this story and all of his anecdotes that I include from time to time), Angela and Mark Craig (my friends, but also my daughter's mother-in-law and father-in-law), James Bambridge, Jane Ashton, Glenys Johnston, Mike Richardson, Mark Birch and Wendi Ogle-Welbourn.

I would also like to thank the brilliant Dr Nat Cary (Forensic Pathologist), Sonya Bayliss from the NCA. The incredible Karim Khalil KC. DS's Nicole Thomas and Jon Walker from the Guernsey Police. Finally but not least Assistant Commissioner David (Chis) Griffith from Barbados.